CHASING ROXANNE

A Book of Fiction

by
Anthony Parran

ISBN: 978-1-4269-4316-4 (sc)
ISBN: 978-1-4269-4318-8 (hc)
ISBN: 978-1-4269-4317-1 (e)

Library of Congress Control Number: 2010913335

*Our mission is to efficiently provide the world's finest, most comprehensive book publishing
service, enabling every author to experience success. To find out how to publish your book,
your way, and have it available worldwide, visit us online at www.trafford.com*

Trafford rev. 09/20/2010

 www.trafford.com

North America & international
toll-free: 1 888 232 4444 (USA & Canada)
phone: 250 383 6864 ♦ fax: 812 355 4082

Author's Note:

Although this is a work of fiction, most of the events are true gathered from my personal experiences, but are a mixture of several events or occurred in different locations.

I have heard the term life imitating art and as you read, you will find this has become true. I never imagined when I started this that there could possibly be a network of drug smuggling in US military aviation. Case in point, the recent find of drugs at the NASA Space Shuttle hanger.

I am a private pilot and hold a US and Canadian private pilot's license.

I was stationed in Korat, Thailand and saw drugs sold openly and freely to American service personal by Thai children. At that time a bag of pure Thai-Weed cost 5-cents.

Unlike the American private pilot, Canadian private pilots are not allowed or permitted to own Jet Warbirds, even American pilots living in Canada

The PZL TS-11 *ISKRA or Spark*, a Polish Warbird I have never seen except in pictures and videos. I have read a lot about what it is capable of, but when it came to getting technical data from several places that imported them, my emails were never returned. Eventually I was able to contact the following and greatly appreciate their time and efforts with their help.

- Mr. Robert Lutz, General Motors vice-chairman.
- Mr. Scott Aston, Mr. Lutz's L-39 plane Captain.
- Mr. Don Foster – A TS-11 plane Captain

As you read this work of fiction and find errors in its operation, I take full responsibility.

CHASING ROXANNE

PROLOGUE - KORAT THAILAND, 1968

AIRMAN MELVIN ANDERSON was in one of hard covers, tending a McDonnell Douglas F-4 Phantom. The electronics bay compartment open. Airman Anderson was supposed to be checking for a minor radar failure, but instead he was looking into the space available behind the bays and taking measurements.

He and another Airman had come up with the idea of sneaking drugs into the US after rumors began spreading that another group had successfully done so in Vietnam. The theory being that returning military aircraft very seldom were searched behind the nooks and crannies of the various bays. So if they could do it, why not them? They wouldn't make millions, but whatever they made sure beat the hell out of $450 a month pay.

Airman Anderson was so engrossed in what he was going; he didn't notice a Captain walking into the hanger.

"Airman, what the hell are you doing?"

"Sir, I had orders to look into a problem in the electronic bay." He said to the officer. The name on his uniform said, 'Washington.'

"Airman, I may look like an ass, but I have never seen someone repair a problem in an electronics bay using a tape measuring roll."

Airman Anderson began to sweat, which wasn't hard considering the temperature.

"Sir, if the Captain will remember there was a new shipment of electronics that came in and I was just making sure that it would fit."

"Airman, don't you think that was taken into consideration back in the land of the Big PX? (Slang for United Stated of America.)"

Melvin began to sweat even more. "You're right sir; I guess I got carried away."

3

Captain Richard Washington, call sign 'Hannibal' just stood there. He too had heard a rumor about successful drug smuggling by Americans in Nam using returning US fighter aircraft as the mule. The individuals were eventually caught, but only after several shipments had already made it through. The fact that they were caught had not been released so as to root out anyone trying to copycat the process and catching the ring leaders.

They never did.

Was Airman Anderson trying to duplicate these efforts? Maybe he was telling the truth. He'd let him continue, but watch him more closely.

"I have already checked the specifications and was even involved with the initial studies. So I doubt you'll have any problems fitting the new equipment into the bay."

"Sir, I'll get right on it."

He put his tape away and pulled out the F-4 service manual. Captain Washington stood for several minutes watching him. Knowing the Airman was only going through the motions of pretending to read the manual, he walked around the hanger area picking up tools here and there as if inspecting them. He went over to the work bench where a lunch box and fruits sat on a clean work cloth.

Without further comment he turned and marched away.

When he was out of sight, Anderson breathed a sigh of relief.

"Hey man, what did that Captain say?" Airman Sam Foster asked walking up to Melvin. He had been in the latrine when Washington had walked in.

"He caught me with a measuring tape."

"Do you think he knows about the deal in Nam?"

"Probably, but I hope I gave him a good answer. He chewed my ass out a little, but I doubt he knew what I was really doing. I think we'd better lay low for awhile."

"We can't man. This aircraft is due to rotate back to CONUS (Continental United States). We have people waiting on the other end."

"Can't we tell them to wait for a day or two? There will be more aircraft going back."

"Man I had to pay those assholes a partial in advance. If the shipment is not there, I lose over $50,000." "Fuck! Man I think that Washington dude is on to us."

"Maybe he is and maybe he isn't. Tell you what, the F-4 isn't going anywhere until the day after. Let me see if I can get Washington involved elsewhere. Will that help?"

"It will, but like what?'

"Don't ask questions if you're not prepared for the answers." Airman Foster said and walked away.

True to his word, Captain Washington was not around when the F-4, stuffed with plastic bags of heroin made a successful landing in the US and Sam, Melvin and buddies each deposited over $125,000 into separate bank accounts under false names. Not much, but a start.

CAPTAIN WASHINGTON was pissed. How in the hell did a colony of fire ants get into his flight suit? He had just returned from the base hospital where he was given medication for the many welts the ant bite had left. His skin looked like he had a bad rash of the measles. He shuttered at the memory of having zipped up his flight suit and almost immediately was hit with the stings. It was several minutes before he could get the suit off with the aid of several members of his hootch that had heard his screams.

Although there were many mounds to be found near the hootch, the Thai grounds keepers made sure that the ones close to any of the hootch's were eliminated. So how did a colony get into his?

When he was back in his bunk he sat on the end applying the cream to the many lumps and bumps he had been given by the doctor. When finished, he was putting the cream away in his footlocker when he noticed something odd. On the floor in the corner, just out of sight was a small tissue smeared with a substance. He bent down to get a closer look. Around the tissue was a colony of the ants. As he looked closer he saw several of the ants had found an opening in the back of his locker and were trooping up the side.

He opened it; following the trail.

At the back inside corner he found the ants not only invading his other uniforms, his flight suits, but his boots and dress uniform as well. In each he found a tissue with the same substance.

This was no coincidence.

Who would want to pull such a prank? To the best of his knowledge he had no enemies.

He was still pondering this when his housegirl and houseboy came in.

He gave his uniforms and boots to his housegirl with instructions to clean everything.

He instructed his houseboy to clean in and around his locker. He took two US $5 bills out of his wallet and extended it to each, but they politely declined.

Damn he loved the Thais and their honesty.

Before he had them start, he took the tissues, placed them in a paper envelope and walked out to the company HQ. There he got permission to take a company jeep back to the hospital. He wanted someone to examine them.

An hour later, Captain Washington had his answer but was again just as puzzled as before.

The substance was a combination of honeydew melon and oils. Where in the world does honeydew melon get onto a US military base? The stuff would have to be imported.

No sooner had he asked the question, he had his answers.

Honeydew was being brought in from Texas as it was the height of the growing season there and served in the mess halls along with apples and oranges.

Just days before he had seen honeydew in the open hanger as an uneaten fruit on a workbench. One of them was Airman Melvin Anderson. The implications were staggering. Why would he smear his uniforms with the stuff unless he had something to hide and wanted him out of the way? Could he really be part of a drug smuggling team such as the ones in Nam?

Captain Washington had to sit down on that thought.

Later, he went to the operations office as he was on medical stand down and would not be flying for a few days in search of some personnel records. There he started going through the records of Melvin Anderson. He had been brought up in Detroit; had joined the Air Force with a friend, Sam Foster before getting his draft notice. He became an avionics tech on North American F-101 Voodoo's, Republic F105's Thunderchief's and later the F-4's. Was considered the best in what he did.

OK, so that seems normal enough, Captain Washington thought. Then he saw a small note on one of his medicals. Melvin had been given the opportunity to join the military after it was discovered he had been arrested with a small bag of heroin.

This was his first offense.

If he volunteered for the military then his record would be cleared of all charges, which it was. As far as Captain Washington was concerned, that was just too much of a coincidence.

So he had a possible motive. But even that didn't add up. He would have needed a small army to carry out the logistics involved in a smuggling ring. Airman Anderson appeared to be more of a loner. Who were his accomplices?

He dug some more in the personnel records and found Airman Sam Foster. Was it him?

This was over his head, but he didn't have any proof to take to the Judge Advocate or Criminal Investigations. He'd have to get more evidence.

Tonight he was the duty officer.

Maybe he'd pay an unexpected visit to the F-4 hanger area.

THE THAILAND night was muggy as usual, although a cooling breeze had brought the temperature down to 90. The humidity was still up around 85%. Armed with a Model 1911 Colt .45 Caliber semi-automatic pistol, Captain Washington hopped into the duty jeep beside his driver; an Airman 2nd Class. In another jeep sat a Thai officer of the same ranks and armed with a Colt .45 as well, but his driver had a loaded M1A1 Carbine lying on the floor between them. Captain Washington's driver had an M-14 rife, although loaded; it was locked down and would be only brought out if the shit hit the fan. Americans were not allowed to use or show weapons as the Thai's did the major patrolling and security of the base. He had instructed the Thai Captain of his suspicions and what he wanted to accomplish. If all went well there would be no shooting, no one would get hurt and everyone would go to bed, well almost everyone, to get some sleep.

He had instructed his driver to turn off the lights when they neared the F-4 hanger, cut the engine and place the gear in neutral, allowing the jeep to coast to the huge opening. The second jeep would do the same.

As instructed, the lights were doused and the engine cut. Since they were on asphalt, the coasting was smooth and quiet.

Just because there were huge work lights on, didn't mean anything.

All of the hangers had lights on, even if there wasn't anyone in them.

This was a round the clock operation in a war time setting and aircraft were always being repaired..

When they had coasted up to the hanger, the driver quietly and expertly applied the brakes, bringing the jeep to a halt in the shadows. There they sat for several minutes, allowing their eyes to adjust to the darkness, but to make sure their approach hadn't been heard.

They hadn't.

Exiting the jeeps, the Thai Captain followed Washington, followed by the Thai driver. He had quietly loaded a round and placed the weapon on safety. The Thai Captain had drawn his weapon, pulled the slide back to reveal the dim glint of brass in the chamber. He left his safety off, but did not put his finger near the trigger.

The weapon looked like an oversized toy in his small hand.

The Thai's signaled that they were going to the back entrance of the hanger as Washington and his driver went to the front.

Lying on the ground, Washington took a peek around the corner and was rewarded with what he saw. Airman Anderson was with another airman. Anderson was placing items in the electronics bay. From this distance he couldn't tell what it was, but he could tell it wasn't items of electronics.

He felt a tap on his shoulder as his driver whispered that the Thais were in position waiting for his move.

Standing, he pulled out his .45, safety off and rushed into the hanger yelling. "Hands in the air. Stand right there and don't move!" His driver followed.

At the back of the hanger, the Thai's came running in, yelling in broken English as well. That did not matter as no translation was necessary.

Taken by surprise, both men raised their hands, heads swiveling back and forth. A plastic bag hit the floor breaking open, spilling a powdery substance. Rushing up to the two airmen, Washington grabbed one and flung him down. He followed him down placing a knee in his back.

The Thai did the same with the other airman. The Thai driver, for emphasis ejected and re-chambered a round.

The ejected round landing just in front of Airman Anderson's nose. A live round in a weapon pointed at you also needs no explanation.

"Hands behind you!" Washington ordered.

With his knee still in Melvin's back, his driver took out his mechanical handcuffs and locked them around Melvin's wrist. Behind him he heard the same ratchet-click as the Thais did the same to the other airman.

When they were secured, Washington and his driver hauled Melvin to his feet and placed him against the back of a large tool chest.

The other airman was placed beside him as well.

Washington gave his driver his pistol, ordering him to watch the two. The Thai driver, stone faced, did the same. These guys never showed emotion.

With the Thai Captain by his side they went over the F-4 and inspected the fallen bag. It looked like heroin but he wasn't about to test it by sticking his finger in the pile and placing it on his tongue.

Maybe one day they'll invent a testing kit.

He picked up the bag; careful not to spill any more of the contents and placed it on the workbench, where he discovered at least four more similar bags concealed underneath a stack of work cloths.

"Well, what have we here?" He then walked over to the F-4 and found a couple of similar bags in a removable electronic sliding tray. He inspected the handiwork. From a distance it looked like an ordinary tray, but now that he was up close, he could see that it was a hollow dummy. There was enough space left for the remaining bags on the workbench.

Washington did not need to see anymore.

He walked over to the two airmen. "Well Airman Anderson, looks like your tape measurements had another purpose after all."

Melvin didn't say anything.

"What's your name airman," he asked of the other.

"Airman Foster, Sir. Sam Foster."

"Are you the mastermind behind this?"

"No sir." Melvin gave Sam a fuck you look.

"I don't believe that for a second Foster. You know why? Anderson looks more like a doer and not a thinker. I bet you set this whole operation up. Did you try the copycat operation in Vietnam? We arrested them you know."

Sam tried to hide his surprise.

"Yeah, caught most of the gang. They're making small rocks out of big ones at Ft. Leavenworth, Kansas. I guess you'll two will be joining them."

"I have no idea what you're talking about sir. I came over to see my friend Melvin and saw that he was at work on the F-4. I wasn't paying attention exactly to what he was doing."

"Fuck you, you liar," Melvin said and spun his ass around, letting his boot catch Foster on the side of the head. Foster shook it off and delivered a kick of his own.

Washington and his driver jumped into the fray, separating the two. The Thai driver placed the carbine once again against Foster's temple. Washington's driver did the same with Anderson.

Both men froze.

Washington chuckled. "Falling out amongst friends? I don't want either of you to move. I'm going to call this in." He turned to his driver, took back his pistol and holstered it, making sure the safety was on. Anderson and Foster weren't going anywhere, not as long as the Thai held his carbine on them.

He spoke to the Thai Captain, explaining what he was going to do and that he was placing him in charge. Since the Captain understood only so much English and Washington only spoke so much Thai he had to get his point across using his hands and pidgin language. The Thai Captain shook his head he understood.

Captain Washington found a wall phone and called the on duty Major at the headquarters of the military police.

It must have been a slow night for within minutes several jeeps surrounded the hanger. Both Thai and US military police were everywhere.

All came to a halt when the base commander, Major General Billy Ray Myers walked in. Taking his time he inspected the aircraft and the bags. It was clearly visible he was pissed. It was one thing to find drugs on an individuals, but to find his aircraft being used as mules was an unforgivable sin.

He walked over to the two airmen, whom had now been well separated and being questioned by the police.

"Which one is Foster?" He asked of Washington.

"He's over there sir."

He walked over to Foster, and knelt in front of him. "Your father named Wallace?"

"Yes sir."

"Damn, I was hoping against hope it wasn't you. You don't remember me do you son?"

"No sir, other than the pictures in the HQ, sir."

The General snorted. "Your daddy and I went to Texas A&M together. Married the prom queen, he did. I had to settle for the runner up. Didn't matter, we were good friends. What the hell were you thinking son? You don't need the money. Your daddy's got enough money to buy a small Texas town."

Foster didn't say anything.

"Well son I wish I could help you, but the evidence is very clear as to what was going on thanks to Captain Washington. My regret in this matter is that I'll have to inform your parents. A task I know that is going to break their hearts."

"Sir, I wasn't doing anything. I just happened to come into the hanger as the Captain yelled for us to put our hands into the air."

Now it was the General's turn not to say anything. He shook his head, stood and walked over to Washington.

"Great job Captain. I'll see that you get a commendation for this."

"I'm not interested in a commendation sir. Just doing my job."

The General snorted, shook his head and walked out of the hanger, followed by his entourage.

A MONTH later, Airmen Foster and Anderson were sentenced to 5-years hard labor at Ft. Leavenworth, Kansas. Airman's Foster's parents pulled strings and Sam only served two years. His records were later "lost." He received a General Discharge.

Airman Anderson served his full term. His records were sent to the National Military Archive center in St. Louis, Missouri. He received a Dishonorable Discharge.

CHAPTER I

McCHORD Air Force base, Tacoma, Washington – March 2012

McCHORD AFB, like all other military airfields take a very dim view of non-military aircraft busting their airspace, regardless if the aircraft in question is a military warbird. Due to the present wars in Afghanistan and Iraq, C-17's Globemaster III military transports are landing and taking off day and night.

There also might be an occasional fighter or two.

On their radar screens, traffic controllers were watching an unidentified aircraft heading their way. Actually they had an idea what it was, but communications with the Vietnam era Rockwell OV-10 Bronco Observation aircraft had been lost. They also knew it was being piloted by a retired US Marine Corp. pilot, which had filed a flight plan for nearby Tacoma Narrows, but the aircraft was well off the mark and too far south, thus heading towards McChord.

SeaTac (Seattle – Tacoma) Air Traffic Control was initially monitoring the aircraft, but when they could not reestablish communications, they alerted McChord, which took over.

"Inbound Bronco seven seven niner niner please be advised you are entering restricted military airspace."

Nothing.

"Inbound Bronco seven seven niner niner, this is restricted military airspace. Change course heading to 330 degrees magnetic."

Nothing.

"Sir, this guy isn't changing, what should I do?" The Airman First Class asked his superior.

"Let's get an alert going. We know this is not an attack, but you can't be so sure nowadays."

"Yes Sir."

Within seconds of being notified, two Humvee's loaded with armed Air Force Security personal were screaming towards the runway.

The fire station had also been put on alert, and two fire trucks took off as well. An official reception committee had been formed to greet the intruder, and followed the AFS Humvee's.

Based on the information they had been given, it was apparent the unknown aircraft was most likely headed for runway 19. One Humvee of AFS unloaded about halfway down the runway and the next about 2/3rd of the way down. The reception committee was halfway in between.

With the naked eye the aircraft could not be seen so the controllers were sending updates on the aircraft's whereabouts as the cloud cover was low, threatening more rain.

Soon they could hear the aircraft over the background noises from local Interstate highway traffic and finally they began to make out the navigation lights of an aircraft in the general vicinity.

Within seconds the aircraft wasn't all that hard to see as the pilot turned on the landing lights.

With perfect precision, the aircraft landed and waited. The pilot started the shutdown procedures and feathered the propellers.

Someone had forgotten to tell the reception committee that the Bronco is a STOL or short takeoff and landing aircraft.

It had only taken up 600 feet of runway.

The reception committee had to regroup and travel back up the runway for its greeting: a somewhat embarrassing situation.

This time the AFS airmen, weapons across their chest, but relaxed, encircled the aircraft as the pilot popped the canopy side doors, pretending that she had not seen the screw up.

Striding towards her was Major Anthony Kenny.

Trying to bite her tongue and keep from smiling, she heard him yell, "I hope you have a good explanation for landing here."

"I do sir," she said saluting. "I lost some of my communication and navigation equipment. My GPS gave me McChord as the best backup airport and I really felt it was better to land here and take my punishment than try at the Narrows. I wasn't sure what emergency services would have been available."

The pilot unfastened her harnesses and climbed down.

"Why didn't you declare an emergency?"

"I tried sir, but I realized I had lost all communications and my options at that point were limited."

"Who the hell are you?

"Celina Majewski, US Marine Corp Retired, sir!"

"You're a Marine Corp pilot?

"Was sir. Captain"

"Where in the hell are you taking this aircraft?"

"To an Air Museum in Texas. At least that was what my initial plans were sir."

"Major. You'd better take a look at this," one of the AFS said.

"Just a second son."

"Sir, I think you'd better take a look at this now."

Major Kenny and Captain Celina turned to see what was so important for a Senior Airman to disrupt their conversation.

He was standing next to the nose of the Bronco and from the front, just below the bulge in the forward section; a fine white powder was cascading to the ground.

The Airman was pointing to it.

"What the hell is that?"

"I have no idea sir."

Both walked over to inspect it. Having seen the substance before, Major Kenny drew his weapon, taking the safety off. "Mam, do not move. Place your hands on your head and get down on your knees. You are under arrest." He ordered. The sound of the safety coming off of the Major's weapon was a signal to the rest of the Airmen to bring their weapon up to the ready.

Celina, slow to obey as she too knew what the powder was; was in shock. She was quickly surrounded and forced to the ground by two AFS personal; her hands forced behind her back and flex-cuffed. Her chin rested on the rough asphalt as she was searched. The searching and rough treatments were of secondary concerns. She could not take her eyes off of the powder as her mind was screaming, "What have I gotten myself into?"

CHAPTER II

EAST OF INDIANAPOLIS AT 15,000 FEET – May, 2012

GENERAL Richard "Hannibal" Washington, USAF (ret.) had no idea what was going on, but whatever it was, it had to be bad. At 15,000 feet sucking oxygen through his mask covered face, his mount, an aging Northrop T-38A *Talon* was sick. Where, he was not sure. There were no warning lights, yet something was not right. Looking at his instruments once again, everything appeared to be functioning correctly.

Below was the town of Richmond, Indiana, sitting on the state line dividing Indiana and Ohio - right smack dab in the middle of corn and soybean fields. Only, Richard "Hannibal" Washington could not see them. It was 22:00 hours, or 10:00 P.M., so he only saw the jewels of the lights far below forming parallel lines on streets. Interstate 70, just north of the city was highlighted with circles of lights for the entrance and exit to an unseen black ribbon running east and west. To the west, there were several smaller jewels of light and then a large cluster of glowing jewels. That would be Indianapolis.

"Indianapolis Center, Coyote T-38."

"Coyote T-38, Indianapolis Center."

"Indianapolis Center, Coyote T-38, is with you at flight level 15, showing 65 miles east GPS of Indianapolis, with information Whiskey." Information Whiskey is information transmitted about the airport condition; the weather and is commonly referred to as ATIS. Pilots entering into a controlled airspace are required to have listened to it.

"Roger Coyote T-38. We have you at flight level 15 - 65 miles east of Indianapolis. What are your intentions?"

"Indianapolis Center got a bit of a problem here. Requesting permission to make a precautionary landing at Indianapolis International."

"Coyote T-38 are you declaring an emergency?"

Good question, Hannibal thought. What if there wasn't a problem. The paper work would be a nightmare. But then what if there was?

"Negative Indianapolis Center. I'm not sure what the problem is so I'm not declaring an emergency at this time, but request permission to enter the Indianapolis TCA for landing at Indianapolis International where I can have someone go over this old bird."

"Roger, Coyote T-38. Squawk-Ident four-zero-five-zero, and stay this frequency." (Squawk-Ident means to enter the numbers given by Air Traffic Control into a special box called a transponder. The "Ident" portion means the pilot is to press a button on the black box, which will make his/her aircraft stand out on radar. Since the T-38 was an older aircraft, it did not have Mode-S capabilities as modern aircraft, thus everything was entered manually.)

"Roger Indianapolis, Squawk-Ident four-zero-five-zero, stay this frequency."

Looking once again at his instruments and running tests, Hannibal could still not find anything wrong. "Maybe I'm being silly," he thought. Maybe it was due to missing the woman he had fallen in love with. She had to leave for Washington, DC as she was an FBI agent. Later she would be heading to Korat, Thailand; a place where he had served a long time ago. But he had no time to reflect on that as his immediate thoughts were his feelings of something was very wrong with the aircraft.

NORTHROP'S T-38 *Talon*, is a twin-seat advanced trainer used by the Air Force. It is a twin-engined, sharp winged, lightweight aircraft. It is capable of supersonic flight and was used by the Air Force for advanced pilot training. It is also used by NASA to ferry astronauts across the country and at one-time, used as the USAF Thunderbird Aerobatic team.

Normally a T-38 does not rust in an Air National Guard hangar, but is sent to the large US military storage center in the Arizona desert to await its faith. This one had a long history of service problems. So it was decided rather than let it age in the desert, it was best to place it on display to some deserving organization or museum. Also not normal for this aircraft was the mounting of Sidewinder missiles on the outboard wingtips.

Hannibal had obtained a special ferry permit to make the final light to the air museum in Texas. The T-38 is a trainer, not a warrior. Its cousin, the F-5 Tigershark was a fighter. Since this was to be a display showing the aggressive role; Sidewinder missiles with their working parts, including the explosives, were removed and the missiles mounted onto the outboard hard-points of the wings.

THE DAY BEFORE was to have been the start of a vacation for General Richard "Hannibal" Washington, USAF (ret.). His soon to be employers, headquartered in Ft. Worth Texas, were a group of Texas military aviation veterans.

As a Captain, Hannibal had flown F-105 Thunderchief *Wild Weasel* missions in Vietnam from a base in Korat, Thailand. Due to an unforeseen incident with some ants, he transferred to F-4's due to a change in mission profiles. Later, as a Lt. Colonel, he flew *Wild Weasel* missions in Gulf War I but from a different aircraft, the Phantom II F-4G's.

He retired with full honors and now he flew a desk.

The company, Advanced Aircraft Restorations (AAR), hired him as a ferry pilot. The fact that he was black didn't matter. One look at his logbooks told them all they needed to know. But it also helped that AAR had heard of Hannibal from other pilots. Anyone who flies *Wild Weasel* missions for as long as he had has got to be damn good.

Wild Weasel missions, developed during the Vietnam era, were designed to force the enemy to paint U.S. fighter aircraft with their radar. The *"Wild Weasels"* usually worked in Hunter-Killer teams of F-4 Phantoms and thus flew right down to the source of the signal; dropping bombs, missiles, or whatever; destroying it. Meanwhile the rest of the teams were all over the sky dodging missiles that may have been launched at them. Living another day took a combination of luck, skill and guts.

Months before his retirement he had gotten itchy feet and wanted to get back into the air where it was thin and you could almost see the curvature of the earth. It so happened AAR had received a call for an immediate ferry flight of a T-38 from Wright-Patterson AFB in Ohio to Ft. Worth's Naval Air Station, Texas, where it would be placed on static display in a museum. Hannibal was the man chosen for the flight.

CHAPTER III

Oliver, British Columbia – Two weeks before

JT was deep in thought. Before him was a customer's PC, and it was a very sick puppy. Although JT suspected it to be a worm, it didn't act like one. Nor did it act like it was spyware. He had run all of the diagnostics, to include an Internet online diagnostic. It didn't add up.

JT owned a hanger out at the airport and that is where his shop was, but he also made house calls. His business office was not all that fancy, but he made enough to pay the bills and then some. His wife Pamela worked too, so they weren't too bad off. They each had hobbies; his was aviation and hers, curling, skiing, watching and/or attending hockey games.

She loved the cold.

JT hated it and looked forward to the lazy days of summer; otherwise just plain warmth would do. Having grown up in Indiana, he was used to the cold. When he lived in Texas he loved every day. British Columbia was a sort of cross between the two. It didn't get as cold, yet in the summer could get just as hot as any Texas town.

During the summer months Pamela ran a houseboat rental center on the lake, along with one of her friends. This was cool because during the Canadian Thanksgivings, several of their friends would get together and rent a houseboat and cruise the several lakes.

JT had been called to this home as the customer owned a business and carried his notebook to and from the office. The customer was afraid that whatever the problem was, he didn't want to infect the other systems.

JT had access from his notebook to the customer's notebook over the Internet using a Microsoft Terminal Server program. No matter how hard he had tried; he could not access the notebook remotely, thus the need to travel to the customer's home.

He had known the customer for several years and in fact his wife and he had helped get his business started. He was trusted to such a degree that he had keys to their home and several other offices and customer homes. The RCMP also got to know him well since he had set off several alarms. It got to the point that if they saw his car near the buildings in question, they'd check to make sure he was OK and leave after a few good natured chuckles and head to the local Tim Horton's donuts shop.

He hadn't been onsite long when his cellphone made a silent buzz. He let it go.

It went to voicemail.

Several minutes later his cellphone buzzed again.

Annoyed he took it off of his belt, "JT's Computer Service" he answered.

"Don't you know how to answer your cell when a long lost buddy is calling?"

"Pardon me. . . Whoa, is this Hannibal?"

"Yep, the one and only."

"What the hell are you doing man? Long time no hear from."

"Well I'm in your neck of the woods, or almost up there looking at an airplane, well a kitplane to build. I'm retiring soon and I want something to keep me busy and also to take me where the fish are."

"Are you down in Chiliwack?"

"Yeah."

"I bet you're at Murphy Aircraft."

"Yep."

A window popped up on the customer's notebook.

"Hey Hannibal how long are you going to be there, can I call you back in a few minutes?"

"Sure, here's my cellphone number."

"That's OK, it came up on my call display. I'm on a service call and I think I'm about ready to wrap it up. I'll call you back in a few."

"OK." The iPhone went dead.

"Oh wow!" JT said.

The program he had been waiting for had finished downloading.

Rebooting the notebook after a few changes to the software; problem solved.

To the customer he said, "Well I better get going. I just received a call from an old friend of mine. He's down in Chiliwack looking at an airplane. Since I have to be down there for a Computer and Electronics Exposition tomorrow, maybe he and I can meet up. It has been a long time since I've heard from him."

Since the customer was under a contract, he did not have to bill them. He packed his tool kit and said bye to the customers, Howard and Rita. Once outside, JT called the number his call display had captured.

"Hey man, what are you really doing in BC?"

"Just as I thought, you're getting old and senile."

"Bite me."

Hannibal ignored him. "Didn't you hear me the first time? I'm buying a plane. I'm going to retire soon and I've accepted a job with a company down near Ft. Worth Naval Air Station. They restore Vietnam era aircraft and put them on display."

"That's cool, but Ft. Worth Naval Air Station? I didn't know Ft. Worth had an NAS. I knew there was one halfway between Dallas and Ft. Worth just off Interstate 30."

"Yeah, you mean Dallas Naval Air Station. You have been away far too long my man. They shut down Carswell Air Force Base and changed it to FT. Worth Naval Air some years ago. Anyway, there is a lot of activity in the aircraft restoration business down there. They even have one company building made to order German Luftwaffe Messerschmitt Me 262jet fighters from World War II."

"Yeah I read about that. So how does this work for you?"

"Well from what I understand, because of my fighter background experience, I'll get a call to go to place XYZ and pick up some old jet; get a one-time ferry permit and fly it down to Texas."

"What about pay; insurance, those things?"

"That is all taken care of. Besides, my retirement takes care of most of my needs. This way I get to fill in the gaps flying aircraft I wished I could have."

"Sounds damn fine if I might say so myself. Say how long you in town?"

"Well I flew into Vancouver yesterday and I'm staying at the Delta Vancouver."

"Yeah, I know where that's located"

"For the past several years I've been reading up on those homebuilt aircraft you've been telling me about in Flying, Kitplanes, and Private Pilot magazine. All of them seem to agree that if you want to go into the outback, then the Murphy Rebel is the one you want to build. So I called them up and they offered me a tour of their facilities. I rented a car, drove up that highway you call the TransCanada, and I had just finished the tour. Pretty nice place and the folks are damned friendly. So I placed an order for a kit to be delivered to my place."

"They had this one monster called the Moose. That thing was big, way more than I needed. The Rebel is just right and the build time is reasonable. The people at AAR said I can have some hanger space to put my plane together and they'd offer any technical advice along the way."

"Damn, and here I was struggling just to get my PZL TS-11 *ISKRA* built by myself."

"You've got a jet Warbird?"

"Yeah, sure."

"Well now, you have come up in the world. I'll have to stop over and you can take me up sometime."

"Ah man, against you, I'd be a bumbling idiot, but sure. Anyway, there's a place in California that sells jet warbirds and imports them as well. They offer advice over the phone or Internet. My other choice was to crate everything up and send it down there. Can you imagine what Pamela would have done?"

Hannibal smiled at the image of a ranting and raging Pamela, a wagging index finger extended at JT· about spending money needlessly.

"Hey, tell you what. I'll be down there for this Computer Convention thing tomorrow and I'll call you when I get there and maybe we can get something to eat if you have time; maybe a Red Robin."

"What the hells a Red Robin?"

"Well it a very nice chain of restaurants. They have huge burgers; big screen televisions everywhere and they play top-40 music."

"Sounds like a plan to me. I can't wait to see you again. Is Pamela coming down too?"

"Naw, she can't get away. She is going to flip out when she finds out you're here and she won't be able to see you."

"Ah man, it would be nice to see her again. Oh well, I guess I'll see you tomorrow then."

"Yeah, I'll call you when I get there. It will most likely be late afternoon before I see you as the Convention starts at 9 AM."

"OK, I'll be expecting you."

Later, when JT arrived home, "You'll never guess who called."

"The Prime Minister."

"No, it was the President. He wanted me to be his Secretary of Information Technology. I told him I was busy."

"Hah!" Pamela said, "In your dreams."

"Thanks for your support." JT walked up behind her, giving her petite ass a quick squeeze and a kiss on the neck. "Hannibal called." He whispered in her ear.

Nearly taking his head off, she whipped around, "He did? Where is he? What is he doing? Has he met anyone yet?"

"Stop!"

"Yes, Vancouver - well Chiliwack, buying an airplane, and I don't know in that order."

"Buying an airplane? For what?"

JT bent down to get a soft drink out of the bottom compartment of the fridge. A hand smacked his ass.

"Do that again and we'll miss dinner."

"You started it. What's the matter? Can't take what you're giving/"

JT watched as she mocked him with her hands on her hips. Her skirt slightly askew; tanned legs ending in feet encased in sandals. Her top made it clear she didn't have a bra underneath. Her face was in a pout.

He felt the beginning of an erection so he changed the subject.

"Well he said he was retiring and wanted to go fishing, but he took a job with a company in Ft. Worth flying airplanes to an air museum. They said he could use their hanger space. Anyway, he was at Murphy

Aircraft, the place I had shown you when we were down there visiting your relatives. He bought a Murphy Rebel kit."

"So is he going home now?"

"No. He's in Vancouver for what sounded like a few days. I told him I was going down for that computer convention. He was really ecstatic. I guess I am too as we haven't seen him for so long."

"Oh damn, and I have to work tomorrow. I'll have to see if I can get off the day after. I'd hate to miss him."

"Yes, well I think he'd be upset if he didn't see you too."

"I'm going to get dinner ready while you pack. Are you flying or driving down?"

"Driving. Let the Jag stretch its legs, blow the carbon out."

"Yeah and get another speeding ticket."

"Naw. I know where they hide."

"Yeah, sure you do. If that was so, how did you get the one in Revelstoke last month?"

"You knew about that?"

"You forget I do your books."

"Uh . . OK. So I got one, but he cheated. Honest! He was in a blacked out car in front of me. He started slowing up and when I went to pass; he put on the lights and pulled me over. He had suckered me!"

"Yeah, right."

"Honest. Boy Scouts honor." JT said holding up his right hand in the Boy Scout salute.

"Go get packed."

CHAPTER IV

THE NEXT MORNING, bright and early, JT showered; put on his traveling clothes, gave Pamela a kiss on her head as she was still asleep, or so he thought. She said, "Have a good trip, and no speeding tickets."

JT snorted, put everything into the Jag's trunk, which wasn't that big, and eventually found himself on highway 97 south, to Osoyoos; catching highway 3 west to Hope, BC and then the Trans Canada to Vancouver.

In Hope he had filled up as the big V-12 engine does not pass very many gas stations. He could actually watch the needle move.

Hope, British Columbia is at the top of the Frasier Valley; still in the winding Trans Canada Mountains but once past there it is flat, level and almost straight stretch until Chiliwack, or about 30 kilometers away.

JT punched the accelerator near a tractor trailer weight station.

The Jag jumped as if it had been scolded; the speedometer hitting 220 km/H in seconds.

The sunroof was open, making a howling noise.

At the end of the weigh station, in the median is a stand of trees; the RCMP were waiting.

A uniformed officer jumped out in a bright yellow vest with red stripes, hand held high. Another one was directing JT were to pull over.

"Ah damn! Pamela going to be so pissed."

Due to his speed he had stopped well beyond the area where they had been hiding. He waited for the Constable to catch up, the necessary documents in hand with the window rolled down.

"I guess you know you were speeding."

"Yes sir."

"What's the hurry?"

"No excuse. I was just a little excited to get the Jag out as it has been stored and needed to stretch its legs."

The Constable hesitated a few second before taking JT's extended documents. He then walked back to his cruiser, punching the information in on his console mounted notebook.

JT waited. No doubt about this one. The fine was going to be huge. Pamela would freak out.

In his rearview mirror he saw that the Constable was obviously finishing his write up and soon the door opened; the Constable exited, walking towards him.

"Mr. Travis, I've reduced your speed to 120 K, or just 20 K over the limit. Be careful next time. Sign here." The ticket, his driver's license and insurance were handed back.

He signed the ticket with relish. "Thank you Constable."

"Have a nice day."

JT put the ticket in his wallet, refastened his seatbelt, took a look in his rearview mirror and inched back onto the highway. The rest of the trip was done at 105K. Over the limit, but not enough to be stopped.

It could have been worse.

CHAPTER V

JT arrived and checked into a hotel. He then attended his advanced Computers and Electronics conference that was taking place in a building near Vancouver International Airport. During one of the breaks he crossed Inglis road and walked down to the restaurants alongside the river.

There he saw two Asian women also standing outside watching the Harbour Air Seaplanes Dehavillland Twin-Otters land on the river and taxi to the floating service stations next to the restaurants.

Being married didn't mean he couldn't take in the view; and what a view it was.

The one that looked Chinese was dressed in a black business pants suit, low heeled pumps, and her dark brown hair with lighter tints, was blown around her face by the prop blast from the aircraft. She wore dark brown tinted sunglasses. If she wore makeup, JT couldn't tell from this distance. Her friend wore a dark business skirt, and cream colored blouse. She wasn't wearing stockings. Her feet were also encased in what must have been 2" black heels. Her jet-black hair was also being blown, but not as bad as it was shorter.

He pretended to turn away from the blast, but this was only to allow him a better perspective of the landscape.

Once the aircraft departed, the two women walked back up the wooden steps; back to the building they had come from. JT didn't miss a step.

When he arrived back at the hotel after his conference, he called Hannibal and asked to meet for dinner. They would meet at a local Tex-Mex restaurant on Bridgeport Road, which he thought was about as close to real Tex-Mex as he would ever get.

Anthony Parran

At the restaurant, he stood by the door waiting for Hannibal. A car pulled up with a rental sticker on it and from the silhouette he knew who it was, went outside to give Hannibal a hug.

"Damn you look good man."

"You ain't bad looking yourself. I see Pamela must be feeding your poor raggedy ass."

"Hah, you're just jealous." They both laughed.

They went inside where they waited to be seated. Hannibal asked, "So what kind of food do they serve in here?"

"The menu is on the wall back there, but when I'm here I always get their ribs, baked beans, garlic mashed potatoes and believe it or not, they serve real cornbread."

"Real cornbread? In here? In Canada?"

"Yep. They call it Johnny cakes here, but brother; it is just as good as home style."

"Well this is definitely my kind of place."

A waitress came over, "Is it just the two of you?"

"Yes"

She took them around a column and up a flight of four stairs. "Will this be OK?"

"Yes, but how about that table next to the rail?" JT pointed.

"Sure. Can I bring you anything to drink?"

"I'll take a Rum and Coke. Hannibal will have . . "

"What kind of beer do you have?"

"Kokanee, Molson, Labatt's, and Coors light,"

"I'll take the Coors light."

"Make mine a Rum and Coke double; no fruit please."

"Sure, no fruit." The waitress left.

"I hear this Canadian beer has more alcohol in it." Hannibal said. I can do without a headache."

"Not true my man. Canadian's like to think that way, but it ain't true."

A waiter appeared with their drinks and a bowl of Nachos and two small bowls of thick Salsa. Picking up a chip, dipping it into the sauce, JT had turned just enough to see two women enter the main door; the same two Asian women he had seen earlier.

They hadn't changed clothes.

JT tapped Hannibal on the arm, "Hey man, see those two women? I saw them at the float plane service next to the airport. Man if I wasn't a married man, I'd be all over that."

Hannibal turned to see where JT was pointing. They both followed them, as they were seated . . . right next to them.

JT was trying not to stare but what the hell.

It was obvious Hannibal liked what he saw too. Over the years he had had a few arms' length relationships, but the military had been his wife. The more he looked at the Chinese woman, the more he fantasized.

'Nah, no way. She's got to be married.' He wondered what her husband looked like. Most likely she drove a Lexus or a Bentley; maybe even a Rolls-Royce.

'She's way out of my league.' He thought. The Chinese woman took off her sunglasses, shook her head, running her hands through her hair before twisting it and placing it on her back.

A waitress appeared; the same one that had taken their drink order. She took theirs as well.

JT and Hannibal were so busy trying not to be so obvious, they didn't see the waiter asking if they were ready to order their dinner.

They placed their orders and then turned their attention back to the table where the women were as their waiter had also taken theirs.

As the evening progressed they relived old times and eventually ran out of steam.

"Hey, let's see if they want to join us."

"You're a married man JT."

"So, I'm not asking them to go to bed. Besides I think the Chinese one likes you."

"Hah!"

JT bet the other woman to be either Thai or Philippine as her skin was darker. They giggled like school girls as they whispered messages back and forth.

"What's the harm Hannibal? I'm going to get those ladies to join us."

"Their old man's gonna come in; see them with us and we'll get our asses kicked. I haven't been in a bar fight in a long time."

"I bet they're not with anybody. I bet they're lonely."

"Not those two. Man I bet they have husbands with gold Rolls and 30-room mansions, at least the Chinese one."

"Trust me. A dollar says they're alone,"

"You're on." Hannibal pulled out an American dollar, placed it on the table and JT pulled out a Canadian Loonie. "I'll give you the difference in exchange later if I lose, but I ain't."

Getting up his nerve, JT stood, walked over to the table, placed his hands together in prayer; the thumbs placed just at chest level, bowed from the waist and said. "**Sawasdee**," the traditional Thai greeting. He then turned to the Chinese looking woman and said hello in "Ne Haw." And to both, "My name is JT."

"Hello to you too." The Chinese looking woman said. "I don't speak Mandarin. I speak Cantonese. Nice try anyway."

"Darn. Sorry."

The women giggled.

The Thai woman said, "Hello you. Where you learn speak Thai?"

"I was stationed in Thailand, actually we both were. I was in the US Army. My friend there, Hannibal, was in the Air Force, and that is where we met."

"You speak other languages?" The Thai woman asked.

"Oh God, here we go." Hannibal said, placing his arms on the table; burying his head.

"Well, let's see, I can speak Russian, Dutch and Spanish." JT said with a grin.

"Are you some sort of linguist?"

"No, not really. I took high school Spanish. I learned Thai in Thailand. Many years ago I was on one of those Russian dating sites and thought if I learned Russian, I would be able to attract a nice woman if she thought I had gone the extra mile to learn her language."

"Were they?" Cindy asked.

"One or two were.   The Mandarin and Dutch I took to keep my mind fresh.   I'm not really all that good and found if I don't have anyone to practice with on a daily basis, I forget a lot."

"Well you did very well." The Thai woman said.

That got a wide grin on his face, so he decided to press his luck.

"Are you finished showing off?" Hannibal asked.

JT ignored him. "Hey, are you guys alone?"

"Well, we're together so we're not alone, but if you're asking if we are meeting other people, then the answer is no," said the Chinese one. "And we're not married." They both giggled again.

"Well in that case, my name is JT or Jerome, and this is Richard, but I call him Hannibal. You know after the dude that was a General during the Roman days."

"Hello Hannibal" They answered in unison.

"And you are?"

"I am Abby. If I told you my real name, you'd only mess it up."

"Well let me at least try. I could speak Thai pretty good at one time." JT said

"OK, it's Pattanapongtak Apsara."

JT thought for a second. "Hello Abby," and put his hand out.

Everyone laughed.

JT turned and said, "And you?"

"I am Cynthia - Cynthia Ng. Can you pronounce that?"

"Let me think, Nah, so I'll just call you Cindy"

They laughed again.

"Well Cindy and Abby, I'll be honest. I'm married, but Hannibal's here is free. He looks mean but in truth he's a kitty-cat. I'll put a leash on him if you'll join us at our table, or we can pull the tables together."

JT looked at Hannibal as he put his right hand up to his head; away from the women with middle finger extended and pretended to scratch his head.

JT in turn, placed his hands behind his back; middle finger extended.

"We'd really like your company."

"You two look harmless enough. Besides, I'm an FBI agent, trained in the arts of kicking ass if you get out of line. She's a special agent with the Thai police force and teaches Thai Kick Boxing in her spare time."

"If I may say so, Hannibal and I were commenting on how great the two of you looked," said JT.

"Kop Khun Mock," said Abby, her head slightly bowed, which means thank you very much.

JT caught Hannibal staring at Cindy, taking her in as if he was . . . 'I'll be damn, he really likes her!'

A smile came to JT's face and said, "You're kidding, right? I mean about the Thai Kick Boxing thing and you being an FBI agent."

"No."

"Assistant Special-Agent-in-Charge."

"So why are the two of you together?"

"Why do you think we were at that conference JT?"

"I don't know. What conference?" He answered.

"Tell you what, we'll sit at your table and tell you. But afterwards we'll have to shoot the both of you."

JT snorted, but he and Hannibal moved the tables closer together.

Once they had the tables moved and the plates rearranged, Cindy sat beside Hannibal and Abby beside JT.

"Have you ever heard of Roxanne?"

Both shook their heads no, but JT started singing, *"ROXANNE,"* imitating Eddie Murphy, which caused a few heads to turn.

"I guess that means you don't know," she said.

"No."

Abby began to explain, "The street name for a new type of cocaine entering the US is called Roxanne. Roxanne is 80% pure. Nothing like it has been seen before. It sells far below street price. If that was not bad enough, it has been seen on Native American reservations."

"Just a second." JT held up his hand.

Their waiter was hailed; he ordered a fresh round of drinks, but not before JT reached over and took his Loonie and the American dollar, which magically disappeared into his pocket.

Cindy said, "I saw you checking us out at the float plane docks. You obviously liked what you saw."

"Shit! I must be getting old. OK, I wasn't that obvious was I?"

"Well, your tongue was hanging out. Were we deserts or midnight snacks?"

Now it was Hannibal's turn to laugh.

"Both, , , neither, , , uh, , in another time maybe, but as I said I'm married. My marriage gets a little stormy now and then, but I love her. So I'm harmless."

Their conversation was interrupted as their meals were placed before them.

When the waiter left, Cindy said "OK, Mr. Harmless and Mr. Kitty-Cat, now that we're here. Who won the bet?" Hannibal pointed a finger at JT.

"You mean you've been checking me, uh, us out too?"

"Yep."

"Well I'll be damned."

"Put your chest back in JT."

"I have to ask one question Cindy," said Hannibal.

"Go ahead."

"Do you drive a Lexus or a Rolls?"

"Neither."

"A Bentley?"

"I wish. I drive a used Honda S2000 convertible. Why do you ask?"

"When I first saw you by the door, I swore that someone as attractive as you drove nothing less."

"Did you make a bet on that too Hannibal?"

"Naw, just a thought."

For the rest of the night they laughed and talked about where they'd been, grew up and all the things people do when they first meet. It was obvious Cindy was taken by Hannibal as he told her about his flying exploits.

JT told them about his, but it was obvious Hannibal was the star.

Another thing that became obvious was that they all felt comfortable with each other, and laughter was easy. JT ventured and asked Abby about her Thai police career.

"I join police. Never knew father well. He Amelican, but sent Guam. He write mother. Send money. He say he trying to get back Thailand, but have to re-enlist. He say he was tired what he see; GI numba Sip Loy (1,000). He no like how GI always mean to Thai."

"Yeah, I know." JT said. "I saw the same thing when I was over there. Dudes would be strung so far out; you needed a rod and reel to bring them back in. I once came upon a dude smoking what looked like a cigarette. I must have scared the shit out of him when I said hi. He jumped about ten-feet in the air, throwing the cigarette down. When he discovered I wasn't an officer or Top (First Sergeant), he gave me shit about sneaking up on him."

"We had another dude that refused to fall in formation. When we marched to work, we'd see him sitting in the middle of a baseball diamond, in his own world, after downing some 'Reds.' Nobody, including the officers, bothered him. That's when I knew it was time to get out."

It got quiet as everyone reflected on this.

JT continued. "Then there was the time right after TET, they sent all of the Vietnam burnouts to our company. I heard a couple of guys talking about putting a grenade under the CO's bunk. Thank God, nothing became of it. I asked one of them why they would do that. He said that they were pissed off about the morning formations, which they didn't have in Nam. So I said, 'What about getting caught?' He said, 'So what? What are they going to do? Send me back to Nam?'"

"That did it for me."

There was about 30-seconds of silence before Abby continued, "Father said he going to get out, start business. We wait. No hear, He never write again. Mother brave woman. I see she broken heart. He became past. With the money he sent before leaving, mother send me best school. I always around military base, I like uniform. Join police. Promoted to Narcotics Suppression Bureau. I sent here Vancouver. Meet Cindy."

Hannibal said, "I saw the same thing overseas, but although we knew some of the enlisted and an officer or two smoked, if they were caught they were gone, no questions asked. High explosives, jet aircraft and aviation fuel just don't mix with weed. I was involved with a minor drug bust. We caught them before most of the drugs left base. Otherwise, I stayed in. Got promoted a couple of times, and recently retired. I've been traveling around to the various schools in low income neighborhoods getting underprivileged kids motivated. I saw what motivated them and it wasn't aviation, or careers at some executive office."

"It was the bling-bling; gold chains, gangsta Rap, big Bentley's and big guns. And yes, there were the drugs. I thought we had cut the supply lines when they busted all those cartel guys in the south. There must be a new supplier in town, cause these kids are still gettin high."

Cindy and Abby gave each other knowing looks.

Hannibal continued. "Gettin old. Thought I'd like to have kids someday and watch them grow up in a quiet neighborhood without all the worry of this crap. Glad I didn't." He looked down at the table as he gave the speech. You could tell he was very passionate about it, which did not escape Cindy's trained eye.

Cindy said, "The thing is, this stuff is so cheap. Why? What is the purpose? It is bound to cause an all-out war on the streets. Forget the prohibition Era Gangsters. That would pale in comparison. That is why Abby and I are here. The new drug; Roxanne is even coming through Native and Aboriginal reservations from overseas." The conference we were attending was attended by several police agencies from Canada, the US and Abby represented Thailand. We're just trying to put intelligence together. Oh you still have your Afghanistan and south of the border stuff, but this stuff is finding places where it has never been marketed before."

"That's a joke, right?" Said Hannibal. "Natives dealing drugs?"

"It's true. My brother died from a drug overdose." Cindy replied quietly.

There were several awkward seconds of silence.

"Wait, you said the drugs were coming in from Thailand? You know the drug bust I was involved in comprised of a couple of Airmen stuffing drugs in the electronics bay of aircraft. But we busted them good. No way could they still be in operation."

Cindy looked at her manicured hands, changing the subject, Cindy said, "So how did you two meet? Isn't it odd for an Air Force officer to make friends with a US Army NCO?"

JT and Hannibal looked at each other, "Go ahead Hannibal."

Hannibal thought for a second, "One of the passing rights of a fighter pilot during Vietnam was when he completed his 100 missions over Nam. The pilot would return; do barrel rolls over the field, ending in a zoom climb. One day when a friend of mine had completed his 100th mission in an F-105 Thunderchief fighter/bomber, he started his roll over the base at low altitude, only he crashed inverted. There was a large explosion and a fireball. The pilot was a buddy of mine and without thinking, I ran towards the burning aircraft."

"Yeah," JT interrupted. "I was in the can, uh, , latrine when that explosion went off. We thought a huge bomb had been dropped on the ordinance area south of us. The walls of the barracks actually swayed from the shockwave. As Hannibal will tell you, when an aircraft returns from Nam with bombs that they had not dropped over the target, they can't land due to the weight restrictions. It would snap the landing gear. So they drop them in this area set aside about a mile away from the US Army side of the base."

"We thought one had fallen too close to the barracks. Everyone ran outside. I ran pulling my pants up and outside we all looked towards the drop zone. Then somebody yelled, 'Over there! Over at the air base!' We turned and there was this large black column of smoke. I ran back inside, grabbed my camera; jumped into the duty jeep and took off."

"Normally we would have been denied entrance for something like this, but I had arrived before the barricades went up. Just parallel to the runway and behind some hootches, I jumped out and ran. There I saw a guy running towards the burning aircraft. That was Hannibal."

"At first I thought he was going to just stop and let the firefighters take over, but he kept going, yelling. I ran an intercept path and tackled him. I had to hold him down. He kept trying to push me off. Finally he gave up and started crying. I saw that he was an officer and let him up, but kept a close eye on him. We sat there, in the grass for what seemed like hours as they put out the fire."

"There was this weird, and I mean really ugly helicopter flying around spraying a fire retardant onto it."

"Yeah, that was a Kaman H-43 Huskie. Great helicopter." Hannibal added.

"Well if you ask me, I'd swear that thing was ugly."

Anthony Parran

"Well it may not have won any beauty contests, but it sure did the job."

"Anyway, they pulled the remains of the pilot out and then loaded the burnt out remains of the F-105 onto a flatbed and hauled it away. There was hardly anything left to identify it as a flying machine."

"The pilot was a very good friend. We had gone to the Air Force Academy together. I knew his wife and kids." Hannibal said. "When JT tackled me, it brought me back to my senses. I can't believe I was going to jump into that inferno to save him. I can still smell the burning flesh."

"So after that, Hannibal and I would see each other from time to time. On base he was an officer and I a NCO, but off base we started hitting the same bars, checking out the same women when he was not on a mission over Nam or someplace."

There were several minutes of silence as Hannibal and JT remembered the needless loss of life that day.

"I think it was ruled pilot error, wasn't it Hannibal?"

"I don't remember, but I think so."

"Hey Hannibal! Remember that damned lizard?" JT said changing the subject.

"What lizard? Oh, you mean that Chinchok?"

"Yeah." And they both started laughing.

"What's so funny about a lizard?" Cindy asked.

"What they talk about is Tokay. Amelicans say same-same cursing them."

"Oh?"

Hannibal leaned forward and whispered to JT, "Fuck You!" Softly imitating the sound the Chinchok makes.

They started laughing.

"Fuck you!" JT whispered back, which caused them to laugh even harder.

"Are you guys going to let us in on what's so funny?" Cindy asked.

"Yeah, well . . .anyway this lizard would say, uh, excuse my French, 'Fuck You'" JT said softly so as to not offend the other patrons in the restaurant, trying to stop laughing.

"Not so. All Amerlicans say numba Sip (10)."

"Well that's what it sounded like to me. One night I was going into the barracks and I heard one. Man I thought somebody was hiding and cursing me out, so I started cursing back. Dudes ran outside to see what the commotion was about and I told them. They started laughing; told me about this lizard and went back inside. Not believing them, I yelled, "Fuck you too buddy and your mama!"

Hannibal said, "Yeah, well I was at this mama-sans place and one of those things started up. When I turned to see where it was coming from, the mama-san started laughing and said, 'GI numba ten. Chinchok no like.'"

"Not curse. Barks." Abby said, defending it. She turned to Cindy and said, "Tokay small lizard; can change colors. This brought another round of laughter.

Several tables of customers turned their heads with disapproving looks.

"Keep it down guys." Cindy said. "Do you want to know why we we're really here Hannibal?"

Hannibal and JT shook their head yes.

"Hannibal, sorry but Abby is here because this new drug is coming, from of all places Korat, Thailand.

"Shit. You're kidding right?"

"Solly JT, It's true."

"OK, so how in the world is this stuff getting past customs? You would think the US customs would know all about the routes into the US and would have closed them down many years ago. We don't have a war going on over there anymore so there is no large US military personnel. Do you think the Thai's have reopened a route and a deal with someone in the US?"

Cindy took several seconds before answering. "JT and Hannibal, what I am about to tell you is confidential, well sort of confidential but I'm going to trust you to keep this to yourselves. It is not a Thai operation, but we think that yes, it is a form of US military operation originating from the Royal Thai Air Force (RTAF) base. We think the drugs are somehow placed on military aircraft, and not just any military aircraft. We think it is being brought in on fighter aircraft. But when we inspected the aircraft, we found nothing. We knew it was there, but where? Think about it. How many fighter aircraft returning from overseas are inspected by customs?"

"Ah man, this has the earmarks of what happened a long time ago. That is going to be a big problem."

"Yes Hannibal, big ploblem." Abby holding up her hands spread apart.

"So what are you going to do?"

"I told you I had a brother." Cindy said. "He died of a drug overdose. The thing is he would never have touched the stuff. But lately this high grade cocaine has been finding its way into Native and

Aboriginal reservations. So the question is why and how. What is to be gained? So for now, we have a lot of questions and no answers. So let's just say we're working on it and leave it at that for now."

"I'm hungry. This is way too deep for me and I've had my share of looking for drugs. " Hannibal said, reaching for a Nacho.

For the rest of the night they talked about other things. The more they talked, Cindy and Hannibal were in their own world, and had moved their chairs closer together. A butter knife wouldn't fit between them, let alone a strand of dental floss.

Abby and JT talked and felt comfortable, at least Abby was.

JT was all too aware of her perfume and the expanse of brown legs showing where her dress had crept to above mid-thigh. The effect it was having was bringing back memories of what it was like to be back in Thailand. He didn't want to move his chair away, but at the same time if he moved any closer, well, , , it would be divorce time.

Abby must have picked up on his discomfort and said, "JT, not ask you bed. We flend. Numba one." She patted his hand, which caused the reverse effect as electricity shot through his arm. He turned slightly sideways to hide the fact another part wasn't going to settle for a no.

They fell into a more relaxed conversation. JT was trying out his long forgotten Thai. She was his teacher, until the waiter came to inform them that they would close soon. Hannibal and Cindy didn't hear it.

"Hey you two, it's about closing time." Abby said; tapping Cindy's on the arm.

"Oh," said Cindy and Hannibal, pulling apart.

"Yeah and you two need to find a hotel room." Cindy started to blush and Hannibal looked at JT. 'Well I'll be damn, he's in love.' JT thought. 'Good for him. He needs somebody to look after him. Cindy looks like a good woman.'

The waiter brought their checks. Hannibal threw his matte-black American Express Centurion card on the table. "I'll take care of everything. JT's so poor with a wife and all, I had to loan him that dollar you saw. He's so poor; he only has the two dollars in his pocket. Ask him."

Once again JT put his hand up to his head, middle finger extended.

Everyone laughed.

When the waiter returned with the receipt and card, everyone stood up and walked towards the door. Outside, Hannibal asked the women, "How did you two get here?"

"Cindy have rental."

"I have a rental too."

Turning to Cindy, "Are you ready to go home?"

"Not really, but I have to get up early. Abby and I have one more day of conferences to attend."

"I'm tired," JT said.

"I have emails. Daytime Thailand."

Cindy reached into her purse and gave Abby the rental car keys. "Don't bend the car."

"Wait. Not sure how dlive car. Thailand dlive diffelent "

"That's right," said Hannibal.

"That's OK; I'll take you where you have to go." JT volunteered.

"I stay Holiday Inn."

"Then I definitely had better drive you there. Make one small mistake on the King George road and you'll find yourself at the Canadian and US border. Besides, I'm staying there too."

"You home by one," Abby said to Cindy, laughing.

Abby turned and pointed towards the north asking, "Why that?"

Everyone turned to look where she was pointing.

Hannibal said, "Now that's cool. Maybe it's a bunch of invading UFO's."

JT laughed and said, "No that's Grouse Mountain. It is a ski resort. At night, the lights appear to just float in the air."

"You ski?" Abby asked JT.

"Well one day I wanted to prove that black people could ski. So I went to Silver Star located in Vernon, which is in the interior and tried. I graduated from the basics to the Bunny hill. Just when I thought I had the hang of it, I dislocated my thumb on a ski pole. I haven't been back. Not that I don't want to, I just haven't found the time. I guess one day, like Hockey and Golf, you'll see a black man hitting the slopes too."

"Amen brother." Hannibal added.

They walked to where the cars were parked when Abby asked JT where was his car.

"Right here." He said, pointing to his pride and joy; his 1984 XJ12 Jaguar.

"Oh, that is nice, but it's old." Cindy said.

"It might be old, but I bet I can pull up to a stop light and kids 17-years old know what it is. Not like the new Jags, which look like upscale Fords."

"Amen again to that." Hannibal added.

"JT is it OK to leave my car here? I'll pick it up in the morning."

"I don't see why not. It's parked near the street and under the light, so I guess so, but I wouldn't leave it there too long as it might get towed. When I go to the conference tomorrow morning, I'll check on it."

"Thanks JT," and she gave him a kiss on the cheek.

"Goodnight," they said heading hand-in-hand towards Hannibal's rental. Using the remote he started the car and then unlocked the doors. He escorted Cindy to the passenger's side, opened the door and she got in. As he walked to the driver's side, he changed direction and went over to JT and whispered in his ear.

"Hey man, this has got to be the best day of my life. I wanna thank you."

"Ah man, don't go getting sentimental on me. You deserve it."

Hannibal leaned over and gave Abby a kiss on the cheek. "I hope to see you again," he said.

"We numba one. You see me again," Abby said returning the kiss.

Hannibal turned and got in the car, backed up, illuminating JT and Abby in the backup lights; put it into drive and drove west on Bridgeport Road. They watched as the car disappeared.

He escorted Abby to the Jag and unlike Hannibal, had to open the door manually. She got in and again her dress rode up. JT tried not to stare, but she pretended not to have seen him stare. She didn't make any effort to correct the skirt.

He drove to the hotel and escorted her to her floor.

Standing by her door, she stood on her tip toes giving him a light kiss on the lips. "You numba one. Kop Khun Mock (Thank you very much)." She turned and unlocked her door, stepped inside and just before it closed, blew JT another kiss.

JT stood there for several seconds. "Hell, forget the cold shower. I'm going to jump into the Ocean," he muttered to himself as he rode the elevator to his floor.

In his room as he took off his clothes, his cellphone rang. It was Pamela.

"Hi sweetheart, what's up?"

"How was your day? Did you hook up with Hannibal?"

"Yeah."

"Great. Anyway I called to let you know I'll be down in the morning. I was able to get off. Arlene is going to watch the shop. I'll be on a WestJet flight out of Kelowna and should arrive by 10. Can you pick me up?"

"Oh shit." JT thought, but said, "uh, sure honey. When is your flight again?" JT asked on a higher note.

She gave him the time and flight number again.

"OK honey, I'm glad you can come down. Hannibal will be happy to see you and you're going to be floored."

"About what?"

"What if I told you Hannibal's in love."

"What!"

"Yeah, her name is Cynthia, well Cindy and of all things she's an FBI agent. She has a friend from Thailand named Abby. They're here on some big drug deal."

"An FBI agent? What have you two been up to?"

"Nothing, but tell you what, when I pick you up tomorrow, I'll tell you all about it. You'll probably meet both of them too. They're cute. The one with Hannibal is Chinese. Actually her parents are Native American and Chinese. The two of them hit it off right away and...

Anyway it's too complicated. You'll see why tomorrow. I have never seen him so happy."

"This I'll have to see." She said.

"Seriously, he had love sick puppy dog eyes and everything. Had they gotten any closer last night, they would have set off the sprinkler system."

Pamela laughed at the image of Hannibal in love.

CHAPTER VI

THE NEXT DAY, JT took a quick drive to the restaurant to check on Cindy's car. It was still there and in one piece. He went back to the hotel, hoping to at least get a glimpse of Abby, but she was nowhere to be found. "That's OK," he thought. "Don't need the strain."

He went to the Conference and later took the shuttle bus the short distance to the Westjet arrivals terminal at Vancouver International, where he met Pamela. She was wearing an old style blue jean dress, which for some reason JT liked. It was a plain front-button down affair, but looked always looked great on her which gave good contrast to her tan. She had only a carry-on bag so they didn't have to wait at the baggage return.

Pamela's face brightened when she saw him, which always made him happy from the first day they had met. She kissed him as if he had been gone for ages. Passengers leaving had to walk around them.

They took the shuttle bus back to the hotel.

Taking the elevator up, she stole a kiss when the doors had closed. They were the only passengers. Opening the room door he let Pamela in, placing her things on the spare bed and went to the bathroom. When he came out, Pamela had closed the curtains just enough to cut down on the sunlight that was filtering in, but not enough to be totally dark.

She had undone the top two buttons of her dress revealing a deep tan down to her breast. She was sitting in a chair facing him; her head slightly cocked to one side resting on two extended fingers. Her elbow was resting on the little table beside the chair. There was enough light that he could see her blue-grey eyes. She was teasing him by batting her long dark lashes with a very devious smile on her face.

She had also spread her legs; feet still in her favorite sandals, revealing beautifully tanned legs ending in white panties.

JT never made it back to the Convention.

Later when they had showered and toweled off, JT called Hannibal's hotel room and made arrangements to meet him and Cindy downstairs. Cindy had retrieved her car that morning; picking up Abby as well. Hannibal said he'd call Cindy on her Sat-Phone and maybe the five of them could meet some place.

Hannibal called back and they decided a trip to Vancouver Island on a ferry would make a great day out.

SINCE HANNIBAL had the larger car, everyone piled in. The three women were in back with JT up front. JT couldn't help but smile as the three sounded like magpies and old friends. They were getting along so well. Hannibal must have been thinking the same as he put his hand out below the dividing console and gave him a low five.

JT directed him towards the parking lot just before the Tsawwassen Bay Ferry dock. It was an all-day lot. To take the car across to Victoria is very expensive, especially for one day. From the lot they took a shuttle bus. Hannibal wanted to take the car, but JT convinced him it was much more fun and he need not worry about it. Besides, he said, you get to see more of the countryside.

As they were walking up the ramp to the ferry, Pamela deliberately slowed her walk, thus forcing JT to slow his as well.

Then the claws came out.

"Ow! Ow! Ow!" JT howled in pain. Pamela had grabbed his right wrist with her left hand and with her right, dug her fingernails into the web between his thumb and forefinger.

"Ow!"

"Abby's attractive JT. Did you screw her?"

"No! Ow! Let go!" He yelped.

Hannibal, Cindy and Abby stopped to see what JT was howling about.

Abby hearing the exchange came to JT's defense by jumping between them, breaking Pamela's grip; putting her arms around them both. "JT numba one. He tell me he happily mallied. He escort me room. Make sure I safe. I give him kiss on cheek."

Pamela looked at her and then at him. "Honest. That's all I did."

"Just checking. I told him you're very attractive. Maybe I got a little jealous."

"You're still number one in my life honey." And he gave her a kiss.

"I'd better be."

A nervous laugh went around.

As the ferry made its way to the island, Hannibal and Cindy went outside and sat on the deck in the sun. It was windy, but where they were sitting they were sheltered by the solid rail. All they felt was the sun. Besides they were in their own world.

JT, Pamela and Abby strode the decks and had a small snack in the cafeteria. Then they too went outside into the bright sunlight and watched as ferries leaving the Island were going the other way.

The ferry wove between smaller islands and they could see exotic homes hidden behind trees.

Once unloaded at the dock, they took the shuttle bus to Victoria, the capital of British Columbia.

The day was spent walking down the streets looking into antique shop windows and for lunch sat on a patio where they could see floatplane after floatplane coming in, landing between the boats.

Later they took a Whale Watching tour boat ride. Hannibal and Cindy sat on the rear seats, again in their own little world. Abby and Pamela couldn't stop talking, so JT went topside and sat next to the boat captain. In the background he heard the radio chatter from the other tour boat captains trying to get into the position to see the Whales. Where he was sitting he could see Cindy and Hannibal and felt like a parent watching their children about to leave home, sprouting their own wings. It was obvious Hannibal was head over heels about her. Hell she was head over heels about him.

The boat appeared to pick up speed and behind them another tour boat was coming up in their wake. This was a boat designed for the more adventuresome people. It was a Zodiac with seating for about 15 – 20; open to the elements. They were all wearing bright orange floatation gear and suits. Digital cameras came out. For almost 5 – 10 minutes the captain of the Zodiac went from side to side in the wake of the boat, getting closer. When he was really close, he broke to one side and passed the boat.

As for finding Whales to watch; they saw them, but nothing like the ones shown up close and personal as seen on the posters. These must have been lazy pods as they were always 300-500 feet away and instead of jumping out of the water; their fins barely broke the surface, a spume of water shot into the air from their blow holes and then they were gone.

For an hour the boat captains chased them. Each time he would slow down where he thought, as well as the other tour boat captains thought, the Whales would break surface; cut the engines and waited.

Soon the captain gave up, started the engines and prepared to return to Victoria.

They stopped about half way and the tour guide called for a couple of volunteers, which JT joined. From out of the ocean she started pulling a long green strand of sea kelp, with the aid of her volunteers. She cut off a length, using what looked like a machete, and then started cutting off smaller section. These she passed around to the passengers. She then explained that sea kelp was used in a lot of ingredients, including toothpaste and told everyone to try it. JT, never one to just up and try odd foods, broke tradition. "What the hell. You only live once," he thought. It tasted flat and salty.

When everyone had sampled their section, the tour guide threw the remaining kelp overboard and the captain started the engines, completing the journey back, dodging those same floatplanes they had seen earlier.

From there they took a bus ride; sitting in the upper level of a double-decker bus back to the ferry.

Pamela sat beside JT. Cindy and Hannibal sat up front with Abby. They were whispering and laughing at some jokes.

Pamela rested her head on JT's shoulder and held onto to his arm.

"He's really head over heels over her isn't he?"

"Yeah, in a way I'm glad to see him so happy, but at the same time I feel as if I've lost my best friend." He started picking at the head of a bolt on the seatback in front of them.

"No you haven't. You've only expanded his world - He needed it. You have to let go."

"I know. I just can't help it. Ever since I first met him in Korat, Thailand that day, I have always felt like a big brother, although we're nearly the same age."

Pamela kissed him. They were quiet for the trip back.

When they docked, Hannibal asked JT what their plans were. He said that they were going to drive home as he had a couple of service calls waiting.

Abby said she needed to pack for her flight home, but wanted to rest for an hour or so first to beat the jet-lag back to Thailand.

Cindy said she had to go to Washington, DC in several days to make a report on an event that had happened at McChord Air Force base, which she couldn't talk about, but if Hannibal wanted, she would stay with him in Vancouver for several days. Damn, the sun must have broken as a grin spread from ear to ear on his face, showing all 32.

Later they escorted Abby to the airport as she boarded a plane for the long flight home. She gave each a hug and looked at Pamela. With a slight nod of approval, she gave JT a kiss on the lips. Then she gave Pamela a big hug. She gave Cindy and Hannibal a hug too.

She turned and waved as the crowd engulfed her.

CHAPTER VII

Over the course of the next several days, Cindy and Hannibal had changed their flights, rented a car and drove to Oliver. They took the Trans Canada stopping in Chilliwack, where he took her on the same tour of the aircraft factory he had just taken a couple of days before. He told her about the kit airplane he had purchased.

From there he drove to Hope, BC where they stopped and had an ice cream at the local Dairy Queen. Above them, a gaggle of sailplanes were using the thermals off of the mountains, climbing higher and higher; the sunlight reflecting off of their white wings.

Hannibal pointed to the nearby mountains and told her that JT had said the first *RAMBO* movie had been filmed there.

After eating, they took off again on the Trans Canada and just north of Hope, took highway 3 east through winding roads, mountains and pine trees. Cindy was the navigator as neither of them had been there before. Along the way, they saw ugly brown, barren pines trees that were infected with pine beetles. At Princeton, they stopped to get gas and use the restrooms.

Back on the highway; it wound through valleys with pine to valleys dark brown and hot. "It was like being in Wyoming," Hannibal said. Soon they reached the town of Osoyoos on the Canadian and US border and turned north onto highway 97 towards Oliver.

JT and Pamela were waiting for them.

As the women did women things, JT took Hannibal out to the airport to see his PZL TS11 *ISKRA*, which Hannibal didn't settle for a look see; he wanted to go flying, which they did. HE even let Hannibal take the controls. Hell that was the best he could do as Hannibal had paid for the fuel.

All too soon, it was time for them to leave. Hugs and kisses went around and farewells given. Hannibal drove north to Kelowna where he and Cindy departed on a flight direct to Chicago. There they wept as they separated; she to Washington, DC and he to Dallas/Ft. Worth.

CHAPTER VIII

RICHARD "HANNIBAL" WASHINGTON had grown up in the rough part of East St. Louis. He had never known his real parents. Hell, he doubted his real name was Richard Washington. He was placed in foster home after foster home. In his final home, his foster mother had so many new boyfriends, he lost count. At 17 he needed to get away and find who he was; not that he would go looking for his parents, but he wanted to find out what he was made of. The Vietnam War was on and the US Air Force was looking for pilots. He didn't have the money for college. He joined anyway and worked his way up to Tech Sergeant. One day an officer had observed his performance and called him in. He told him that he had been watching him and had taken a peek at his test scores. He said that he would help him brush up on his grades and maybe get a scholarship into the US Air Force Academy. Richard wasn't sure and expressed that he didn't want to disappoint the officer. The officer told him he wouldn't. So Richard took the test; passed and was accepted into the academy. The Air Force became his wife.

CHAPTER IX

WITH HANNIBAL back in Ft. Worth, his kitplane parts started arriving. As they had promised, his new employers allowed him a corner of the hanger to start his project. Then came the assignment to ferry the T-38, located at Wright-Patterson Air Base, in Ohio.

Before he left, he received a call from Cindy. She was being sent to Korat, Thailand. She and Abby; constantly emailing each other, were close to finding the bad guys behind Roxanne, but needed confirmation. The only way to do that was for her to go to Korat and set up surveillance of their suspects.

Hannibal had already agreed to the ferry flight and could not back out due to the time frame. They were to have taken a few weeks off and just disappear someplace. That wasn't about to happen. So he told her he loved her several times and expressed how much he missed her. She too said she loved him.

The next morning she was on a flight to the West Coast and he flew commercial to Wright-Patterson.

The museum for the an interim destination located just south of DFW, Dallas/Ft. Worth on highway 360 not too far from the old Bell helicopter complex where wealthy businessmen, each with a military background, wanted to preserve a piece of aviation history. To date they had built an outstanding museum and stocked it with some of the latest fighter jets and observation aircraft from the Vietnam War. Coyote T-38 was to be the latest acquisition.

The T-38 had been in storage in a National Guard hangar at Ft. Wayne, Indiana. From there it had been sent to Wright-Patterson AFB, Ohio for basic refurbishment. It was flagged as unfit for continued service within the military, so it took some hard talking to get the ferry permit. The only other way it would have gotten there was on the back of a semi-trailer. Not a good way for an aircraft to finish its career. Besides, that would take too long.

It was only a three or four hour flight from Wright-Pat to Ft. Worth. Those Texans with their slow talk, big cowboy hats, flashy belt buckles, and diamond rings that made the Queen's tiara diamonds pale, weren't all that dumb. They knew where the money was and it wasn't all in oil; the Dallas Cowboys, Dallas Stars hockey or the Texas Rangers baseball team.

CHAPTER X

ON THE Ground – Indianapolis, Indiana

MARCUS Fredrick's the III was a small time drug pusher and pimp. He drove the streets in his custom made 5.8 liter, V-12, 400 hp Mercedes S-Class. Tonight was as usual; time to check up on his drops, and make a showing on the streets. Although his ride was first class, his home was a run-down shotgun next to an empty lot. He stepped out, locking the door. Inside were two Great Danes that were really wimps when it came to protecting things, but who was gonna argue with dogs the size of small horses?

His neighbor, whom he rarely saw, except when peeking out of the blinds, was an old woman. He often saw a gangsta wannabe kid from across the street visiting her from time to time. The kid lived with strict relatives so he was told. He'd see him pull up in his highly polished black Honda. Kid wasn't hardcore yet, so he never could understand why he was trying to act like one.

Marcus had grown up hardcore. This kid had not. The kid was intelligent, not like some of the other assholes around. As a businessman he could see it. He wanted to sit down and take the kid under his wing, but his relatives would rat him out, as they have warned, if he came anywhere near him. Well that was their problem and not his. The kid would just have to pay his dues.

Across the street the other neighbors also kept to themselves, at least those that felt they were better off and turned their noses up to people like Marcus. There were a few school age kids Marcus saw when he came home standing at the school bus stop. Some of the older kids had erected a pole, tacked a 4X4 sheet of ¾" plywood, painted it white and added a hoop. At night you could hear them playing ball under the glow of the street lights.

Those that didn't play ball; the gangsta wannabe's, hung out with their various rides. Now and then there was the occasional loud talk and semi-automatics magically appeared. After a couple of these and several funerals, the gun play continued, but the fingers were not as fast to pull the triggers. After all, the bigger the gun one displayed meant you had the bigger balls to back up what you said. Titanium gold .50 cal. AE Desert Eagles always won arguments, fired or otherwise, and got everyone's respect.

On the other side of the empty lot was a time worn strip mall of sorts with a 7/11, 24-hour Laundromat, hair salon, a pizza shop and a pharmacy run by an old Chinese couple.

The sidewalk was cracked and chucks of concrete went missing. The parking lot had been dug up so many times to add new sewer pipes, power lines, and what not that the asphalt looked like a bad idea of a quilt, only in various shades of black.

Litter from the 7/11 and the corner McDonald's was everywhere. A track of bare ground ran from the McDonald's through patches of tired grass to the strip mall adding to the worn out look.

Since just about everyone had cellphones, an old graffiti covered phone booth still stood, without phone or glass as a monument to a time long since past but made a nice place to take a late night piss.

One did not have to walk past to smell the urine.

An old homeless guy slept with his grocery cart behind the dumpster on the side of the 7/11. Most likely it was he that used the old phone booth as his choice of toilet as the McDonalds people had been told to keep a watchful eye on him. He was a harmless old dude and like now, as Marcus watched, made his way towards the phone booth.

The empty lot was a reminder of the city's progress to improve living conditions on that side of town, but progress was politically slow.

CHAPTER XI

HIGH ABOVE, in the night skies of Indianapolis, Indiana

DEEP inside Coyote T-38, located just below the left wing, was a rivet working its way loose, a minor but soon to be costly oversight by the inspection mechanic and refurbish team. The rivet, suffering from fatigue aging, was vibrating and chaffing a wire bundle that ran to the left engine, shorting it. At first it was gradual, so nothing was registered. Had the fuel pump a brain, it must have wished the idiot in the cockpit would make up his mind; either on or off. When the rivet finally came loose; jamming upwards into the wire bundle, it shorted the engine and fuel pump wires. The pump must have thought, "Well it's about time!" The pump's manufacturers would have been proud. It performed as specified. It quit: stopping all fuel flow to the engine.

What Hannibal had experienced before and had given him cause for concern was small engine fluctuations caused by the loose rivet. Now he had major warning horns, and a female voice in his headset he had an engine failure. "No Shit," he said.

Trouble lights were flashing everywhere.

"MAYDAY, MAYDAY, MAYDAY!" Hannibal shouted into his mike. "Coyote T-38 has an engine flame out "MAYDAY, MAYDAY, MAYDAY!"

"Coyote T-38, Indianapolis Center, understand you have an emergency, squawk, seven-seven-seven-seven. You are cleared for immediate decent into the Indianapolis TCA. Say your height and speed."

"Why do those guys sound so cool?" thought Hannibal. "Indianapolis Coyote T-38 descending through 5,000 feet, course heading of 275 degrees, 10 miles GPS. I have lost my left engine."

"Roger Coyote T-38. Understand you have lost your left engine. Continue if possible on course heading 275 degrees and descend for a straight in approach. BREAK! All aircraft in the Indianapolis TCA we have a declared emergency. All aircraft are to maintain their present positions for further instructions. BREAK! Coyote T-38 change frequency to Indianapolis Tower, one-two-zero decimal niner. Good luck sir."

"Roger Indianapolis Center, descending for straight in approach, frequency change to one-two-zero decimal niner. Thanks."

Making the frequency change, Hannibal wasted no time in contacting Indianapolis Tower. "Indianapolis Tower, Coyote T-38 is with you on one-two-zero decimal niner."

"Roger Coyote T-38" We have you on a course heading of 275 degrees, squawking seven-seven-seven-seven. You are cleared for an emergency direct in approach to runway 32 right."

"Roger Indianapolis Tower. Cleared for direct approach Runway 32 right."

Below him, Hannibal could see the multi-colored, jeweled lights of the Indianapolis west side. Looking further to the west he saw the approach lights had been turned on, guiding him to the runway of Indianapolis International slightly to his right.

Seeing these lights cheered Hannibal. "Soon I will be on the ground." he thought.

Coyote T-38 had other ideas. The loose rivet had worked its way further into the bundle, further shorting it out causing a small fire, causing the right engine to fail as well. The nose of the little dart like airplane plunged downward; its tiny wings unable to provide even the remotest idea of a power off glide.

Without wasting another moment, General Richard "Hannibal" Washington USAF (ret.) aimed the aircraft to what looked like an open lot and pulled the ejection handles.

Kicked in the ass by the explosion from his rocket-powered seat, Hannibal was slammed downwards as his seat accelerated upwards though the canopy, broken by his seatback. In the time it took to blink an eye, Hannibal's spine was compressed by the acceleration and within seconds he was free falling through the night sky. Released from his seat, Hannibal's chute opened. He was snapped upright.

Turning in his risers, he frantically looked to see his tiny airplane plunge downward. At first it aimed for the dark spot he had selected, which he prayed was an unoccupied lot. But the nose dipped a fraction and aimed for the street just before the lot. "OK, so it's going to dig a hole in the street first."

Nosing down even more, and traveling at over 280 knots, the wings, so thin they are like high-speed butcher knives; the aircraft severed a light pole, causing the aircraft to swing slightly to the right. Next it struck the ground, ricocheted off the pavement and back into the air aiming for an occupied telephone booth cutting a human in half.

Blood and body gore followed the stricken aircraft as it tumbled through the empty lot trailing sparks and burning aviation Jet-A fuel.

The aircraft hit a mound of dirt and rock, becoming slightly airborne again, and with its bloody package in trail, slammed into a home, instantly incinerating everything.

CHAPTER XII

Marcus, while standing on the porch watching the old man, could not will his body to move as he watched the fighter hit the pole and then spun through the phone booth. One of the Sidewinder missiles detached from the already detached wing.

Just as sure as if he'd been harpooned, he was nailed to his front door by the pointy end of the missile. The force of the impact caused the missile to split along its sides. A fine white powder began to rain down onto his shoes. As he was dying, he recognized the powder for what it was and thought how ironic that here he was, tacked to his door and had just made the biggest score of what was left of his life.

The gangsta wannabe's having heard the initial explosion of the ejection seat. Looked up and had long since run for cover. Burning aviation fuel melted cars including the Class-S belonging to the dying Marcus.

Neighbors that had gone to bed were running outside and then back when they saw the destruction coming their way. But it was over. The little aircraft was no more. All that was left was the burning house, cars and the soon to be discovered body of Marcus Fredrick's the III.

"Coyote T-38 Indianapolis."

"Coyote T-38 Indianapolis." The anxious controller called again.

"Indianapolis Delta 353 heavy."

"Delta 353 heavy Indianapolis."

"Indianapolis we see a large burning area right about where that T-38 was."

"Delta 353 heavy Indianapolis. Thanks. Out."

"Indianapolis Mooney 22 Tango."

"Mooney 22 Tango Indianapolis."

"Indianapolis, we just saw an ejection seat . . . Yeah, there's a parachute opening right above the area where there's a big fireball. I think that's your T-38."

"Mooney 22 Tango Indianapolis - understand you see a parachute in the vicinity of Coyote T-38. Thanks. Indianapolis out."

ABOVE and watching the trail of destruction, Hannibal prayed the damage was minimal. He landed; falling as his legs gave out, which his compressed spine had suffered from the ejection, sent a message loud and clear to his brain, he was in trouble.

Cars stopped at the lights were astonished; first from the destruction they had witnessed to the white apparition that had descended from the night skies. Those that realized what had happened ran to Hannibal's aid, untangling him from his parachute lines, helping him to stand.

It took a lot of will power, but once free of his lines and standing, he limped to where his aircraft had blazed a path of destruction; gagging at the blood-smeared telephone booth remains, and lower body torso.

Moving towards the house or what was left of it he came upon the next house with a body harpooned to the front door by the missile. "What's the hell is that?" Hannibal asked as he watched a fine powder spill from the split sides forming a mound. Realization dawned and all he could say was, "Oh God."

As if his body functions had totally shutdown, he collapsed on the edge of the porch, unable to believe what he was seeing. Cindy's Roxanne was true and now bigger than shit, he was literally right in the middle of it.

He turned to look at the dead body and the blood still flowing down the remaining parts of the missile. He could hear dogs behind the door; growling, howling and scratching at the coppery scent. Hannibal had seen death before, but nothing like this. The blood was forming a tiny river beside the powder, dripping off of the porch, being soaked into the dirt.

He reached over and pinched some of the powder. The light from the fire gave the powder an orange cast, but it was not hard to identify it for what it was.

Before he could get a closer look, there was a loud "WHOOSH." Hannibal fell to the ground. To his right a few people had started to walk cautiously his way, but dropped as well.

The remaining fuel had ignited, sending more broiling red and black clouds into the night sky.

Soon sirens, screeching tires, screams, and the sound of burning fuel all added to the surrealistic and chaotic scene of a major battle zone.

Several of the neighbors finally made it to where he was and tried to help him up but saw the powder as well. A young teen looking dude with baggy pants several sizes too big and no shirt, dropped Hannibal's arm and stooped to get a better look at the powder on the porch. "Ah man! Fuck me! Is this what I think it is?"

"Maybe it is and maybe it isn't. Either way you just stand back." Hannibal said struggling against the pain in his spine, stood and tried to back the kid away.

"Fuck you man," the kid said and pulled out what appeared to be a Smith & Wesson chrome hammerless revolver.

Instinct took over; Hannibal delivered a kick to the back of the kid's leg with his right foot. *BANG!*

"Fuck!" Hannibal yelled as the bullet grazed his left leg and buried itself into the dirt. Someone in the small group had seen the gun come out and tackled the kid from behind. There was a small scuffle as the kid tried to scramble for the gun. Hannibal fell on it as others joined into the action to subdue the kid.

When they had him under control, a couple of Indianapolis police cars had come roaring up the street, dodging debris. Officers jumped out of cars and reached the scene with weapons drawn as they had heard the shot. They fanned out in a semi-circle, but made sure they were not in the direct fire of their fellow officers.

"Everybody! Show your hands now!" An officer yelled.

Hands went up. Hannibal, on the ground pulled his from under him; gun in hand.

"Gun!" Yelled one officer.

"Drop the gun!" Another yelled.

Hannibal let it go.

"Everybody down on the ground now!"

The kid, already on the ground rolled over onto his stomach; hands spread and flat. He'd done this before. His head was turned towards Hannibal, giving him the evil stare.

Hannibal mouthed, "Fuck you." He then turned his head and tried to talk to one of the officer near him. "Officer. I was the pilot of that there airplane. . . ."

"Shut the fuck up." The officer yelled, his gun aimed steady at Hannibal, moving cautiously close, and kicked the gun away.

"Officer I can explain. Shit!!." Hannibal howled as he was given a kick in the ribs – the wind knocked out of him. "Shut up!" The officer yelled again.

"Officer, that man is innocent . . . Another person tried to come to Hannibal's defense and he too received a reward for his efforts.

"Hey Jerry look at this." Another officer was pointing to the mound of powder.

The officer turned to see the blood and powder.

"Jerry it looks like this stuff is coming from that missile that must have come from that airplane."

Jerry turned and stepped over Hannibal to investigate.

Hannibal became aware of the yells and shouts of orders being given to firemen, dragging hoses over to what remained of the house and his fighter.

Mist from the water hoses blanketed them.

Officer Jerry returned.

"You! In the flight suit. I want you to get up on your knees, hands on your head." An officer yelled. Hannibal tried as best as he could to follow orders. Another officer ran over, grabbed one arm and placed a cuff on one wrist and then the other.

"Officer, I'm shot." Hannibal said. Another officer grabbed the space between the cuffs and tried to pull him up, up Hannibal stumbled from his injury.

"Jerry, he needs medical attention. His right leg is bleeding." The first officer said.

"OK, let him stay right there. Check his pockets. You got anything on you that you don't want us to find?" He asked Hannibal.

"No officer." Hannibal said and was searched. His wallet, portable Aircom radio, damaged cellphone, and PDA that contained an electronic record of his flight logs were removed and taken over to a police car hood where it could be caught on the dash cam. The gun was placed there as well.

The police began to order each of the people on the ground to get on their knees and place their hands on their head. They were searched and then cuffed. A spot had been picked on the curb where they were placed and watched by a couple of officers with riot shotguns and automatic weapons.

One by one, another officer hauled each one up and took the individual a few steps away and questioned him.

Their attention turned to Hannibal. He was rolled over and an EMT called.

His flight suit pants leg was soaked in blood. With latex gloves on, they unzipped his leg pulling the fabric out of the way to examine the wound.

"He'll live. Mainly a flesh wound. The bullet only grazed his leg." The EMT said.

They bandaged his leg, closed their kits and let the officers have at him and then proceeded to assist with helping get the guy tacked to the door down.

Not much they could do about the other house as it was still smoldering. Crime scene tape had gone up while Hannibal had been lying down. Flashes were going off as the CSI guys made measurements and placed ID plaques at each point of interest.

"OK, we're going to sit you up," which they did.

"Who are you and what the fuck happened?" The officer known as Jerry asked.

"I'm retired General Richard Washington of the US Air Force. I was ferrying a T-38 aircraft when I experienced a flameout in both engines. That means the engines quit." Hannibal said.

"I'm not stupid sir; I know what a flameout is. I was in Iraq at Rasheed Air Force Base and saw several myself."

"Well I had a flameout in both engines and had to eject. When I landed I came over here to determine what had been destroyed and see if there was anything I could do. Not much I could do about that house, but I found this guy with a missile in him and then I saw this powder on the porch. When I sat down some people came over to help me. That kid over there with the pants around his ass pulled a gun.

I kicked him and the gun went off. That's how I got shot. Then you guys came."

"Do you know what that powder is sir?"

"I have an idea. I think it is cocaine."

"You think?"

"Jerry, may I call you Jerry?"

"Go ahead."

"Jerry, about a week ago, my girlfriend who is an FBI agent , ," This caused Jerry's eyebrows to arch. "She told me about a drug smuggling operation that involved Vietnam Era jets. Anyway, I retired to Ft. Worth, Texas and went to work for a small aircraft restoration outfit. I was sent to pick up this aircraft at Wright-Patterson in Ohio.

That hulk over there is what's left of it.

Anyway those missiles were supposed to be dummies. I never bothered to check them other than to insure that they were firmly attached when I did my pre-flight walk around. My girlfriend Cindy, said a new drug was hitting the streets called Roxanne and that she and a Thai police officer were investigating it as it appears to be coming in from a US Air Force base in Korat, Thailand. I guess it's true as you can see over there. Honest. I had no idea what was in that missile."

"I'd like to believe you. I think I know you sir. Would your nickname be Hannibal?"

"Yes, that's me."

"Ah damn, sir." Jerry put his gun away. "If it wasn't for you sir, I wouldn't be here."

"Excuse me?"

"I don't know the whole story but in Iraq, I heard that low on fuel from one of your missions, you had taken a different route back and discovered that portable Scud missile launcher that had somehow slipped past a flight of McDonnell-Douglas F-15 Scud hunters. I heard without any support you took out that launcher as it was in the final stages of being launched right at us. You got some kind of medal."

"Air Force Cross. No big deal. Anybody could have done it. I was just doing my job."

"That might be true, but sir you were the only one there. You became an overnight hero when we found out. Maybe you don't think it was a big deal, but my wife and I were expecting a baby. Every day I look at him and feel grateful to the man that allowed me to return home and see him born."

Another officer came over. "Hey Jerry, those guys over there say that the kid with his pants around his ass pulled a gun on your man here. They say he kicked him and when he did, the gun went off."

"Thanks. What about the others?"

"We questioned them and their stories match. The kid didn't wanna talk. So we let the others go. We're going to take him in and see what information we can dig up on him."

"OK." Jerry said. The other officer walked away and assisted the others in placing the kid in the back of a police car.

"Well at least that part of your story holds up, but damn sir, I'm gonna have to place you under arrest until we can get more information on your story about this Roxanne drug. I'll take the cuffs off though as a courtesy. Can you stand?"

"I understand and appreciate you taking the cuffs off. I think I can stand." Hannibal said, struggling to get up. Jerry helped. He was led to another car and placed in the back seat. A camera crew from the local television station had arrived.

"Well here's my 15-minutes of fame."

There were several officers standing around Jerry's car, some of them from the Marion County Sheriff's office and he could see some distinctive hats, worn by the Indiana State Police. They seemed to be discussing Hannibal. Officer Jerry took one of the troopers aside and spoke to him.

A few minutes went by and Jerry came over, the trooper following, unlocked the door and asked Hannibal to get out, helping him.

"Sir, it seems that due to the nature of this being a military aircraft involved in what looks like a drug smuggling operation, I have to turn you over to the State Police. I told them I know of you and your background. "

The State Trooper said, "Sir, I'm really sorry about this, but my hands are tied. I'm taking Jerry's word that you are who you say you are. I won't put the cuffs on you, but I will have to take you in until we can get to the bottom of this."

"No problem. You're just doing your job. What about the guy on the door?"

"That's a good one. We know him as a drug dealer of all things. I guess that missile was his final score."

"Yeah. Oh yeah, I heard some dogs inside when I was over by the porch."

"We'll check it out later."

"Was there anyone in that house that got incinerated?"

"We think so, but we'll know more tomorrow."

"One more thing, you probably saw that phone booth."

"Yeah. Not a pretty sight." Jerry said. "Well I think you should go with Mack here. Like I said, I'll try to get you some help. I know of a trooper up north at Schererville, Indiana post. He was in Iraq with me. He'll remember you too."

"Thanks." The State Trooper led him to his car, where he was placed up front this time.

The gun was placed in a plastic bag and given to an Indianapolis Police Officer. Hannibal's personal items were placed in another bag and given to the Trooper.

As Hannibal was led away the powerful lights from the camera crew followed them as he was driven away.

CHAPTER XIII

Oliver British Columbia Canada

SITTING at the breakfast table, enjoying a cup of tea and munching on a slice of bacon and cinnamon toast, the term UFO, or Unidentified Flying Object was not new to JT. In fact when he was a little boy growing up in Indianapolis, he swore he saw three of them one night in perfect formation flying over his home. In this case, this UFO was inside the house and thus not unidentified, but it all honesty it was an honest to God flying saucer.

What was once an object at rest was now flying at warp speed towards his head; his peripheral vision had seen it coming. By just turning his head, the flying saucer missed its intended object - shattering against the wall into a thousand pieces in a perfect starburst pattern.

"I hope you don't expect me to put that back together again," JT said trying to lighten the moment. Another IFO, Identified Flying Object, came his way. Ducking, he grabbed the remaining toast running out the door, brushing the remains of the IFO from its top.

What could he say? Sorry?

The truth be known, Pamela had a right, well at least to be angry but not to throw the saucer. He shouldn't have bought that Garwin GPS for his airplane as she had asked him to wait. She was a hockey nut and as far as she was concerned, the BC Lions were king. But with age, she needed glasses and they only had a 27" flat screen television set.

He on the other hand was a Hamilton Tiger Cats hockey fan, but preferred his NFL Indianapolis Colts, and Dallas Cowboys. He had been living in Dallas when Troy Aikman and team were winning Super Bowls in the 80's; that is until Troy got his bell rung too many times and the Jerry and Jerry management team split.

Pamela would take command of the remote controller if a game was on, and it didn't matter if JT was watching *Dog the Bounty Hunter*; that was just too bad. Pamela couldn't see the hockey puck, so she wanted one of those 52" HDTV's that you hung on the wall and had to sit outside to watch. He tried to tell her that, but she was adamant; she wanted this monster. So JT had tried to let the conversation die, hoping it would go away. Not so.

When a special on the GPS came up, he bought it telling her later as in that morning. That is when the IFO's tried to rearrange his facial structure.

Two saucers meant she was really pissed.

As any man would do in his shoes, he made himself scare. What he hadn't wanted to tell her was that he had found another HDTV, with the same qualities, but he had to order it in.

He wanted it to be a surprise.

Anyway he'd come back later when the dust had settled and the house free of IFO's but first he had to make an unscheduled stop at the nearest RCMP (Royal Canadian Mounted Police) post, as it was requested that he identify the remains of a dead computer.

At first he thought this was a joke, but the "BLOCKED" call display could have only come from an official place or a creditor. When he answered, it wasn't a creditor, but an RCMP Constable requesting his presence.

So, today, full of "What the hell" questions he drove to the post. Through a glass sliding partition, he identified himself and was buzzed in and escorted to a side room. There on top of a table was, as sure as shit, the remains of a computer with his company logo. He recognized the computer as one he had made several modifications to the weeks before. The customer was new; a woman working on a book, so she said.

The Constable asked if he recognized it. "Yep, what happened?"

"From what we gathered, the woman to whom the computer belonged had called in a domestic disturbance in progress. When we arrived, we watched in awe as the husband, axe in hand, whacked the computer several times and then tossed it into the nearby lake. He was arrested and a dive team brought up the remains of the computer, which you see on the table."

Holding a bundle of cables, JT made a joke by saying, "Well it's dead all right." At least the Constable had a sense of humor and thought it was funny.

The Constable went on to tell him that the customer had asked for him specifically not only to identify it for insurance purposes, but to see if the data could be retrieved from the hard drive. It was not hard to see that the memory chips, which had become dislodged were most likely still on the bottom of the lake, also the CPU chip had lost its cooling fan. Again no big problem, but one look at the hard drive left any guesses as to the present state of the computer.

The axe had hit a corner of the drive, not only taking out the corner of the case but nicked the inside disc as well. Yep, it was truly and honestly dead.

JT told him so.

Signing a release form, JT was given a box, which he placed the computer remains in and was escorted outside.

Driving to the airport down highway 97, which is only a hop-skip and a jump north of the 49th parallel better known as the US and

Canadian border, JT parked his XJ12 Jaguar outside his hanger door, unlocked the entrance door and proceeded to raise the bio-fold doors flooding the interior with sunlight.

To the south of Oliver is vineyard country and to the north, beautiful bluffs and further north, the pristine lakes of the Okanagan and Shuswap. Go even more north and you run into a huge snowcapped wall called the Canadian Rockies. The airport is to the south of Oliver, but still within spitting distance of downtown. Since it was still early morning, the air was still cool and dense enough to make take off and landings a breeze.

CHAPTER XIX

IN RECENT years Oliver, British Columbia had become home to a warbird group that specialized in rebuilding Chinese made Nanchang single engine, low wing CJ-6 Trainers. Although a very stable flying platform, JT wanted something a little faster and a little more unstable.

During an airshow he had flown in the back seat of one, flying in formation with another and thrilled at its performance. The cost of one was around $60,000, the same as owning an *ISKRA*. The *ISKRA* won.

While traveling through the back roads of Washington State several years ago, he had come across an airfield with old warbirds to be parted out. Through a series of written letters to Transport Canada, he received special permits and finally become the proud owner of a Polish PZL TS-11 *ISKRA* or 'Spark' in Polish or Sparky..... Well at least a non-flying assembly of wings, fuselage tail parts, landing gear and a couple of engines in various stages of bits and pieces. Just as he had rebuilt his Jaguar and built two other aircraft, over time he built the *ISKRA*.......A very long time.

There are only ten know examples still flying. JT's made it eleven.

As the doors allowed the sunlight into the hanger, the *ISKRA* was bathed in the sunlight and gleamed: he smiled. It had a low stance. Standing beside it, the canopy sill came to about his waist. It was a tandem configuration; the pilot in front and passenger behind. A tail boom extended over the jet exhaust. The main wings protruded at mid-fuselage level. Under each wing root was a small air scoop for the single turbo-jet WSK-SO-3W engine of 2,425 pounds of thrust. There had been several upgrades but JT was just happy to have this one and a few spare parts.

She could cruise at around 478 knots maximum for about 783 miles. She was fast on landings; like any fighter, but very forgiving. She was also called in some circles as a *motor-glider,* due to the excellent engine-out characteristics. Maybe too forgiving as he often saw many of them up for sale as trade-ins for something faster or sexier on the Internet like the Delphin.

The front nose gear gave it a pronounced kneeling, nose down look, very close to the ground.

This was the same aircraft to which he would soon install the GPS but not today. Today he just wanted to strap himself in and fly high above the mountains, doing nothing but burn aviation fuel, but first he had to call Eileen, the owner of the dead computer. Before he could do that he had to call for a fuel truck if he wanted to get up in the air anytime soon.

Behind the *ISKRA* and to the side was a modified Cessna 152. The original engine had been replaced with a one of 150 HP. The owner in his younger days did banner towing, thus requiring a heavier engine. About three years ago he retired as an executive from an electrical supply company. One day while he was fueling the *ISKRA*, the 152 owner approached.

"Hey nice airplane."

"Yeah, got it as a pile of junk out of Washington State. Put it together myself."

"Wow. Anyway, the reason I am here is that I heard you take care of airplanes real well and I have this Cessna that needs a little bit of

TLC. You can fly it all you want, as long as you pay for the fuel and I'll pay for the insurance and annual inspection."

"You're kidding, right?"

"Nope. Here's the keys." With that he reached into his pocket, pulled out a set of keys, and then handed him a leather bag, which he had been holding. Inside were two pair of headsets, a handheld Aircom radio, owner's manuals and logbooks.

"I want to play golf and not worry about the airplane." He said. And just like that he was gone.

JT just stood there. Only once before had something like this ever happened and that was down in Texas when a female pilot, going in for surgery, asked him to take care of her airplane.

"Must be my good looks."

Flying the Cessna was fun. Due to the larger engine, he could do things, such as almost aerobatics, at least that is what he called it as a 'normal' production aircraft like the Cessna 152 is banned from such flights, although most pilots know, in the right hands, it is a very capable aircraft for performing some of the simple maneuvers.

What gave JT the most fun was taking kids and parents up for their first flight. He went beyond what's called for by Transport Canada and the FAA to make sure a passenger knew how to exit the plane in an emergency. He wanted his passengers to feel comfortable about him, but also about the plane. He made a game of it, especially with kids. What he would do is have them walk around the aircraft with him during the pre-flight; showing them the various control surfaces, and the things that held them together. What to look for and then had them raise and lower the control surfaces. He had them take the fuel sample bottle, push the sample tube into the hole and drawn a small amount of blue colored aviation fuel.

He then asked them, "What are we looking for?" Their little faces would scrunch up as they thought; then they'd wring their hands, "I don't know." So he told them, "We are looking for tiny bubbles. Airplane engines," he said, "don't like bubbles. It gives them really bad hiccups. Do you like hiccups?"

"No," the child would usually respond.

He went on to say, "If there are no bubbles then there is no water in the fuel and it is safe to fly the airplane. If there are bubbles then we need to keep taking samples of the fuel until the bubbles go away." Then JT would sing, "Tiny Bubbles," an old Don Ho song.

"Well I don't see any bubbles now." The child would usually say.

"And that means we can go flying! Yea! " JT would jump up and clap his hands, which usually got the kids jumping and clapping their hands as well.

Once in the air, he did a few mild turns and dives to let the child get used to the unusual attitudes. Then he'd ask if they wanted to try it.

Most of them did. Most interesting was the girls were more willing to explore their limits. Regardless, he'd place the aircraft in level flight; made sure the trims were set and then got on the radio giving out his location for other pilots to avoid. He then instructed the child on how to hold the control wheel.

Their first reaction was to grab the wheel too harsh and off they'd go up, down, left or right, which scared them. Meanwhile JT would have his left hand within inches of the wheel on his side. The child would let go of the wheel, but he would slowly talk them back into holding the wheel. He knew that the airplane wasn't going anyplace.

"See there, what did the airplane do?" "Nothing," they would answer. "So you see there is nothing to be afraid of."

Before long, each child would overcame their fears; becoming more adventuresome and explored their limits. When they were satisfied they gave him back control of the aircraft, which he never gave up in the first place, and returned to the airport.

Only once did he met a child that was so bored she wanted to return right away. When JT asked why, the little girl said, "What about all of that turning and burning stuff you see on TV."

"You want to turn and burn?"

"Yes."

"All right!"

He reached over and pulled her seat belt and shoulder straps tighter.

"Here we go," JT checked to make sure no ice had been built up in the carburetor by pulling the mixture control several times. Satisfied, he pulled the throttle back to idle, which decreased power; pushed the control wheel forward, which dropped the nose and far below they were looking at the lake, dropping like a stone. After dropping about 1,000 feet, he hauled back on the control wheel, while applying power and the little Cessna started clawing upwards like a home sick angel.

Blue sky filed the windshield.

Gravity pushed them into their seats with about 2G's of pressure; or they were weighing 2 times their body weight. Hoping she wasn't going to get sick, he looked over and had his answer.

She was grinning from ear to ear. After a few more of these and a few power stalls, they landed. When he shut the engine down, the little girl jumped out and bounced around the airport.

When her mother asked her what had happened, she was told and feinted.

JT shook his head at the memory and laughed. Anyway, he still had Eileen to call, so he might as well get it over with.

She answered on the second ring as she had been waiting for his call and the truth came out.

All the time she had told him that she was writing a book was a smoke screen as she was actually been online dating an American. Her husband had somehow found out.

JT didn't know what to say or make of the situation so he didn't say anything. He told her about the hard drive and heard the disappointment in her voice, but from what he gathered, she was happy that her soon to be ex was out of her life.

He didn't know much about her ex but when he was at the home servicing the computer, he stayed in the living room; hacking and coughing his lungs out. He never said a word and JT felt as if he was being scrutinized. Not hard to understand, considering what Eileen looked like.

Now he understood why.

She might have been looking for love in cyberspace, but she never made a pass at him.

Eileen thanked him and hung up. "Now if that don't kick all ass," At least when he returned home he could honestly say, "Hey honey, you'll never guess what happened today!"

Maybe that would brighten Pamela's day.

Once again he shook his head laughing to himself and began the task of performing a pre-flight of C-CDY or Charlie-Charlie Delta Yankee, the *ISKRA*.

He had to roll the aircraft outside to perform the pre-flight in the morning sunlight.

Attaching the tow dolly, he rolled the aircraft out just as the fuel truck rolled up.

"Good morning JT, how's it going?"

"Hey Mike. Good morning to you too."

"How much fuel you gonna need?"

"Not sure yet, I haven't had a chance to check my bank account. I'm only going up for maybe 30-minutes, so I'll probably only need half tanks. Give me a sec."

Pamela did the books and made sure he only used the credit card for emergency purposes. Flying the *ISKRA* and Cessna was not an emergency.

"Sure JT." The driver attached a ground cable to a grounding stud in the ground and then to the *ISKRA*. Then he unrolled the fuel cable.

JT pulled out his iPhone, brought up Safari and checked his bank account. "Let's see, the car loan is due along with the insurance and hanger rent." He mentally added it up. He could afford about 400 gallons of Jet-A. "Hey Mike put 200 gallons in each wing." JT yelled.

"OK, how's the oil?"

"I had some spare oil from the last time. It's OK."

When the *ISKRA* was fueled, JT gave Mike his ATM card, which he swiped on his portable terminal. JT could only watch as his bank account drained when he hit the OK button and the words 'APPROVED' appeared on the display.

Just like his Jag, it was not the cost of the vehicle or jet, but the maintenance and fuel. Since he did most of the maintenance himself, that only left the fuel and there was not a lot he could do about that.

The *ISKRA,* he could fly about once every two months.

The Cessna 152 he could fly at least once a week. The Jag with its V-12 engine, he could drive every day, but it never passed up very many gas stations. If he kept his foot out of the tank, he could go about 500 kilometers, but why have a V-12 engine car if you can't use all 12 cylinders? "What's that saying about men and their toys?" He thought. Some Jag owners had converted them over to Chevy V-8's through a company in Dallas. As far as he was concerned, that was not a pure Jag.

"Here you go JT. Have a great flight," Mike said, handing back his ATM card and receipt. He didn't want to see it and spoil his day so he folded it over and put it into his wallet for Pamela to add to the bookkeeping.

Mike stood by as he commenced his walk-around preflight. When he was finished he checked the windsock and saw that he would be using runway 18, which was right up the valley.

To the left of the airport was a series of tall mountain bluffs and for reasons unknown, he always had the feeling someone would turn the runway right into them.

When using this runway he made sure he held just to the right more than required for takeoff and launched himself straight down the valley.

The *ISKRA* had not been flown in over two-months so JT had to perform a pre-flight ritual and that was to pre-lube the bearings with a hand crank. A pain in the butt, but what the hell?

He suited up in his flight suit; one of two given him by Hannibal and his old Vietnam era combat boots with green canvas webbing.

An invention he had come up with was several removable sections of ballast mounted on a platform, controlled by an electric motor from the cockpit. The guns had long ago been taken out so to get the correct center of gravity, he had installed the platform. The ballast could be removed by section or entirely if needed.

Although not really tall at six-feet, the canopy came to JT's waist. He hung his helmet, electronic and mechanical plotting gear and bag containing the iPhone, wallet and other personal items on the front console. Grabbing the sides, he carefully placed his combat boots on the seat, careful not to dislodge or accidentally move switches and climbed in.

As he settled into his seat he moved his butt from side to side to get it settled in and comfortable. He also moved his shoulder blades back and forth.

The dry air of lower British Columbia also caused his back to itch.

Making sure he hadn't dislodged anything, he put his helmet and Nomex flight gloves on.

Next he put his other gear away.

Mike backed his truck away a few feet and although not needed, as a courtesy he stood by as JT started the engine with a portable fire extinguisher.

He turned on his battery switch and then his generator.

He then made sure his fire detector and extinguisher controls were on.

Looking outside he watched his wing trailing edges as he set the flaps.

Ignition – On.

Ground / Airborne – Ground.

Fuel pump – On.

Low Fuel pressure light – Off.

Fuel Shut-off – Open

He then opened and closed his speed brakes to reduce the hydraulic pressure.

Satisfied, looking to his left and then his right, JT cleared the aircraft. "Clear!" He yelled.

As is a habit, he left the canopy in the up position.

He depressed the start button and watched the turbine temperature climb. He had set his clock and had hit the timer at the same time he had hit the start button.

As the temperature increased and since he was on battery power, at 800°C he then depressed the overflow button to drop the turbine temperature.

At 4,000 RPM the low oil pressure light went out.

He had a good light off.

Only once did he have a bad light-off but caught it before the allotted 20 seconds and shut everything down.

He spent the next week going over the engine to determine the cause, which he found to be a blade from the first-stage compressor had failed, taking out a couple of others. Due to his quick actions the engine was not a total loss. He replaced the blades with spares. He then sent the engine to an aerospace company in Seattle, not too far from the Boing plant, and had it certified.

They proudly sent him the bill.

Crap! There was a lot of zero's after the comma. His only saving grace from Pamela's wrath was a large contract he had landed.

Since then he watched the over-temperature indicators like a hawk.

He let the engine idle at 6,000 RPM and the temperature drop down to 660ºC.

He gave the thumbs up to Mike, reached up and pulled the canopy shut.

Once again, looking to his left and right, he inched the throttle forward, released the brakes; the *ISKRA* began to roll.

He had long ago given up on the idea of getting a snappy return salute like the Thunderbirds or Blue Angels flight crew.

Mike waved back, got into his truck and drove off.

Over the Unicom radio he got and received permission to taxi to the active.

Turning left onto the active, he applied full throttle and was soon skimming the earth at 100 feet. He retracted the landing gear and with a little back pressure on the stick the valley, bluffs and mountains soon looked like Google Earth.

CHAPTER XX

PAMELA had no problems with his flying; in fact she often took up a wrench helping with minor repairs. Her concern was the money aspect. They weren't poor and far from being rich. They lived comfortable on what they made together, but she recognized his need to have a few boy toys. When she helped, on those days life was good.

When she had time from her busy schedule, he'd take her over to Golden, BC down Roger's Pass between very majestic, snow covered mountain peaks, or over to Delta, BC near Vancouver to see her parents.

Some of the guys at the airport were jealous.

That was their problem.

Although she'd never win a Miss Universe contest (Being that she's a Mrs.), to him she was his fantasies all rolled into one. She had a great body and a voice that would make angels sound like bullfrogs.

She was born under the sign of a Taurus and had a mean streak that would, from time to time, show up like this morning.

She also had a couple of friends that would also qualify as Miss Universe runner ups, all blondes, and they too would come out to the airport just to have a day out, thus putting JT at the butt of some very interesting good natured jokes.

The women knew this and made things interesting when the hanger doors were closed. They would make groaning noises, yelps and giggles as if in the death throes of a passionate love orgy.

JT left when they started; grinning and shaking his head. Doesn't mean he didn't think about it though.

The other pilots had to wonder just what was going on in that hanger. To make matters worse the women would come out pretending to straighten out their clothing.

JT as a visible minority; black-American, thus as one can imagine the stories got even spicier.

Fellow pilots took to grabbing their cohonas and gave him a thumbs–up.

CHAPTER XXI

Pamela had grown up as a single child. Her mother had passed away when she was a little girl. Her Father remarried to what Pamela described as a witch with a mean daughter. At first JT thought this is what most children think of their step-parents and their off-springs. Later, he found this not to be so.

The daughter was a mean bitch and the mother, soon to be blind, a very mouthy. . . . Witch. She told him that one day her mother-in-law took a spiked high-heel and whacked her father over the head with the pointy end. He had an image of a high heel sticking out of her father's head. Spiked high heels were no longer his favorite woman's shoes.

Later she said, her father died and left her with an inheritance of nearly a million dollars. When she reached her 21st birthday, through some craftiness on her mother-in-law and step-sister's part, the money was gone.

JT made himself scarce when they came to visit, which got him in trouble as Pamela wished she too could escape. He soon stopped hiding and sat beside his wife, holding her hands as they endured the sarcastic remarks; a lot of it directed at him.

When the Witch and Bitch left, Pamela sat, wrung out crying.

CHAPTER XXII

THE Polish PZL TS11 *ISKRA* JT was flying was originally built in 1973. Following a series of exchanges, it made its way to the shores of California in a crate. The owner from Washington State felt that the Aero L-39 Delfin was more to his liking, thus the *ISKRA* was relegated to remain in parts and sentenced to a slow death in the back woods of a Washington State junk yard, until he stumbled on it.

The *ISKRA* might be as glamorous as the Delphin, but it is a more forgiving and deemed a good step up aircraft for aspiring jet warbird owners.

New engines for the *ISKRA* were found in Ft. Worth, Texas by his friend Hannibal. The latest in navigational equipment was installed, minus the GPS, and then painted green with executive stripes down its sides. The paint was the latest in paint technology; it always looked wet. The long canopy was polished to a crystal finish.

Today he was staying near the airport, and was only going to go up for 30-minutes to keep fresh.

He missed a couple of entry points as he did his usual turns and burns so they did not come out as perfect as the ones seen in the movies. "OK, so the Thunderbirds won't be handing me a contract." He thought. At least he got his heart rate up and that was worth any day at the gym.

"*ISKRA* Charlie-Charlie-Delta-Yankee, Oliver Unicom."

"Oliver Unicom, *ISKRA* Charlie-Delta-Yankee."

"JT, Pamela just called and said for you to call home when get down."

"Did she say it was urgent?"

"No, she just said for you to call home."

"Uh . . . Roger. . I should be down in a second."

"I wonder what that's about."

"Roger JT. Oliver Unicom Out."

JT keyed the mike twice in the universal method of message understood and acknowledged.

"Oliver traffic, Charlie-Charlie-Delta-Yankee is descending from 8,000, direct enroute to Oliver International for a full stop landing." The 'International' part was his doing to get a laugh out of a few pilots that might be listening.

When he had taxied to the hanger, he undid the belts, removed his helmet and dug out his cell phone.

Pamela answered immediately. "JT, I received a call from Indianapolis, but I didn't recognize the number on the display. When I asked who it was, they said something about the Indiana State Police. Oh JT, I hope it is not your mom or somebody." Pamela sounded worried.

"Do you still have the number on the display?"

"Yes it's here."

"OK, write it down, I've got to put the *ISKRA* away. This might be an emergency and I'll need that number.

ONCE THE ISKRA was in the hanger, and the doors closed, JT drove home, his mind full of what ifs.

Pamela was waiting for him, handing him the paper when he entered. Taking his flight jacket off, he placed his flight bag of log books under the computer desk. To his iPhone he plugged in the USB cable to sync with his notebook and get it charged.

Using the cordless phone he dialed the number on the display.

"Indiana State Police. Corporal Walter Harris."

"Corporal, my name is Jerome Travis, someone called this number maybe an hour ago." JT looked at Pamela for confirmation. She shook her head yes. "Do you know what this is about?"

"Hold on Mr. Travis and I'll let you speak to someone."

"He's getting someone." JT said to Pamela. She was close to tears with worry.

A few minutes went by. "Mr. Travis?" A new voice was on the line.

"Yes?"

"Mr. Travis, my name is Colonel Frank Branson. Have you seen the news yet?"

"No."

"Well last night we had a plane crash that took the lives of several people."

"Was my family involved?" JT asked, steeling himself for the worst.

"Uh. . . No, at least not a direct member of your family that I know of. As I was saying, we had a plane crash last night. The pilot was a retired General Richard Washington."

"Oh no!" JT said. He put his hand over the mouthpiece and gestured to Pamela to turn on the news.

"Sir, he's not badly hurt. He was shot, but we have a very serious situation and he asked for you specifically."

"He was shot?" JT could only imagine Hannibal lying in a hospital bed, tubes sticking out everywhere. By now Pamela was in a fit to be tied; wringing her hands.

"Yes. He said you were the only family he has."

"I guess that's true. What happened?"

"Well sir. . . . ." Colonel Branson began to explain. When he was finished, JT hung up.

He heard Pamela gasp and turned to the television to see smoke and a large blacked area that could have been a scene in any war torn country.

The news was already in progress.

"I'm at the site of a jet crash last night and as you can see there is very little left of the small U.S. Air Force F-5 fighter. You can also see a small section of the left wing over by that fence and what looks like a missile of some sort that had come lose and really nailed this guy to the door."

"Have you been able to get any more information on exactly what happened?" the anchor in a studio asked.

"Jim when I got here, the police had roped off the area and wasn't allowing anyone close, but I was able to get a few people to tell me that they were asleep when it happened.

From what they said, the pilot, a retired Air Force General Richard Washington, was arrested. General Washington got into a scuffle with the police and was shot. They said the police found large quantities of cocaine on him.

"What!!??" JT and Pamela yelled in unison.

Trying to do a one-legged jump out of his flight suit he grabbed the remote and accidentally turned the volume up past ear-splitting levels.

Damn remote.

Turning it down to a comfortable level he hung onto every word the correspondent was saying.

"From what I did gather talking to sources at Indianapolis International Control Center, the pilot was experiencing engine trouble and then the engines quit altogether. The pilot ejected but his plane crashed, taking out a phone booth. Another spectator told me that someone was in the phone booth at the time.

From here there appears to be blood and body parts everywhere. I am also told a woman lived in the house that was flattened. It's a pretty gruesome sight."

The camera panned behind the news commentator to zoom onto the remains of the phone booth and destroyed home.

"Behind me you can see several military personal vehicles, Indianapolis Police, Indiana State Police and members of the Marion County Sheriff's office walking around the wreckage. This area looks like a war zone

The view is switched back to the main studio.

"OK keep us posted. Again, we would like to repeat for our viewers who have just joined us with what we know at this point. First, the model of the aircraft involved in last night's crash was a T-38 Talon, not an F-5 fighter. It crashed on a quiet rural street of Indianapolis, Indiana killing

two; possibly three people. The identity of the victims cannot be released until the next of kin have been notified.

The T-38 had left Wright-Patterson Air Force Base in Ohio and was enroute to Ft. Worth, Texas. The pilot is General Richard Washington, a highly decorated retired United States Air Force officer of the Vietnam and Gulf War. He experienced an engine malfunction and ejected. He got into a scuffle with police and was shot. They found large quantities of a controlled substance on him when he was searched. That is all we know at this time. Stay tuned for more updates as they happen."

"Holy shit!" JT said. "At least Hannibal wasn't killed."

"Yes, but what about those people on the ground?"

"I don't know. I guess it could have been a lot worse considering the area where the aircraft went down."

"What are we going to do?"

"I don't know. I need to think this through."

Dinner was a silent affair.

CHAPTER XXIII

That night, as they lay in bed, Pamela, as she usually does, turned to JT and placed her head on his left shoulder and crossed his body with her left leg and arm.

"What are you going to do?" She asked again.

"I don't know. I don't have any major service calls. Maybe I should go home and see what I can do. Hannibal getting arrested for smuggling drugs is a major offense. My sister is an attorney. Maybe I can get her to help. You and I are the only family he has. I just don't know."

Pamela's head suddenly rose, "Oh, no, does Cindy know yet?"

"She's in Thailand so I doubt it. Ah hell, this is going to break her heart." JT said stroking her hair.

Pamela turned away from JT onto her left side. JT spooned and threaded his right arm through hers, brushing her breast. She held onto his arm tightly.

"I'm sorry about the plate this morning," she said.

"Ah, that's OK, I knew you weren't really that mad. Although I'd hate to find out what you'd do if you really were mad though. I wasn't going to tell you but I actually ordered the HDTV. I was going to make it a surprise, but if I go to Indianapolis, you'll have to be here when it arrives."

"You're kidding, right."

"No."

"I love you." Pamela said kissing his arm.

"I love you too." He kissed her neck.

"Hey I almost forgot. Are you ready for this?"

"What?" She asked in a sleepy voice.

He told her about the rescued computer from the bottom of the lake. She started laughing. After a while JT could feel her breathing grow relaxed and she started to make tiny snoring noises.

JT removed his arm and turned with his back to hers; he was wide awake.

CHAPTER XXIV

Korat, Thailand

CYNTHIA "Cindy" Ng was born in Manhattan, Montana to a Chinese father and Native American mother. Her brother, Daniel was found dead several months ago from a drug overdose near a dumpster. That is when she first heard the name Roxanne, the drug she was trying to bring a halt of its importation into North America.

She wanted to get to the bottom of her brother's death.

She stood looking out of her hotel room window of the Royal Princess Korat Hotel. Below were modern paved roads and cars. It was hard for her to imagine this very same city as described by Hannibal and JT who were stationed here and the conditions back then, but they had shown her the pictures and told her stories about how, a long time ago, elephants ruled the streets as there were very little vehicle traffic on the hard dirt packed streets.

They told her that during the rainy seasons, the streets turned to 12 inches or deeper mud trenches, mixed with the waste that came from the small klongs, or canals, that paralleled the streets. They said that in those days, the Thai samlors, a sort of three-wheeled bike, were the only mode of transportation, outside of the elephants and trucks. The Thai peddlers, with bulging thigh muscles, tried their best to go from point A to B. It was easier to get out, pay the guy for his efforts, hop from one spot to the other, hoping that by the time you reached your destination you only had ankle thick mud clinging to you.

They said you could always tell how many Americans missed their intended spots or made a mistake as four letter words rang throughout the streets. The Thais on the other hand, simply took off their flip-flops, packed them away and walked through the sticky goo. When they arrived home, most Thai homes main living quarters were upstairs, it was a simple matter to take rain water, wash their feet and head up.

Cindy had arrived at Don Muang Airport and once cleared customs, showing her ID, took a taxi to the Amari hotel on Petchburi Road for two days of winding down from jet-lag. From there she took a bus to Korat, which was only several hours, to the province of Nakhon Ratchasima, or better known as Korat as there was no direct flights. There is the Royal Thai Air Force Base (RTAF), built in the 60's to support the Vietnam War. Most of the highway she traveled were built by American military funding and was the most modern even then. It is called *Thanon Mittraphap*, or Friendship Road.

To the south of the RTAF is Camp Friendship, where Hannibal and JT had been stationed. It is still being used today as a training base for Americans and Thais in modern warfare.

Hannibal and JT told her that a squad of Thai's could out-perform a company of American's as they were mean bastards and took no prisoners. They also told her that in those days, Americans had no local protection as they there were there as guest of the Thai government. Thus if a GI got into trouble with the local Thai government, he or she was at their mercy. JT said one night he had watched a friend get slapped several times by a Thai police Captain. In those days, a man, married or not, could not show affection in public. The guy was caught holding his girlfriend's hands as they stood outside a local bar. The girl was arrested and thrown into the monkey house, or jail and the Captain proceeded to teach the GI Thai customs. Shouts from other GI's begged him not to strike back or do anything stupid. So he just stood there; head rocking back and forth from the blows. Eventually the Captain stopped and he was allowed to leave. The girl too was eventually released.

"My how times have changed," Cindy thought. Although still frowned upon, more and more Thais were breaking from that tradition. It has always been acceptable for same sex persons, like two men to hold hands. Hannibal and JT said this would send the Americans up the wall and they would shout at the Thais, calling them Queers, or Gay. Hannibal had no comments, but JT said he tried to understand the Thai traditions and at times he was embarrassed to be an American.

Hannibal and JT had shown her a picture of a very modern looking hotel in downtown Korat, which back then, was the only multi-storied structure around. Today it is no more as in 1993; it collapsed, killing nearly 100 people.

JT had made friends with another US Airman named Martin and together they dated the daughters of a mama-san, who ran a very respectable diner. Hannibal said he didn't remember it as an Officer and a Gentleman; he avoided places like that, which brought out JT's finger.

Later JT was invited to Martin's wedding held in Muang Phayao, Thailand well to the northeast, within spitting distance of Laos and China. The wedding was actually the second part as the first, a Christian one, was held at the USAF chapel to get her American citizenship. This one would be the proper and traditional Buddhist wedding. JT told her that he never understood how Martin and Penoy communicated as JT spoke and understood enough Thai for the entire American group going up.

They had taken a train from Korat to Bangkok and from there to Chaing Rai, Chaing Mai and then a bus the rest of the way. JT celebrated his 21st birthday on the train somewhere between Chaing Rai and Chaing Mai.

Although the Thai are a very friendly and open people, Hannibal said he never feared for his life. JT on the other hand said there were only three times he had feared for his life. The first was when the bus they were riding was stopped and boarded by a band of insurgents; holding what looked like ancient bolt action rifles and automatic weapons. The mama-san had instructed that he, Martin, and Dave, another of Martin's friends keep their heads down and not took look into their eyes.

The insurgents strutted from back to front as if they owned the bus, which he guessed at the time they did. They stopped at the seats where

JT, Martin and Dave sat and stood for several minutes, which seemed like hours, scrutinizing them.

Nobody looked up.

JT said he needed a change of shorts.

When they were satisfied with whatever it was they were looking for, only then was the bus allowed to depart and continue its journey deep into the very rugged beautiful jungle mountainside.

The second time, JT said was when he had just steeped off of the local bus which served Camp Friendship, RTAF and Korat, heading towards the diner and was immediately grabbed by a muscular Thai who forced him against the side of the bus with a semi-automatic pressed against his forehead. The Thai held up a picture beside his face, decided there wasn't a match, let him go; boarded the bus looking for the face to match the picture.

Meanwhile another Thai stood outside yelling and screaming, which a lot of it JT did not understand in words. In meanings though, whoever it was, it was obvious that person was going to have an extremely short life expectancy.

If he found him, he didn't know as he had made himself quietly disappear; 'exit stage right.'

The third time was when he attended a traditional Thai dance hall, and always asked for one of the beautiful Thai dancers to sit at his table, which he had to pay for her time. Being an American, well he could have paid for her time and all of the others as well. I guess this pissed off some of Thai men.

One drunk Thai on the other side of the room stood up, pulled out a revolver, emptied the shells, putting one back in and played Russian Roulette, aiming the gun at him.

The Thai dancer disappeared.

CLICK! The sound was loud as even the Thai band had stopped playing and every one froze.

When the gun didn't go off, the Thai threw the revolver on the table and went into the men's room where he commenced to beat the shit out of the porcelain urinals. Meanwhile JT was either stupid; frozen or both, stayed as if nothing had happened.

He said he was never threatened again.

Maybe they thought he had magical spirits.

From then on, he was greeted at the door as if he was an International celebrity and allowed to talk to any of the beautiful women he wanted, but he always chose the first so as not to press his luck and piss somebody else off.

He told her that when he had time on his hands and nothing else to do if Hannibal was out and about dodging missiles or blasting up the jungle, he took Huey helicopter flights from RTAF to places far to the east near Cambodia with black and white Americans dressed in civilian clothing.

He could only assume these were CIA spooks. They kept to themselves during the flights and only whispered to each other and not over the inter-plane headsets.

He said that his only regret while stationed there was not being able to travel to Kanchanaburi, where during World War II; the Japanese had built a POW camp and a railway bridge linking Burma to Thailand. A fictional movie was made about the POW camp and bridge called "The Bridge over the River Kwai." JT, having seen the movie so many times wanted to see what it really looked like.

CHAPTER XXV

CINDY sighed at the memories of Hannibal and JT and the tall tales they told of Korat and what it was like to be here 45-years ago. She started smiling at another thought they had told Abby and she. They said back then; apples and oranges were considered contraband and any US military personal caught with them were arrested as sometimes there were surprise road checks conducted by the US and Thai military. They said that a man could make 'arrangements' with a woman of interest with just such an apple or an orange. This she found very funny, but the look on Abby's face confirmed it. The guys quietly let it drop.

"Hannibal and JT would have coronaries if they saw how cosmopolitan Korat had become since their absence." She thought. Now all a woman had to do was go down to the large shopping mall and buy that apple or orange.

Turning from the window she thought of her upcoming meeting with Abby. When Abby, Hannibal and JT had met at the restaurant and she told them about the drugs, what she hadn't told them was that two weeks before a Vietnam era OV-10 Bronco had made an emergency flight into McChord Air Force Base, and Captain Celina Majewski, USMC (ret.), was arrested. They found large quantities of drugs in several electronics bay boxes. Cellophane bags were hidden under dummy circuit boards. During the ferry flight one of the bags had ruptured from the sharp component pins projecting from the circuit board, and the spilling powder had insulated several electrical contacts casing a communications failure. Cindy was called in because she was in the area on another assignment that she was bringing to a close. After lengthy interrogations, Captain Majewski's story remained the same. She had been hired by a restoration company to ferry the aircraft, end of statement.

Nothing seemed out of the ordinary.

The weight and balance were correct, which she had shown them the log books. The communications gear worked during her pre-flight communications checks, so why should she open the electronic bays? As she had told them over and over, there wasn't a problem until she lost communications northwest of Seattle. Had she known would she have landed at a very large, very on the alert military installation?

They couldn't argue with that.

Captain Majewski was released to a private room with an AFS guard standing outside her door for several days. Later she was given a conditional release; she had to be available if and when they needed her as in don't leave the country.

During this time Cindy and been allowed to look at the boxes. Where they were from and what about the dummy circuit board? The boards were cut down PC mother board so that wasn't much help. She then took a closer look at the boxes. The one thing she noticed was that the serial numbers, when entered into the military online logistics database, all had shown them to have been sent to Thailand as replacements for the ones there.

So how in the hell did an electronic box from Thailand get into the bay of an aircraft that had never left the US? Not only that when a search of the Captain's name was made, she too had not left the country within the past year. It was for this reason they had to let her go.

Captain Majewski unfortunate landing had opened a lot of 'boxes.'

Cindy called her district office with her findings; they were not surprised and that threw her. "What are they not telling me?" She thought. She was ordered back to the office and allowed to see a classified "Secret" file. The file had shown that this was not the first incident. The FBI was also working with the Federal Marshal's office, Texas Rangers and CSIS or the Canadian Security Intelligence Service.

Because she was able to break the link, she was placed in contact with the local branch of the Thai police Narcotics Suppression Bureau and met Abby. Over the phone and through emails, Cindy discovered she liked Abby very much. A meeting was set up with the FBI, the Fed's, CSIS and the Thai government. Abby was flown to Vancouver, and that is where they met JT trying hard not to be so obvious. She laughed at the thought. I guess that meant she was still attractive. But JT almost got into trouble with Pamela over Abby looks as well. Although taught the possibility of using it, she had never seen someone tear up like that when she pinched JT's hand.

But Pamela was attractive as well and could understand if JT had been fooling around.

Cindy was the first to identify that the serial numbers of the boxes should match equipment still in Thailand. When they started looking into the serial numbers of the other equipment from the other aircraft, they too should have been in Thailand, most specifically Korat.

Her mind was swirling with all sorts of what ifs, how comes and where from. She had no answers but she needed them soon. Besides, she was getting a headache trying to make the puzzle fit.

Her thoughts went to a recent and very annoying television commercial. *"Head On!"* it screamed. Well she wished she had some *Head On* right now, but would settle for just a simple aspirin. She also needed to purchase a few items from that very same shopping mall she had seen. She went over to the bed far from the window where she had opened her cases. She had laid out some of her clothes from one case, putting her underwear, stockings bras neatly away in the drawers of the credenza, which only took up one drawer of the six. She hung the rest of her clothing up. It was from the second case that had drawn her attention and sent her to the window in the first place. Actually it was what she had forgotten to bring.

On the bed was her netBook, Wideye Sabre I satellite communications device and her Iridium Sat-Phone. The item missing was a voltage and outlet converter; the only place that might carry one was the shopping mall. During her many stops on the flight over, and to pass the time, she answered emails, watched a couple of videos; *Transporter III* with Jason Statham, and *The Bank Job*, again starring Jason. She was a Jason Statham fan. She also listened to iTunes she had downloaded onto her netBook; all on battery power. So when she pulled everything out, the netBook refused to power up.

OOPs.

Her Sat-Phone was also showing a low power indication, so she had turned it off to conserve power. With her right hand she hit her head. Must be old age creeping up.

How could she have forgotten? She put everything back, except the Sat-Phone, into the room safe, locking everything away. Dressed in jeans, sneakers; no socks, navy blue loose fitting blouse, with pink flowers, she grabbed her purse, keys, and the Sat-Phone, satisfied everything was secure or put away, she tossed her hair back, installed a brown plastic comb, pinning it back.

The purse she carried was a Jessica Simpson Latitude Tote knockoff, which she had purchased in Bangkok. Looking around once more, she grabbed her things, locked the door and headed for the elevators.

Cindy had not brought a handgun. That was too messy with customs. She knew Abby had one of those Springfield Armory XD semi-automatics manufactured in Croatia. She had once told her that she could shoot the heads off of thumbtacks at 50 paces. "Go on girl," Cindy had said. When back in the US of A, Cindy carried a 45 cal. Semi-automatic pistol. A little heavy for her, but it was far better at stopping someone than the Glock Model 19 her fellow agent's carried. It was also proven to be more trustworthy. She wasn't good, but she wasn't bad either. Most importantly, she wasn't afraid to use it.

CHASING ROXANNE

CHAPTER I

Los COLINAS, Texas

HANK MARSHALL looked down into the plaza from his 5th floor office in concentration. One part of his mind was split in thought listening to the members of the Retired Transport Pilots Association (RTPA) file into the conference room this warm sunny Texas day; the other part was of the galloping Mustangs, frozen in time by a sculptors hand far below. How real they looked galloping through a water bed. Tourist with cameras had other family members pose at various points to maximize their faces with those of the horses. A smile came to his face as he remembered years before he had done the very same with his kids and more recently with his grandkids.

Behind him was the buzz of conversation as each member greeted the other, catching up on the latest family and friends stuff, which had been updated just last month. Hank had called this meeting to discuss the recent events, which was major to the survival and reputation of RTPA and the various enterprises, of which included Advanced Aircraft Restorations (AAR) had to be protected.

The Texas Rangers, Homeland Security and FBI had suddenly taken an interest into their activities. As far as he knew they had nothing to hide. If his aircraft were being used to transport drugs, he was not aware of it and frankly was pissed that the Texas Rangers would even suggest such. Yet he couldn't deny the evidence found on both aircraft. But why would anyone within AAR, as it was their responsibility for maintaining the arriving aircraft, involve the organization in drug smuggling?

He turned to face the conference table, walking to his seat but did not sit down. He stood behind it, his hands resting on the back. Gradually conversations died as each realized Hank was waiting.

He was not given to cursing and wasn't going to start now, "What the hell is going on?" A question he just threw out to anyone in general.

There was only silence.

"I ask once more, what the hell is going on? Can anybody even remotely guess?"

Several seconds passed still with no answer. His gaze only fell on downcast eyes as each sought to move an imaginary dust particle from the notepad or twirl a pencil in their fingers. One of the women took a special interest in her polished nail.

"OK, let me put it this way. Within two months I've lost two aircraft and in each, some sort of new cocaine called Roxanne was found. The first was in Washington State at a US Air Force base of all things. The second was a crash in Indianapolis, killing three people and my pilot, General Washington was arrested. So what is going on? Why is the Texas Rangers and FBI beating on my doors? Sam, you're the man I hired to make things work, what do you know?"

"Well I have some ideas but nothing concrete Hank?"

"Like what?"

"Our problems did not start until you hired that General Washington."

"Whoa, hold on Sam. Washington is a retired and respected General in the US Air Force. You had better have something far more than concrete to make that kind of statement."

"Well I did some checking on, uh, General Washington and to be honest, his background is a little shady Hank."

Confusion and amusement appeared on the faces of the members of the conference, except for Hank. On his was anger.

"All we can get on him is that he was born in East St. Louis one of the biggest and dirtiest drug infested places in America. I'm not saying anything, but once in the ghetto, you can't get away from it."

"I wasn't raised in the ghetto Sam, but that does not mean I haven't lived my life with my eyes closed."

"I know that Hank and my comment was not intended that everyone raised in the ghetto is bad. Like I said, I've been doing some background research ...."

"I don't think I like the way this is going."

"Look Hank, I'm not a racist. I know you hired Washington on his merits, but I also think you've been blinded by the stars he wore."

The members of the board wondering where he was going with this,

"Remember right after you hired him he bought that airplane? Yeah you asked if Melvin and I knew him. We did but only remotely. We gave him room in the hanger to assemble it as you requested. Well it was right about time that things became strange. Things went missing. I didn't tell you as I had hoped they were only misplaced by the workers, but I started finding some of the missing items in his locker. You can ask Marvin. He and I also found traces of a white powder on the floor as if someone had spilled it and then tried to clean it up. At first I didn't know what to think and didn't have it tested. So to be honest I don't know what to tell you. I think someone is playing with our shipment of aircraft parts. We've never had anything like this before. It's not hard to put two and two together. With his background I bet he's setting up drug networks with is brothers in the hood."

Hank quietly simmered. He may be from Texas and his old man might have been a member of the Klan handing out leaflets in full regalia on Richardson street corners, but he had vowed that he would treat all men and women of color equally. As a former American Airlines pilot, his most trusted second in command was black, and he had proved himself time and time again. "I suppose you can back up what you're accusing General Washington of?"

"Sure can. In fact I was going to ask you for some time off and travel to Indianapolis to gather some evidence."

"What makes you think you're going to find something that the FBI, Homeland Security, and the various police agencies haven't?"

"I don't think they know where to look."

"And you do, how?"

"Look, you know me, and you know my background. I was raised in Detroit and saw how they operated. In each and every case, I saw them arrested only to come back selling the same shit. They will never change, just like Washington will never change."

Containing his anger Hank walked from behind his chair, and paced the area behind. Was he so, as Sam said, blinded by Washington's military career that he could not see beyond it? What if he was right? It would be the first time he had ever made a mistake. Mistakes are what other people made.

Does anyone else have anything of value to add to this meeting?

"Yes sir."

"What Melvin?"

"Sir I agree with Sam. I like Washington, but I also have had the opportunity to work with him and yeah, he knows plane, but I find him closed and aloof."

"Since when does being aloof account for drug dealing?"

"Well I mean he is not all that friendly. I don't know maybe he does have something to hide."

Several seconds passed. Hank turned to face the other board members, "Apparently I've wasted everyone's valuable time by calling this meeting. Meeting adjourned. Sam you and Melvin stay."

The other board members scattered like mice.

When they had left, Hank stood within Sam's personal space. "You had better tell me what you expect to find. You're really starting to piss me off. I have always considered myself a good judge of character and you're telling me I've made a grave mistake in hiring Washington?"

"I'm only saying that maybe you had made a bad decision."

"Washington was arrested and then released, so I'm told."

"And that is my point Hank. He gave them enough bullshit and they released him. I'm willing to bet now that he's free he will somehow try to pin the evidence on us. That's why I think I can find what the others couldn't."

Collecting his thoughts. "I'm going to give you that leave to prove me wrong and by God you had better come back with some solid evidence." He turned to take Melvin as well. "Or the two of you can forget setting foot into the conference room or this building again."

Without waiting for a reply, he stormed out of the room. The door wouldn't slam they were on a pneumatic hinge.

CHAPTER II

AS SAM FOSTER and Melvin Anderson walked across the open plaza past the galloping mustangs; from above they were being watched. Hank had known Sam a long time. It was never spoken, but he knew he had served in the US Air Force alongside Melvin. His records had shown he had a served but he had received a General Discharge. What the hell is a General Discharge? Sam never told him; he never pushed the subject. His side-kick Melvin Anderson had served a five-year sentence for something or other. Sam had vouched for him: the two were inseparable. He hired them for their extensive knowledge on jet aircraft. So far he had not heard anything wrong or bad about the two. But something wasn't adding up. It had started when he had interviewed Hannibal Washington. Although they were not on the interview, he had shown them a copy of his service records and asked for their input as it seems they had served at the same military installation in Thailand. Both gave Washington a nod, but nothing more. That could have been for several reasons. Maybe they knew him, but only remotely. Not unusual during a war where personnel rotated on a constant basis.

But why make a sudden about face in character on a person of Washington's brilliant career and as far as Hank could tell, integrity? Had he really been that far taken by the glitter of his service record and not looked deep enough? It just didn't add up.

Hanks continued to watch Sam and Melvin in animated conversation until they disappeared around the column of the next building heading towards the parking lot. He looked up. A typical crystal blue Texas sky. CAVU or in aviation terms Clear Air Visibility Unlimited. To the east he could just make out the cluster of building that signified downtown Dallas. From this height the view has not changed little over the years.

He brought his attention back inside the conference room and circled the huge table of waxed imported African wood. Each piece had been put together and placed in a database so that if a section was ruined, it was only a matter of calling up that data base and find a matching piece from the warehouse where extras were stored.

In front of his chair was a conference phone, mike and a notebook, mounted below a glass partition. A touch screen to the right gave him access to the functions that he needed. He pressed one.

"MaryAnn?"

"Yes sir?"

"How hard would it be for you to get some military records for me?"

"Wow, it depends on what you're looking for Hank."

"I'm looking for a match between General Washington, Melvin Anderson and Sam Foster."

"Anything specific?'

"I guess if they served in the same outfit; maybe on the same dates."

"That shouldn't be too hard. It might take a day or two."

"See what you can do. Also get me an update on the Washington crash. Especially what exactly happened and what was the substance on the T-38."

"Do you want me to go through the FBI, the Indiana State Police or the military?"

"Well if I remember it was the city police that arrested him, before being turned over to the State. Start there."

"Yes sir."

She broke the connection.

Hank had no idea what he was looking for but he had to start someplace and fast before his organizations came tumbling down around him.

He pressed the touch screen again.

"Yes sir."

"Find out what are the reasons a person would get a General Discharge from the military."

"On who?"

"Don't need names, just reason for."

"Yes sir." Once again she broke the connections.

Sam and Melvin walked across the plaza.

"Melvin I need you to watch things while I'm away. Let's start keeping a low profile until this blows over."

"Do you think he suspects anything?"

"About us? Maybe. That's why we need to lay low. I think I can pin this on Washington. This will take us off the radar screens. We'll have to change a few things, but for now we've done well for ourselves. A few more months isn't going to matter."

"Do you think he's watching us now?"

"I know he's watching us from that big window of his. Just keep it cool."

"Right, you're the one that doesn't have anything to lose. I can't get another job like you."

Out of view from the conference room window, Sam stopped, causing Sam to do likewise.

"Look Melvin. You and I go back a long ways. I've always been here for you. We're like brothers."

"Yeah only your military record was cleaned. I don't have your rich parents."

"Come on man, when have I ever let you down?"

Melvin didn't answer.

"Just lay low and keep it cool. This will all be over soon. Trust me."

Melvin snorted.

CHAPTER III

O'Reilly Raceway Park – West of Indianapolis

THE BILLBOARD SIGN SAID 15.43 seconds – 112 MPH. Not bad Terrell "T-Boy" Jefferson said to himself. Tonight was Tuesday Street Legal racing. Not one Tuesday over the previous two years had T-Boy missed the event except two weeks ago, when that brother from the airplane dissed him in front of his crew. Every time he thought about it, all he could think about was putting a bullet in his ass instead of his leg. Since then he has been tryin to figure out how he's gonna get his due. That nigga cost him two weeks of his life.

He was released as he had no priors, not even a speeding ticket. He told the judge that the gun belonged to his uncle. When he heard the explosion, he didn't know what was going on, grabbed the gun in case he needed it to defend his family. Then this brother came over, pushed him down, and the gun accidentally went off.

The judge assigned him to 50 hours of community service and was fined $500.

The 50-hours meant helping clean up the mess the airplane had caused. Oh, he wanted him bad.

Completing his community service he was released and his first priority was to get into his black Honda Civic dx, with gold rims, ground effects, and black bra. He had had the interior redone in a blood red fabric. He repainted the plastic trim using the new Krylon Fusion paint. He had made some basic engine modifications like adding a Nitrous Express NXT 100-shot direct-port wet kit, fuel rail, and two

5lb. bottles, otherwise everything was stock. He drove aimlessly around for a while trying to think of something to do, somehow finding he had driven to the Raceway, and of all things it was Tuesday night. That was what he needed. A couple of runs would replace the anger he felt.

When he had completed them, he drove outside the gates, pulled to the side where he got out and carefully put his racing gear away.

A man approached wearing a black Stetson hat, a shirt that was cream colored on one side, black on the other, blue jeans and tan cowboy boots.

"Mr. Jefferson?'"

"Who askin?"

"My name is Sam Foster and I am here to make you an offer." He said, sticking out his right hand.

T-Boy looked at the out stretched hand. There might be a black man sittin in the White House, but out here, in reality when a white man stuck his hand out, calling you '*Mister*', and on top of that making you an offer, as a black man you took off for the hood.

But T-Boy was curious. This cracker was wearing a big belt buckle with the letters 'AAR' over an aircraft emblem, but even without the belt buckle he could tell his accent was Texan or somewhere from the south. T-Boy stuck his hand out, shaking the stranger's.

"You can call me T-Boy." He said. "My ride is not for sale."

"I don't blame you. I saw your times. Nice, but I'm not here to buy your car. It seems you and I have a common problem. You obvious know a Mr. Washington."

"If you're talkin about the nigga that I busted a cap in his leg, yeah I know him. Wish I'd busted one in his ass. Nigga made me look like a bitch ho in front of my crew."

"Well. . . uh. . . yes, we're talking about the . . .uh, same person. I represent a company willing to correct a problem we have with Mr. Washington. My concern is can I trust you and can you keep this conversation private."

"I know how to keep my mouth shut if that's what you're askin." T-Boy responded.

"Well Mr. Jefferson, I hope you can appreciate and respect my concern. I know all about the problems you've had since uh, Mr. Washington put you in an unfortunate situation which sent you to jail. I can't erase the jail time, but I can offer you a way to get back."

"You remember that cocaine on that airplane? It was ours and Mr. Washington was stealing it. Obviously we can't go to the police with that information. So here's what I'm offering; I want Mr. Washington to hurt a little. I don't want him killed, I want him to suffer. He's causing problems with our operations. What if I offer you $20,000; $10,000 now and $10,000 when he is out of action."

"$10,000? You gonna roll up on a brother, thinkin I'm stupid enough to do a hit for you? You ain't even got $10,000. Yeah, you got a fancy belt buckle an all, but that don't prove nutin."

"I'm not asking to make a hit on Mr. Washington. We just need him out of the way for awhile until we can complete some arrangements. If we wanted him dead, that would be taken care of with, uh . . someone with a little more professional abilities. You fit the bill for what we want as you have a reason to be angry and want revenge. We're just offering you a little something to help you along. Reaching inside his attaché case, Mr. Foster pulled out a thickly padded brown envelope; opened it, displaying a wad of $100 bills.

"You sayin all I gotta do is scare the shit out of the nigga?" T-Boy said

"That's right."

"For $20,000?"

"The money is a sort of arrangement. You don't tell anyone and you keep the money."

"What kinda business ya'll runnin?"

"If I told you, then I'd have to kill you, wouldn't I?" Sam smiled at his own joke.

T-Boy looked at the envelope. $20,000 would make a lot of upgrades for his ride.

"Can I think about it?"

"Sure." He reached into his case again and pulled out a business card with the same logo, RTPA, as his belt buckle, giving it to T-Boy.

"I check my email everyday. But, and this is important, if I haven't heard from you in 24-hours, then the deal is off."

"You'll hear from me. I just have to take care of some other business."

"Good. I'll be waiting."

Sam closed the attaché case.

"Oh yes. Mr. Jefferson, there's one more thing I want you do."

"What?"

Sam reached into his shirt pocket and pulled out a bag of white power, handing it to T-Boy. "Whatever you do, I want you to put this where it will be found on Mr. Washington."

T-Boy took the bag. "That's the same shit I saw the other night."

"Yes it is. It is very important that it is found on Mr. Washington."

"Oh, I get it. You want him to get busted with the shit. Man you don't even have to pay me for that."

"I trust you'll do it right." Sam said and walked back to the gates of the Raceway.

T-Boy watched him leave and got back into his car. He sat there thinking about the money and drugs. He wasn't into shootin up so that wasn't a problem. And if putting the stuff on Washington was all he had to do, that nigga was going to jail for good. He looked at the card again and put it into his wallet.

He left the Raceway; Busta Rhymes, *Back on My B.S,* was pumping from a set of Polk DB-6500 component speakers in front, DB-690 three-ways in back, and dual DB-104 subs.

From one of the brother's he was sharing a cell with; he learned that the name of the old man that had brought shame and disgrace to him was retired Air Force General Richard Washington. He was being held in a Hotel room. They didn't have enough information to charge him with anything, but they couldn't let him go either. He wasn't under arrest, but if he went anywhere he was escorted by a plain clothes cop.

He told them that he was going to get his due, but he didn't know how. His cell mates just laughed. "Man you better let that shit go." They said. "That man is a genuine American Hero and you don't fuck with a hero."

"That's an old man. He ain't gonna be so hard to take down." T-Boy said.

The brothers only laughed even harder. Well he'd show them and now he had the money to do it. He'd only told that cracka he needed time, when in fact his mind was already made up. He just wanted to see if he was for real.

CHAPTER IV

Oliver, BC – That Morning.

AT 3:45 Pamela awoke to find JT was not there. In her sleep her hand had reached over to touch him. When it did not find him she came awake disoriented. Sitting up and pulling the hair from her face she turned on her small high-intensity reading lamp next to her side of the bed. Where JT should have been, the blanket was thrown back and his pillow ruffled. His robe, which normally hung over the end of the bed, was not there. Getting up, she put on her terry cloth robe and went into the hallway. There was no light in the computer room, but there was a soft glow coming from the kitchen. She followed it where she found JT sitting at the dinner table, starring at a cup of tea. On a plate were the remains of cinnamon toast.

"Are you OK?" She asked.

"Oh I guess so. I couldn't sleep and didn't want to wake you." He said.

"Well you know when you aren't in the bed; I miss you and wake up anyway."

"Sorry," he said.

"Oh, don't be. I was going to say you look as if you've lost your best friend, but I guess that is not the right thing to say right now."

"Hah, yeah." JT responded with a small laugh.

"JT I guess we have an emergency right?" She asked.

"I guess, why?" He asked.

"What I'm saying is that we have an emergency and we should treat it as such. You can take the *ISKRA* down. You can use the credit card but only on one condition."

"Oh, and what condition is that?"

"I go too. Hannibal is family and as family we have to do this together."

"But how are . . ." JT didn't get to finish. Pamela put her hand on his.

"Sweetheart, I can get off work. I have some time coming and as I said, this is an emergency. Hannibal comes first." She said. "But you need to get some sleep. I can't let you fly the jet on no sleep."

"Just a minute," she said. She got up, went over to the range, and turned off the exhaust fan light. Then she walked back to the table and pulled one of the chairs out into the middle of the floor. She then took JT's hand and led him to the chair. She opened his robe and massaged his chest working her way down. JT was getting stiff. She then took his member and massaged it as well, leaning close to him and let it rub it against her tummy. She then pulled his robe off and took hers off as well. Underneath she was wearing a short silky night slip. She pulled off her panties and pushed him backwards slightly, sitting him down. Kneeling before him she continued to stroke his member and then took it into her mouth. When he was nice and hard, she stood, straddling him and then put it into her. JT groaned from the heat and pleasure. Rising on the balls of her toes, she began to rock back and forth. She then put her arms around his neck, pulling him into her breast. She felt him began to release and increased her rhythm. When he came she drew him to her and kissed him hard.

Resting for a few minutes, she got up, took him to the bedroom, leaving their clothes in the middle of the kitchen floor. In the bedroom, as he headed towards his side of the bed and she hers, JT turned, grabbed her, picking her up placing her lovingly in the bed. He spread her legs and starting at her breast, tracing a pattern downwards. She moaned when he stuck his tongue in her massaging her clit. When it too was stiff, he put himself in her and made long slow strokes. When she came only then did he come again, collapsing on her. She felt him sobbing.

"Are you OK," she asked.

"Yes sweetheart. I needed that more than you'll ever know." He answered.

"I want you to sleep now." She said.

JT rose allowing her to move to her side of the bed and turned over on his back. She placed her head on his shoulders and they both fell into a deep sleep.

CHAPTER V

JT had met Pamela many years before. From day one it was like God had given him a new life. She had had problem with their previous computer service person and called JT's Computers. When he walked in his heart did a flip-flop when she made eye contact. He felt like a ten-year old, caught admiring his grade school teacher. Later she would tell him the same thing. For the first several months they kept their feeling secret until they were brought together though a series of events. One night he had to make a late evening service call. As she stood watching, he took a gamble and revealed his desires for her. She told him that she was interested in him as well. He asked if he could do something he had never done before and that was to touch her just below her neck and above her breast and that it was not intended to be sexual. That is not the way it turned out. He touched her and if felt as if he had received an electric shock. When he started to take his hand away, she put her hand on his and kept it there. No words were needed as they looked deep into the eyes of the other. He moved her against a wall and gave a deep kiss, which she returned. She took him to a small room where they made love on a small cramped sofa. From that day not many verbal words of love had to be spoken between them. All each had to do was touch the other and it was transmitted.

They were married a year later.

In his life and as she told him, they had never felt such deep love for another person. He made himself a promise that no matter the events of their lives, there would never be another woman in his life that could equal what she meant to him.

CHAPTER VI

THE SUN WAS SHINING when JT awoke. Pamela was awake, watching him.

"How long have you been awake," he asked.

"About 10 minutes. I was watching you sleep. Did I tell you I love you?" She asked.

"Gee, only about a dozen times. I love you too." And he kissed her, feeling himself get hard again. She put her hand on his member and squeezed. "Ow!" JT said.

"You've got other things to do besides lying in bed. You have to conserve your energy. Maybe I'll let you join the Mile High Club."

"We're already members of the Mile High Club." JT reminded her.

"Yes, but only in the Cessna. Not the *ISKRA*."

"We can't join the mile high club in the *ISKRA* as only one person can sit up front." JT said.

"Then I guess you'll have to dream about it." She said, pushing him out of the bed with her feet laughing.

JT hit the floor with a thump. Looking up, he saw her laughing and started laughing too.

She got out of the bed, crossing him. He got a long look up her night shirt, getting him hard again. He just laid there admiring her tanned legs as she headed for the bathroom. He got up following her; his penis pointing the way.

"If you don't make the water too hot, I'll join you," she said.

"But you like it cold." He answered.

"I do not. I like it warm."

"Feels like it's cold to me." He mumbled.

He ran the water and she joined him, but kept him at arm's length when he tried to place his hands between her legs, allowing him to only touch her breast.

"No fair," he mumbled, wondering what he was going to do about the baseball bat between them.

She laughed, pulled the curtain back a little and got out. "Don't you dare do what I think you'll do," she said.

"Ah damn, no fair you leaving me like this."

"You'll live." She said, and with that turned on the overhead fan and left.

JT looked down and said, "Down boy!"

ONCE HE WAS DRESSED in jeans and shirt, he padded through the house to the computer room and called up the latest weather reports from British Columbia to Indiana for the next 24-hours. He then set about getting out the appropriate maps and plotted his course. He had installed the GPS, but had not had the opportunity to learn all of its functions. "Besides," he said, "it is always best to make a manual calculation first." Weird things happen to electrical devices. The electron Gods took no prisoners. With Pamela flying with him on their first long International flight, he was not taking any chances.

Once he had plotted his course; he determined he'd need to stop at Great Falls, Montana, clear customs and refuel. Another refuel stop was needed at Denver, Colorado, Kansas City, Missouri; landing at Indianapolis Eagle Creek. He figured on an hour to clear customs in Butte and about 45 minutes at each stop. JT then called flight service and filed a flight plan.

In the bedroom, Pamela was dressed in a skirt, blouse, and flats. JT had never been fond of them. He liked her sandals when she wasn't dressed up.

Pamela had packed a special baggage case JT had splurged on to fit the storage space for the ISKRA not realizing he'd actually need it one day. "Better now than never," he thought.

He loaded everything into Pamela's car. She drove them to the airport.

"Did you call Gail?" Pamela asked.

"Yep. She said no problem." Gail was his computer backup person. She had taken a maternity leave from her regular job and JT employed her from time to time when he was swamped or out of town.

Pamela had never flown in the *ISKRA* as she considered it his toy. Rolling out the aircraft, he parked her car inside. They performed the preflight together. When it was complete, he called Mike over to top off the fuel tanks and oil.

From a locker in the back he retrieved his flight suit and Vietnam Era, green canvas combat boots. He stripped, placing his clothes on a chair, and put them on. Pamela had gone to the toilet with stand-up shower JT had installed early on because he never knew how long he'd be there on a service call.

Mike arrived and grounded the aircraft with the cables. "How much you want this time JT?" He asked.

"Top up both tanks."

Mike looked at him in mild surprise. "What did you do, win the lotto?" Mike asked.

"No. Pamela gave the OK to use the credit card."

Pamela came out right at that moment and said, "You didn't tell him I kept you from using the card did you?"

"Well. . . . yes." JT said.

"You make it sound like I'm a tyrant." She said, punching him on the arm.

"Yes Mike, he can use the credit card today." She yelled.

"OK," he said and began the task of filling up the tanks.

"Oh, Mrs. Travis?'

"Pamela please." She said.

"Uh, Pamela, who do I see about renting a houseboat?"

"Well whenever you're ready, let me know. If I'm not there you can see Arlene."

"Isn't she the other woman I see with you and JT?"

"I think so."

"OK, thanks." Mike returned his attention to filling the tanks.

"I have a surprise for you," JT said. He took Pamela's hand and guided her back into the hanger. From the locker he pulled out another flight suit, a helmet, and a pair of black boots.

"What's that?" she asked.

"It's your flight suit," JT said, holding it up. I had hoped one day you'd go flying with me in the ISKRA, so I picked this out for you."

"JT how am I going to wear that? I've got on a skirt!"

"Yeah I can see that. Well you can always take those off and fly in your panties and bra." JT said with a grin.

"Ha. Ha. Nice try." She said.

JT walked back to the locker and pulled out a hanger with a pair of pants covered by a flannel shirt, and a pair of socks.

"There's my pant's JT! I've been looking all over for them. What are they doing here?"

"Well I took the liberty of placing them here for a special day. Today is that day."

"And the socks?" She inquired.

"Well you know how cold my feet get? I went to the hunting outlet store and purchased a pair of heated thermal socks for you and me. I modified them so that instead of the bulky "D" cell batteries, they plug into the *ISKRA* electrical system.

"Yuck." She said holding them up and headed for the toilet. She returned and posed for JT. "Well how do I look?"

"You look like a famous female blonde aerobatic pilot in a flight suit." He said.

"Who is she?" She asked.

"Don't worry, you'd like her."

"What are all of these pockets for?" She asked.

JT walked over and touched her left breast pocket. "You put your lipstick in here and your makeup kit in this pocket." He said touching her right breast.

She smacked his hand saying, "Stop."

"Hey JT, she's fueled and ready to go." Mike said, having walked into the hanger.

Pamela blushed.

JT fished out the credit card from his wallet and gave it to him. This time when it said 'APPROVED' JT didn't even blink at the $975 total.

As JT was loading the aircraft, Pamela took out what she thought she'd need. A couple bottles of water went into each leg pocket and a paperback novel into the waist pocket. JT helped her put on the helmet, trying to keep the hair out of her face.

"Did you try and call Cindy again?" Pamela asked.

"Yeah right before we left the house. I keep getting her voicemail. Maybe I should try one more time. I'll tell her to call me as soon as she gets my message."

"What if she calls while we're flying?" Pamela asked.

"I doubt it as it is early morning over there. She's asleep and probably turned off her phone."

JT made the call, but again got her voicemail, but told her of their plans to fly down to Indianapolis and take care of Hannibal.

He installed Pamela in the back seat, insured her straps were secured and got into the front seat. Startup was simple and they were soon taxing out to the runway. He announced his intentions over the radio and with a shove of the throttle, they were gone.

From the back over the intercom, he heard Pamela, say, "Heeeeee Hawwww. Indianapolis here we come!!"

CHAPTER VII

THE SHORT FLIGHT to Great Falls, Montana was uneventful. When they landed they were instructed to park near a terminal and not leave the aircraft. JT opened the canopy and waited for the CBP (Custom and Border Patrol officer with Homeland Security.).

After 30-minutes of waiting Pamela said, "JT I have to use the bathroom."

"I thought you went before we left?" He said.

"I did, but I got thirsty and drank both bottles of water I had placed in my suit."

JT started laughing.

"That's not funny. If that CBP person isn't here soon, I'm going to pee all over your airplane." She said which made JT laugh even harder.

"Just wait a little longer" he said. "We can't leave the aircraft."

Just as he said that, he could see the officer approaching the aircraft with customs forms being fanned by the wind that was attached to a clipboard. JT got out first, greeted the officer and then helped Pamela down.

"Officer, can I go to the bathroom?" She asked.

"Not until I've inspected the aircraft mam," he said.

"Sir, I really have to go." She said bending over, putting her hands between her legs.

He said, "Mam, over there is a terminal, you can go over there, but don't make me come looking for you."

"Over there?" She said pointing to the terminal about 200 feet away.

"Yep."

"I'll never make it." With that she took off for a picnic table beside a small tree and trash bin. She was running in slo mo, the boots weighing her down. By the time she reached them, she was already pulling zippers down to get out of the suit. With what must have been the exact moment, hiding and squatting; JT and the CBP officer saw a stream of water trickling towards the sewer drain.

The CBP officer and JT watched; chuckling. JT turned to the CBP officer, "I guess she really had to go, huh. Damn a Kodak moment and I missed it."

"Yep, she really had to go. Tell you what; I'll just go quietly back to my office and pretend I didn't see that, besides if you had a camera, she'd probably kill you. My wife would. Here's your paper work and have a nice flight," he said, patting JT on the back, leaving the same way he had come.

JT pulled out his cellphone and called for a fuel truck. He had to go to the men's room as well, only he'd use the men's room in the terminal. He waited for Pamela and when she emerged, she was carrying the boots, with her flight suit over her shoulders.

"So you think that was funny?" She asked.

"Well you have to admit, that it was. You should have seen yourself." JT said, starting to laugh again.

She thought for a moment, "I guess I did. Do I have to wear this thing?"

"Yes you do. These suits are made to keep you warm and they are practical as they act as a fire retardant. I don't expect anything to happen, but if it did and I lost you for a simple thing as not wearing a flight suit, it would devastate me." He said looking into her eyes.

She looked at the suit, "Well as long as you put it that way." JT helped her get back into the suit; kneeling down to lace up her boots and pulling the zippers shut. "Hey I bet if I stuck my tongue in this one . . ." He said unzipping instead of zipping the one in front.

"Stop JT somebody might be looking. Do you remember the scene in 'Something about Mary' where Ben got his balls stuck in his zipper? How would you like your tongue stuck that way?"

"You're a cruel woman. So let them look." JT said.

She pulled away and did the rest of the zippers herself.

"Ah, you're no fun. Where's your sense of adventure? How many opportunities are going to come along like this?"

"Not here and not now." She said.

"I need to use the restroom myself. Wanna walk with me?"

"No, you go ahead. I need to get a bottle of water out. I promise only one this time." She proceeded to climb back into the aircraft.

"Do you want anything?" He asked.

"If they have a strawberry yogurt, I'll take one of those." She said.

"OK."

When he returned with the yogurt, Pamela was standing beside the aircraft as the fueling truck had just completed topping off the tanks.

ONCE THE AIRCRAFT was fueled; Pamela and he got back into the aircraft. JT made sure she only had one bottle of water this time and gave her the yogurt. He started the *ISKRA*; received permission to taxi to the active, was wished a good day by the controller and once again they were off. Six hours later, JT, coming in from the west spotted Indianapolis International and to his left Eagle Creek Airpark.

"Indianapolis Approach *ISKRA* Charlie Charlie Delta Yankee." JT announced.

"*ISKRA* Charlie Charlie Delta Yankee Indianapolis Approach."

"Indianapolis *ISKRA* Charlie Delta Yankee has information Bravo at 5,000 feet inbound on course heading 110 degrees 15 miles west of the airport VFR for Eagle Creek."

"*ISKRA* Charlie Delta Yankee Indianapolis understands you are 15 miles west of the airport at 5,000 feet."

"That's affirmative Indianapolis.'"

"*ISKRA* Charlie Delta Yankee Indianapolis altimeter Two Niner decimal Niner visibility 25 miles. Reduce speed to 180 knots indicated. You're cleared for VFR direct to Eagle Creek. Frequency change approved to One Two Two decimal Eight."

"Indianapolis *IRSKA* Charlie Delta Yankee altimeter Two Niner decimal Niner, reduce speed 180 knots, direct VFR Eagle Creek, frequency approved One Two Two decimal Eight. Requesting my flight plan be closed. Good day sir."

"IRSKA Charlie Delta Yankee Indianapolis flight plan is closed. Good day to you too."

During the exchange, JT could see Pamela in his rearview mirror trying to get a better view of what was ahead. Due to the narrow canopy, her vision was limited and to the side, the wings blocked her downward view.

JT changed frequency. "Eagle Creek Unicom *IRSKA* Charlie Charlie Delta Yankee."

"*ISKRA* Charlie Delta Yankee Eagle Creek Unicom.'"

"Eagle Creek Unicom *ISKRA* Charlie Delta Yankee is inbound VFR crossing midfield for runway 3 full stop."

"*ISKRA* Charlie Delta Yankee, you're number one in the traffic. Altimeter Two Niner decimal Niner winds are calm. Your rental car is waiting."

"Roger that."

"JT I can't see anything." Pamela said over the Intercom.

"I guess we'll have to fix that." He said. He reduced power and pulled back on the collective, applied left aileron and left rudder going into a barrel roll."

From the back he heard Pamela go, "Wwwwwwooooooooooo!!"

He held it inverted for five seconds, in which her paperback novel fell to the top of the canopy. He completed the roll, when his wings were level kicked left rudder and aileron again; making a knife end left turn upwind of runway 3. Pamela's novel first hit her on top of her helmet and then flew sideways.

Once level again, from behind his shoulder he felt a hand tapping and looked in the rearview mirror. The other hand was being held up for him to see, with a perfectly manicured pink fingernail, the middle finger, pointing straight up.

JT chuckled. He taxied the aircraft to an open tie down spot. A small crowd had gathered to see the *ISKRA*, which JT found was the usual case when he landed at different airports. He opened the canopy and started shutdown procedures. When he was finished he turned to get out and was whacked on the back of his helmet with the paperback.

"Did you have fun?" Pamela asked.

"Well you said you couldn't see anything." JT responded.

"Well I wasn't prepared for that. I almost pee'd and pooped in your airplane. Don't you ever do that again without telling me first."

"Yes dear." JT said in a mock contrite voice. Here let help you down."

When she was out and JT was handing down the specially made flight bag, she asked, "Do I need to keep these boots on?"

"No."

"Thank God for small miracles." She said.

She dung around in the flight bag and pulled out her sandals. She took them to a grassy area next to the tie down area, sat down and proceeded to unlace her boots.

Meanwhile JT went into the FBO and retrieved the keys to the car. Several of the onlookers wanted to know more about the jet. JT gave them his prepared speech. Normally he would have taken them on a tour, but it was late afternoon and they still had a lot to do, like contacting Hannibal. He finished signing the final forms, and asked for a fuel truck. He got into the car and carefully backed it up to the *ISKRA*. He opened the trunk and placed the flight bag, Pamela boots, helmets and his flight case inside. From the nose of the aircraft, which had once housed the radar and other military gear, he grabbed the wheel chocks, covers for the exhaust, bright orange engine intake plugs with long red streamers and a pitot tube cover.

The fuel truck arrived and topped off his tanks. He placed the canopy in the down position and locked it. It took 15 minutes to install the covers, chock the wheels, and tie the aircraft to the ground. When he finished, Pamela was already in the car, engine running and the AC going full blast.

When JT got in she said, "How can you stand this heat?" She asked. She had a line of perspiration on her upper lip, which JT took his thumb and wiped away.

"It's only 87 degrees," he said. I guess because I was raised here it feels normal."

"And the humidity!" She said unzipping her flight suit to mid-stomach. Somewhere along the flight she had taken off her blouse and was only wearing a black bra.

"Ah, come on it's not that bad. You'll get used to it. You should be here when it gets 99 degrees and 100% humidity. Did you take your pants off as well?"

"No way!" She protested. "And yes I took them off and put on a pair of shorts."

"You are the most sexist woman I have ever seen in a flight suit." He said.

"I thought you said I looked like that blonde aerobatic pilot whatever," she said.

"I have never seen her in a flight suit." JT responded.

"Thank you." She said. "I'd hate to think I had competition."

"You know you're always number one in my heart." JT said.

Changing the subject she said, "See JT, I only drank half of the water," Holding the bottle up.

"You're a good girl and for that I give you a kiss," which he did by leaning over the center console.

CHAPTER VIII

JT HAD MADE reservations at the Residence Inn in the upper northwest corner of Indianapolis. They drove north on I-465, following it around towards the east, exiting on highway 421. What are those buildings JT?"

"Those are the Pyramid Office Complex. I once maintained their computers years ago. That's a manmade lake in front. You should see it when the clouds are low and the early morning sun hits the windows. It is a heavenly sight." JT said.

Pamela and JT must have made a sight as they walked to the reservation desk. People hid their amusement as they watched a six foot black man in a flight suit, Vietnam Era combat boots carrying two overnight bags, accompanied by a petite 5'3" white female in a similar flight, the lower parts of her suit legs rolled up revealing tanned legs with bright pink toenails encased in tan sandals. The top of her flight suit was unzipped revealing tanned cleavage.

When they were in the room with everything unpacked, JT called the number where Hannibal was being held. He was told that he had been transferred to a hotel room.

Hannibal answered on the second ring. Pamela could hear Hannibal's excitement. They made arrangements to meet the next day. They still had to cover some missing points on the investigations. Once again he expressed how happy he was that they had made it and hung up.

While JT ordered room service, Pamela took a shower.

By the time the both of them had eaten and JT had taken a shower, the reality of the day hit them. They were on one of the beds, watching television with the volume turned all the way down.

JT said, "Thank you for letting me come down and thank you for coming with me."

"I told you that we were in this together. Hannibal is family and I'm glad we came. Believe it or not, I actually had fun. Maybe when this is all over, I'd like to go up with you again without a crisis." She turned her head and gave him a kiss.

Did I ever tell you how much I love you?" JT said.

"Well you did this morning, but you can tell me again." She said."

"I love you."

"And I love you too."

They fell asleep on top of the covers.

Somewhere in the early morning hours, they awakened and climbed under the covers, staying that way until the sunlight came streaming into the window bathing their faces in its glow.

CHAPTER IX

Crown Hill Cemetery – Indianapolis, Indiana, The next day

The Reverend Allen Michaels stood in his pastoral robe surrounded by the Church Choir. The choir was swaying to the hymn *'Just As I am.'* Before him was a dark wood casket with gold handles sitting on the catafalque soon to be lowered into the grave. In the casket were the remains of Sister Ester Jefferson one of three people killed when the T-38 dropped from the sky that faithful night.

In the front row of seats reserved for relatives was the grandson, Terrell 'T-Boy' Jefferson. He sat with his aunt and uncle and their children. He was the sole survivor of his immediate family. He was an only child as not too long after he was born; his parents were gunned down in a drug theft gone badly. They were visiting an old family friend when two gunmen entered, unfortunately the wrong house, seeking what they thought was a stash of crack, cocaine, meth, and ecstasy. When they had entered they tied everyone up and started ripping the place apart.

Multiple gunshots rang out; shooting everyone one by one in the hope someone would tell them were the drugs were.

Nobody knew.

The victims slumped where they sat. When the gang left, a fire was started to hide the evidence.

The gang members were never found.

T-Boy's aunt and uncle took him in and raised him with their daughter and two-sons. They were as strict with him as if he was theirs.

Rev. Michaels, in his rich baritone Baptist voice, sought forgiveness for any sins Sister Jefferson might have committed and prayed that her soul be admitted into Heaven.

T-Boy was hard. He sat up straight. He wasn't going to cry. Not in front of the Church members, especially the neighborhood families that had come to pay their respects and the television cameras held back at a distance by barricades and police to allow privacy.

When Rev. Michaels finished, several Deacons of the Church, started lowering the casket, the little cranks making tiny squeaks.

A tear came to T-Boys eyes. He fought it back. Just as the top of the casket traveled below the dirt, streams of tears come from his eyes; he began to cry in earnest. The Sisters of the Church tried to comfort him. One large bosomed Sister held him close, burying his head between two large breasts, nearly smothering him.

Rev. Michaels didn't help much either. "Let it out brother Jefferson, let it out son! There is nothing to be ashamed of. Let it out!" He preached.

The Choir, which had been humming, now broke out into loud praises of God with the members shouting, "Amen and *Hallelujah!*"

For ten minutes Brother Jefferson did exactly what he said he wasn't going to do.

Finally, drained of all emotion, as he stood he was offered a rose, which he threw on her casket and walked away.

Somebody was going to pay.

CHAPTER X

HANNIBAL WAS BEING held at a hotel room in downtown and was released to JT and Pamela, described as family members. They left downtown headed back to the Residence Inn, northbound on I-65. By coincidence, T-Boy had left the downtown area of Indianapolis, traveling west on 38th Street, taking the entrance onto Interstate 65, when he spotted a rental car with what looked like the nigga General in the front seat. Another brother was driving and a white woman in the back.

T-Boy held back, letting his anger build slowly. There was very little traffic and he doubted they would recognize him as he had tinted windows that just barely passed State laws. He had an idea. They were in the left lane. Maybe he could do one of those PIT maneuvers he had seen on the COPS shows. If a cop could do it, he could too. He'd simply come up in their blind spot on the right side and tap his bumper to the left. That should send them off the road into the medium.

He punched the accelerator just as they were coming up on the Lafayette Road exit and the Interstate started curved to the left. He was almost upon them, when he saw the woman in back turn and scream.

HANNIBAL was up front and Pamela in back as JT drove the rental car. There was very little traffic and he was in the right lane. Mainly because he knew from experience that there was an exit coming up and if he was in the right lanes, there might be a slow car making the exit and he'd have to slow down.

"Hey JT, isn't this where you told me you lived?"

"Yeah."

"Isn't the Indianapolis 500 Race Track down that way?" Hannibal asked pointing to the left. "Have you ever seen the Indy 500 Race track? I know Pamela hasn't."

"No," he said. "Other than the sports channels highlights."

"Well I'll show you my old stomping grounds on Georgetown Road." JT said.

"Ah shit, I'm in the left lane. Hold on." JT looked in his rearview mirror where there was a black car about 50 feet back in the same lane. He put on his turn signal and headed for the exit when Pamela screamed. "JT look out!!"

Out of nowhere the black car had accelerated to the right lane and he was about to hit it. Although not a professional driver, he wasn't a slouch either. He quickly corrected while slamming on the brakes and when the black car had passed, slammed hard over to take the right side exit.

Pamela screamed again as she was thrown sideways. Hannibal had grabbed the "Holy Shit" handle.

"Damn JT you almost hit that guy," Hannibal said.

"I didn't! He just came out of nowhere!"

On the exit ramp he brought the car to a halt. They got out inspecting it for damage,

"Honest Hannibal, the guy was behind me when I put on the signals. But out of nowhere he was right beside us. Had it not been for Pamela, I'd have nailed him for sure!"

"Give me your cellphone and I'll call 911." Hannibal said. "Mine was lost in the crash."

"Man, I bet that guy is pissed. I honestly never saw him."

"I didn't see him at all." Hannibal said.

"Are you alright?" Pamela asked JT.

"Yeah I'm OK, just a little shaken. That was really close. Are you OK?"

"I'm OK. Like you said he came out of nowhere." Pamela added.

Above them and on the highway, they saw several motorists had stopped where the black car had come to rest at the end of the guardrail. It was not hard to see the damage to the passenger side from where they stood. The driver was obviously unhurt as he was standing in front of his car checking the damage. They tried yelling at him to see if he was OK. He must have been as he just stood there. Then he did a strange thing, he pointed his finger at them as if holding a gun and pulling the trigger.

"JT. Pamela. Get into the car now. I don't know what's going on, but that's the same kid that shot me."

"What!!??" Pamela and JT said in unison.

"Get in the car," Hannibal said again.

They got into the car and drove north on Lafayette Road. JT made a few wrong turns as it had been many years since he'd been in this area, but eventually he made it to the Residence Inn.

"DAMN! What the fuck! Where's he go?" T-Boy yelled. The car he was trying to do a PIT maneuver on flew backwards and behind him off the ramp. He was so busy watching the other car pass; he forgot to pay attention to what was in front. He hit the guard rail on the passenger side with a glancing blow. But instead of bouncing off, there was a loud bang and screech, the rail acted as a guide forcing him around the bend, but at least not over the overpass.

He came to a stop, jumped out running to the passenger side to inspect the remains of his car. It was heavily damaged, but drivable. He looked over the rail and saw that the other car had stopped as well; the three of them were looking up and him. They were waving and yelling something, which he couldn't hear because of the distance.

All he saw was red. First this nigga dissed me and now he crashed my ride. That nigga is gonna pay. I don't need no money. This nigga is mine and that asshole with him and that woman. I'm gonna teach them a lesson they'll never forget. He pointed his finger at them, pretending to have a gun and pulled the trigger. They got in there car and took off. "Yeah, you'd better run!" He yelled.

Several people had gathered around to look at the damage. "Get the fuck back," he said.

He got into his battered car and drove away.

AT THE RESIDENCE INN, JT found a parking spot and they walked through the front doors and to the reception desk.

JT said to the receptionist, "I'd like to book a room for my friend," he said.

"No you aren't. I'm very happy to see you guys and I know you two are on a budget."

JT started to protest, but Hannibal pulled out his matte-black American Express Centurion card, trumping their VISA, which the attractive young thing behind the desk took no time in picking it up and running it through the data terminal.

"Show off." JT said."

Pamela grabbed JT's arm giggling like a school girl and led him to an over stuffed leather sofa in the waiting area while Hannibal filled out the forms.

What should we do about that guy that tried to run us off the road?" Pamela asked JT.

"I don't know. We could call the police and file a report, but that guy came out of nowhere and we really can't prove that he tried to run us off the road." JT said. "But my question is what the hell was he trying to do? He shot Hannibal right? But why the attitude?"

JT was still pondering the question when Hannibal came over. They stood up and he picked Pamela up giving her a big hug. She squealed. "I love you guys'" He said. Putting Pamela down he turned to JT and they hugged as well. "We love you too, you old fart."

"You're as old as me." Hannibal countered.

They took the elevator up. There was an empty room directly across from theirs. Hannibal didn't have much with him as everything that he had was destroyed in the crash. JT opened the room to theirs as Hannibal checked his room.

"Your room OK?"

"Yeah."

"Well come over to our room for a few minutes. I know you'd like to have some peace, but man it feels like years since we last saw you."

Hannibal closed his door and joined JT and Pamela in theirs. He sat in the chair next to the window. It was night outside so all he saw was night lights of various buildings.

Pamela had gone to the restroom, which reminded JT of something. "Hey Hannibal, it's a good thing you're sitting down, you're gonna love this!" JT said.

Pamela came out of the bathroom and stood behind JT.

"Anyway, we landed at Great Falls, Montana as it was the Port of Entry. During the flight, Pamela drank two bottles of water."

"JT don't you dare." Pamela protested.

JT looked at her and continued, "She had to pee so badly, when the CBP officer pointed to the terminal, she took off. . . . . ZOOM!"

JT never finished his commentary as Pamela punched him in the ribs, shoving him backwards onto the bed and jumped on his chest. She was trying to cover his mouth with one hand and hold his hands down with the other.

" . . . . She . . . . Stop it! . . had . . to . . pee. . . so bad. . . . Ouch!"

Hannibal starting laughing.

"She . . peed . behind a . . garbage can . . . . .Mummmfff!"

Pamela covered his mouth with hers; sticking her tongue in as far as it would go.

"Mumm . .??" JT managed to turn his head sideways. "You should have . . ."

She tried to tickle him.

"Stop! . . ."

Hannibal was really laughing now. "Will you two get a hotel room?" He said.

"Uh, Hannibal, this is a hotel room." Pamela said.

JT had laid his cellphone, keys and wallet on the credenza. His cellphone started to buzz, turning it around in a circle. Everyone stopped to watch.

Pamela stood letting JT up and he answered it.

It was Cindy.

"Cindy, oh my God how are you! Are you OK? We've been trying to call you all day!"

"Yeah, everything is OK here. No, Hannibal is here too."

"Well, yes he was shot, but it was minor wound in the leg."

"No the police didn't shot him, and no he wasn't in a fight with them."

"Tell you what; I'll let you talk to him now and tell you what happened."

"Hi Cindy," Pamela yelled into the cellphone standing beside JT.

"She said hi back."

173

"Here's Hannibal, its Cindy." He said handing Hannibal the cellphone.

"Hey cutie. Yeah I miss you too." Hannibal said.

"Come on sweetheart let's leave Hannibal alone. I'm hungry. He can join us downstairs." JT said.

JT mouthed that they were going to eat, grabbed Pamela's hand and together they left.

CHAPTER XI

The Hood, Indianapolis, Indiana – Two days later.

T-Boy had changed into his street clothes. Going to the bathroom; standing to take a piss, he looked out the window at the black scar of last week's destruction and the remains of his grandmother's home, which was soon to be leveled as well. The drug dealer was long since gone and his house was soon to be leveled. The two dogs were taken to the Human Society; their fate unknown.

He sat in the backyard on the remains of an old lounge chair. The chair was from the drug dealer's home. In several places, the stuffing had long since been either ripped out or chewed away by one animal or another.

It was comfortable.

Next to him was a can of beer sitting on the grass in the shade to keep it cool. Before him was his Honda. He could see his reflection in the mirrored gloss of the black paint.

Perfect!

From this side his ride looked as if nothing had happened. He had backed into the yard with the damaged passenger side hidden from view along the hedge row that separated his aunt and uncle's home and the neighbor. On the ground before him were several stacks of $100 bills, held down by a .45 cal ACP Baby Desert Eagle, which he had purchased using some of the money that Texan had given him.

The police had kept his uncle's gun.

He was going to kill the General. He had made his mind up hat morning after the funeral. But killing him wasn't going to be easy. The white woman with them must be their bitch ho. His best plan was to shoot the bitch first and then that wimp-ass nigga brother. That should shock them enough; giving him time put a hurt on the General. He'd shoot him in the leg again to paralyze him with fear then he'd put one in his other leg and watch him beg. He wanted him to suffer and then he'd put one in his heart. When he was finished, he'd put the bag of cocaine in his shirt pocket.

He thought if he carried out this mission properly, maybe they'd let him in on some of the shit they were pushing and become a heavy hitter; that he wasn't afraid of nothin. He'd heard some brother's in his cell talking about this new cocaine called Roxanne that was 80% pure and selling below the street price of the other shit out there. This must have been the shit he had seen on that porch and what was in the bag. Maybe he was their mule and had fucked up. That's a laugh, cause he sure did, and took the life of several people; his grandmother included.

He had taken $5,000 of the money he was given and placed it in his uncle's closet, above the door where he had discovered a hole in the plasterboard. How it got there he has no idea, but he had been hiding things in there every since and no one had found it. On the ground was $3,200. He had paid $500 for the gun from a brother down the street and $1,300 down on a used car that morning. When he completed his mission he'd have his car fixed with the $3,200 plus the extra $10,000 he had been promised.

He took a sip of beer, daydreaming what it would be like to have $15,000 for a few hours of work. He had to do this right. He had to think of all of his options; how he would fuck up the woman up first. "Won't be flyin them fancy jets hurtin people." He thought out loud.

He had never shot anyone before. He knew several brothers that had. The brother's in the cell told him it was easy, but they hadn't shot anybody either. The hard part they said was not getting sick, but keepin your cool. You just walked up behind your target and popped them. POW!

He had been canvassing the northwest side of Indianapolis and once again by accident had found out where they were staying. He had scoped out his hiding place in the Inn. There was a room where the ice maker was kept along with a drink dispenser. He'd just walk in and wait. He had an ice bucket all ready and some change in case somebody wanted to know why he was there. There was also a set of stairs next to the alcove. He'd be down the stairs and out the door before anyone knew he'd been there. He also had a pair of hospital scrubs, which he'd wear over his street clothes. A cap and shoe covers from the nearby hospital and a pair of surgical gloves. Yep those CSI shows were a real help. The only thing he wasn't sure of was if there were any hidden video cameras.

When he was finished he'd throw away the gun he'd get rid of the gun by throwing it away in the nearby manmade lake. Too bad; it was a sweet looking gun but couldn't take any chances.

Sure he had everything covered, he poured the remaining beer in the grass, collected his money and bag of cocaine from the ground, putting everything in his pockets. In between a wad of money he placed the business card so that when he was finished, he'd call the cracker Texan and demand the rest of his money. He didn't want to waste any time as he might have to go into hiding. He placed the gun in a plastic bag along with the gloves.

Earlier while at the nearby hospital to the Residence Inn he was dressed in the colors of a hospital housekeeper and walked into a closet. How many people are going to question a black man in a utility closet with a bucket of water and mop? He pulled on a set of gloves he had taken from conveniently and strategically placed dispensers around the hospital hallways; placing a set of scrubs, cap, and shoe covers and an extra set of gloves in a plastic bag as well. Can't be too sure nowadays what they'd be looking for if he was stopped. He exited the closet, pushing the mop and bucket to another closet where he left them. A housekeeper with gloves on was not necessarily an odd sight. Germs can spread with housekeeping staff too. The plastic bag was hidden inside another green trash bag draped over the top as if he was throwing away some trash he had found.

Once in the second closet, which was by the service elevator, he removed the gloves and placed them in his pocket, but the housekeeping colored uniform he placed in a chute that fell to the basement into large laundry bins. He entered the elevator riding it down and exited the staff side door.

NOW IT WAS TIME to put his plan in motion. He went into the house, throwing the beer cans into a recycle bin. His aunt was hell bent on being Green. He then went to his room, making sure that there was nothing to incriminate him; locking his room he left using the front door. A few neighbors were walking to the 7/11; saw him saying how sorry they were about his loss. He got into his replacement car and drove north.

He arrived at the Residence Inn with his package now in a gym bag and took the stairs to the next floor. Now for the tricky part; he had to be fast. He checked the hallways for guest. They were clear. He took out the hospital clothing and quickly dressed. He put the gloves on and the put the gun under the ice maker on the floor in case someone was to walk in. He then took out the small ice bucket and some loose change for the pop dispenser and waited.

He didn't have to wait long. The elevator bell chimed announcing its arrival. He heard them before he saw them. They were all laughs. Let's see how long the General laughs when he blows his friends brains out. T-Boy took a chance to look around the corner. They must have been shopping as the bitch had a large bag with what looked like decorations sticking out. They were too busy talking that they did not see him. He picked up the gun and moved behind the wall hiding and waited. The white bitch was between the brother and the General. First he saw the General and the bitch pass the entrance. Knowing that the brother was not too far behind; he timed it, stepping out and drew down on the back of their heads.

CHAPTER XII

JT, Pamela and Hannibal walked towards their rooms. They had just been shopping at several malls and department stores in downtown, near the Lucas Oil Stadium. Pamela had purchased a bag of several tops, some wrapping paper and a purse. At least that's what she called it. JT called it a shopping bag. JT pulled his cell phone out as was vibrating. "Maybe it was Gail in need of help on a service question," JT thought.

It saved their lives.

He had just started slowing down his pace, turning to his left to get a better view of the call display; Hannibal and Pamela were in deep conversation about Cindy. They had just passed an alcove containing a soda machine and ice maker. To his left, JT saw an arm come up holding a semi-automatic pistol.

"SHIT!!" He yelled.

He lunged forward, shoving Pamela into Hannibal, while at the same time, pushing the gun hand down, grabbing the arm. The gun fired. From his right he heard Pamela scream. Using the momentum he continued to pull the arm, dragging the gunman out of hiding. The gun fired once more ripping a hole in the floor.

His momentum caused JT to fall, banging into the opposite door frame. Using an overhead swing, he tried to slug the gunman with the cellphone in his hand. Over his back he felt a body go over his left shoulder and saw arms wrap around the gunman's neck.

It was Hannibal.

Together they fought the gunman to the floor, but he would not give up the weapon. He was trying to bring it up between them. With JT holding the gun arm and Hannibal on top, JT tried once more to pull it from him when once again the gun fired and there was a scream from the gunman as a bullet went into his front right side.

JT yelped as the hot ejected shell hit him in the face.

The gunman went limp, causing Hannibal to fall. The weapon came loose and JT threw it across the hall.

Blue smoke and the smell of cordite was everywhere.

Hannibal rose, "Ah Shit," he said. It's the kid again." JT looked, but his thoughts were elsewhere.

He turned to his left for Pamela. She sat on the floor, slumped against the wall; a smear of blood followed the path she had taken when she fell, and a large wet puddle was forming on the floor; the new purse spilling its content everywhere. Over her head was a bullet hole. He could see body tissue and a gray flannel material where the supersonic bullet had taken stuff with it.

JT went crazy, scrambling on all four's towards her. "Pamela!" He yelled.

Guests, getting up their nerve to see what the commotion was about, peeked around the corners of their door frames. Several ran towards them.

JT yelled, "Call 911!"

He gently laid Pamela on the floor; she was breathing. He ripped at her clothing trying to find where she had been hit. He could see that the bullet had hit her in the hip area. Her grey light flannel skirt had a hole it where she was bleeding.

He had seen her do it so many times, and even had done it with ease during their many playful intimate moments but now he all thumbs as he tried to turn her skirt around so that he could get at the zipper.

"Piss on it." He said. He pulled her skirt up above her waist to expose the wound. She hated stockings. Her legs were always tanned, but now her skirt, legs and panties were soaked with blood oozing from ripped flesh on her hip.

"Pamela!" He yelled again.

On her left shoulder he saw the beginnings of a bruise. That must be where he had pushed her.

"Somebody call 911!" He yelled again. Even with the wound, he could not understand why there as a large wet spot. And then he saw her bottle of water, or what remained of it. It had taken the round as well, the contents mixing with the blood.

He ripped her shirt and stuffed the material into the wound. Behind him he felt someone push him out of the way.

"Move!" A woman's voice commanded. "I am a nurse from the hospital down the street."

JT moved as she was joined by another woman.

"We'll take over here; go see about that other guy." He was ordered.

JT returned his attention to Hannibal and the gunman. Hannibal and another man were stooped over the body.

"What the fuck is going on!" JT yelled in a shrill voice crossing the hall, arms flapping like a bird.

"I have no idea JT." Hannibal replied

"What the fuck you mean you don't know? What did you do to this kid?" He yelled again. He ran towards Hannibal grabbing his shirt, pulling him sideways; delivering what he thought was a knockout punch.

Hannibal yelled, "What the hell is wrong with you!?" He delivered a punch of his own.

JT rolled over the guest who had stooped to help taking Hannibal with him, "You motherfucker, you just got Pamela shot!" He screamed.

Grunting, he was about to deliver another punch when he felt several hands pull him backwards, pinning him to the floor.

Behind them they heard a voice croak, "JT! Hannibal! Stop it!"

They both looked to where Pamela lay.

"Let me up!" JT yelled.

"Only if you behave Mister." One of the people that had jumped him said.

"JT?" Pamela croaked

"JT? Settle down. I'm OK . . . I think . . . I'm not dead anyway." She said weakly.

"You gonna calm down now?" The man asked.

"Yeah, just let me see my wife." He said.

They let him go. He ran to her side once more. She was pale, but her eyes were open, staring at him.

"Why did you hit Hannibal?" She asked.

"I'm sorry sweetheart, I just saw you lying there and I thought I had lost my whole world and just went crazy. Do you know how much I love you?

"JT what happened?"

"Some fucking kid tired to blow us away." He said.

"JT."

"What!"

"Stop cursing. What kid?" Pamela asked.

"Remember the kid that shot Hannibal? He's the same one that tried to run us off the road. He's also the one lying on the floor over there."

Pamela tried to look where the body lay. The nurses had raised her on her right side to treat the wound.

"Is he really dead?" She asked.

"Yes I think so, Hannibal's checking him now."

Tears started to well up in her eyes. "A kid? What for? He looks to be in his teens."

"I don't know."

He brushed the hair from her face and took one of her hands.

"I think I hear an ambulance and the police coming." Someone said.

"Is she gonna be alright?" JT asked one of the nurses.

"I think so, but she'll be hurting for awhile. The bullet took out a small section of the fleshy part missing the bone. She's also got a nasty bruise on her shoulder. How'd she got that." The nurse said.

JT said, "Uh, she got that when I shoved her out of the way."

The nurse gave him a look that could have meant anything.

As JT watched, he tried to remember when he had seen her hurt.

Never.

Once she broke a fingernail, which hurt JT more than she. To see her lying there, he wanted to hurt someone or something. This was so alien to him as he tried to understand what forces had brought this beautiful woman harm.

He gave her a light kiss and told her that he loved her again. She said she loved him too.

"These ladies are going to take care of you until the Paramedics arrive. I'm going over to see what Hannibal is doing."

"JT."

"What?" He said softly.

"Apologize to Hannibal."

"I was going to." JT said.

He brushed the hair from her face one more time and returned his attention to the kid and Hannibal.

They heard a commotion coming up the stairs and the elevator bell dinged at the same time. Blue uniforms began to match the number of guests standing around.

"OK, if none of you are involved in this please clear the hallway, except those that saw what happened." An officer ordered.

"Officer I didn't see what happened, but I was one of the first to come to help along with those nurses." One of the guests said.

"You stay. Anyone else see what happened?"

Two others raised their hands.

Hannibal turned to the voice and said, "Hey Jerry."

The officer turned to get a better look, "Damn, not you again sir."

"Fraid so. Jerry this is my friend Jerome, we call him JT, and that's his wife Pamela over there."

"His wife, geez, what happened? Jerry asked.

"Look at the face over there and tell me if you recognize it." Hannibal said.

JT was not tracking with what was going on and it showed.

"JT, meet Officer Jerry Parker. Jerry as I said this is my friend JT. Jerry was the one that arrested me after the jet crash. He also arrested the kid over there. Jerry was also instrumental in vouching for me during the investigation."

"Hi, JT said," putting out his hand.

Jerry took it, "Please to meet you I guess. What the hell is going on?"

Hannibal said, "Jerry, JT I've got something to show you."

"Just a minute, here come the Paramedics." Jerry said.

Jerry walked towards them. "We've got a wounded woman over there and a dead kid there," he said pointing.

"There ain't much we gonna do about him," one said and pushed their equipment laden gurney over to Pamela. They took over from the nurses, who had written down what treatment they had provided. Once she was on the Gurney, they started putting IV drip needles in the back of her hand. JT winched. He watched as they too checked her over for any other wounds. "She's got a hell of a nasty bruise on her shoulder one said."

JT rolled his eyes. He waited until they finished, and went to her side.

"Sweetheart, you're going to hospital now. I'll be there in a minute, but I've got to find out what's going on. Love you OK?"

"Yes, I'm OK. Love you too." and they kissed.

JT walked back to Jerry and Hannibal just in time to hear Hannibal explain . . "Jerry, JT look at this," he said. Hannibal gave him a business card and a bag of white powder.

"So, it's a business card." Jerry said. "And that's a bag of cocaine; just another street junkie. I bet it's that Roxanne."

"Jerry this is the people I work for. . . Well not exactly. These are the people that front the money for the Aircraft Restoration place I work for. The 'RTPA' means Retired Transport Pilots Association."

"What the fuck are you talking about Hannibal?" JT cursed again.

"JT, I said stop cursing." Pamela said as her gurney was being taken away.

"Yes dear, we'll see you in a few minutes." JT said sheepishly.

"I'm saying this kid had one of their business cards in his pocket and look at this. ." Hannibal said.

From the front pocket, careful not to touch the blood where the kid had blown a hole in right side he pulled a wad of $100 bills, placing them next to the one's he had already taken out.

"I counted over $2,000 and there's still more. He said.

Jerry said, "I don't like the way this is heading."

"I don't either Hannibal. Are you saying someone hired this kid to kill us . . you?"

"That's what it looks like." Hannibal replied.

"For what? What did you do to them? How do Pamela and I fit into this?"

"JT you know as much about this as I do. I have the feeling that you and Pamela are just in the wrong place at the wrong time. I don't know anything. I accepted a job, that's all. Then the T-38 crashed and since then all hell broke loose and none of it is making any sense! When I took the job, I met a couple of guys in a boardroom. They went on to state that they not only restored aircraft but had recently expanded into importing rare Vietnam Era aircraft to preserve. They said that a lot of old parts are still in Southeast Asia. The parts are brought back to make whole flying examples. Some of them are still flyable anyway. It's just a matter of configuring them to the needs of the museum. There were a lot of Air Force and Army bases all over Thailand supporting the Vietnam War. You know that JT. Assuming that this group is importing drugs from there in concealed compartments . . . ." JT remembered. Remember Cindy had mentioned something happened at McChord Air Force Base, but she wouldn't go into detail."

"Yeah, I remember that too," JT said.

"I'm going to tell you something else JT. You may as well hear this too Jerry. I've been thinking about what Cindy said and an old event came back. When I was in Thailand before I met you JT, I had to participate in a court martial of two airmen. One was sentenced to hard labor for five years and the other to 90-days extra duty and 90-days restriction. Both were reduced in rank. The reason I remember it was that in Nam, a couple of successful flights into the US had been made smuggling drugs secreted in fighter aircraft. These two had tried the same in Thailand. I'm beginning to believe that someone has started the ring again."

"Wait a minute; I guess I should tell you something we came across last night sir." Jerry said. "Let's go over next to the ice maker." They walked the short distance into the room.

"This is where the kid was waiting Jerry." Hannibal pointed out. "JT saw his arm, pushed his wife out of the way, and grabbed the gun, which went off, one of the bullets hit her. Anyway you were saying."

"Before I tell you what I have, I think you should know something else. Remember when you crashed and a house was flattened with a woman inside?'

"Yeah, I'm very sorry about that." Hannibal said.

"Yeah, but what if I told you that the kid lying over there is the grandson of the woman that died and he was the only surviving member of his family? His parents had died years ago." Jerry explained.

"Ah fuck!" JT cursed. "No wonder that kid wanted you so bad."

Anyway, the rest of this might involve your Roxanne and didn't you say your fiancé is an FBI agent?" Jerry continued.

"Yeah, why?"

"Uh . . Something happened in Thailand about a drug agent getting shot or killed. It came over at our intelligence office and passed on to us because your aircraft was carrying the same stuff they found on another aircraft in Washington State. Somehow this is all tied to what happened over there."

Hannibal was pale. "You said an agent was killed?"

"That's what I'm told but the information is sketchy right now."

"You don't have a name?" JT asked.

"Nope, not yet."

This knocked the wind out of Hannibal and he sat on the floor.

JT went over to his side, "Ah man, not like this. We don't need this. Not Cindy." Hannibal buried his head between his legs.

"I don't know what to say." JT said. "This is way over my head."

"Jerry did you say it was one or two agents?"

"I only looked at the printout briefly, but I think it said one agent. Why do you ask?"

"Because Cindy and a Thai Drug agent, named Abby were tracing a lead they had from Thailand."

"I'm sorry if it was her sir, but there might be more information since then. All I know is that someone died in an explosion. Can't you get a hold of your fiancé?"

"My cell phone was destroyed in the crash. It's night time over there now, so I doubt we'll get anyone with information. Cindy and I only got engaged recently so I doubt even the FBI will share its information with me."

"Sir, I'll see what I can get for you. Maybe speak to someone at State. They get the same intelligence as we do, maybe even more."

"I'd appreciate that." Hannibal replied.

JT went over and picked up his iPhone from the now covered body of the kid. "Well we aren't going to be making too many calls from this thing either," holding it up showing the shattered display. "At least the SIM card is still intact. I can buy a new phone from a local shop on the way to the hospital. God I hope it wasn't Cindy," and then he thought, "Oh no, not Abby either."

Jerry said, "Well sir, you're welcome to ride with me downtown, and see what I can pull up."

"OK, but can I ask you to meet me at the hospital? We need to check up on JT's wife."

"Sure, no problem."

"Do you need us for anything?" JT asked.

"Naw, this was a clean shooting from what I can see. Besides, the kid shot himself when you tried to disarm him and you have witnesses. I'll see you over at the hospital. You two go ahead."

Once outside, JT said, "Hey man, I'm sorry about back there."

"JT had that been me, I'd have done the same thing. I know how much you love her. I hope that God will let me love someone that much someday."

Hannibal put his fist out in an Old School dap; a handshake once a greeting common in a black community. They ended with back-handed slaps, clinched fingers tips and drew each other into a hug and pats on the back.

"God I hope that wasn't Cindy. If it is, promise you'll put me out of my misery."

"I don't think it was Cindy. I just hope it wasn't Abby either." JT said.

"Yeah. You know, I think I need to start taking a closer look at my employers."

"How you gonna do that?" JT asked.

"I guess I'll take a commercial flight down to Texas pretending I don't have the slightest clue what's going on and do some digging." Hannibal responded.

"Tell you what, if you pay for the fuel, we'll both go down in the *ISKRA*. It's been a long time since I've been to Dallas and Ft. Worth. I'd like to see it again. I think Pamela is going to be in the hospital for a few days and unable to travel. If they release her early, I'll put her on a commercial flight back to British Columbia. I took out medical insurance before we left, so all of her medical bills will be paid as will the flight and ambulance ride home." JT said.

"No problem, but you had better check with Pamela first. She might want you to wait and go down too." Hannibal said.

"No way man. I thought I'd lost her back there. I am not about to put her life in danger again. Besides she'll most likely agree I should go along with you to keep you out of trouble." JT teased.

"Ha!" Hannibal snorted. "Sounds good to me I guess but whatever you do, don't tell her about Cindy and Abby. Agreed?"

"Yeah, that would really kill her." JT agreed.

As they left the building, JT saw a strip mall across the street, with a wireless sign above a door.

"Hannibal there's a wireless store across the street. We can get a couple of cell phones there."

"Sure, let's walk."

They crossed the street and entered.

Whereas Hannibal saw what he wanted and purchased it, JT was wowed by all the gizmos, bells and whistles the Androids and Blackberry's we're offering, but then an image of Pamela entered his thoughts.

Damn! He chose a replacement a new iPhone 4-32 GB model. It still beat the crap out of a lot of the new Blackberry's and Androids. So why change? They had a buy one, get one free, so he got Pamela one as well.

If they were going to leave her in Indy, they needed a way to communicate. He pulled out the plastic and paid for the purchase before Hannibal had time to throw down his matte-black.

From his old phone he pulled out the SIM card and placed it into the slot of the new one, powered it up and prayed. After a few seconds it gave a musical chime and started searching for a network. He was rewarded with 5-bars and the words, 'ROAMING.'

He looked at his old phone with the damaged display, gave it a pat on the shiny backside, before tossing it into the trashcan along with the packing material. He made sure the sales slip was tucked safely away in his wallet because as sure as crap, Pamela would ask for it.

They left, headed back across the street and took the rental to the hospital getting lost once before finally locating Pamela's room.

JT peeked in the door to see if she was awake. She wasn't, or so it seemed. He pushed the door open slowly and both walked in. Hannibal went into the small restroom, shutting the door.

JT's heart filled with sorrow as he watched all of the monitors surrounding her bed. Some were going beep and the others showing an electronic representation of her life in lines.

JT walked over to her bed and saw she had needles taped to her hands. A metal tree had fluids bags of this and that with tubes running to the needles.

Bending over he kissed her forehead. She woke turning her head. She opened her eyes and was rewarded with a return kiss.

"Hi Sweetheart," he said.

She tried to answer but could only croak. She gestured towards a picture of water and a foam cup of ice. After drinking nearly all of the water, she said "Hi dear."

"How are you feeling?" He asked.

"OK, I can't feel anything on my left side right now." Pulling the sheets back to expose her hip, which was covered in a light gauze and some sort of cream.

Looking around to see if it was all clear, he put his hand on her legs and slowly worked their way upwards. He leaned over and said. "I love you," kissing her.

"JT . . umph.. stop." She said.

When he found what he was looking for, he massaged it. She stopped protesting. Her eyes closed as she helped guide his hand.

Just then the toilet flushed.

He removed his hand and repositioned the sheets as Hannibal opened the door. He walked over and gave her a kiss too. "Hey beautiful! How's it hanging?" Hannibal asked.

"Very funny," she laughed. "But I'm feeling fine. How did it go at the Inn?"

JT and Hannibal gave each other looks. "Uh, everything is fine baby. You know the kid is dead. A police officer that knew Hannibal told us it was an accidental shooting, so we're free and clear but was unsure why the kid would have chosen us to ambush."

"Did he have a family?" She asked.

JT waited for Hannibal to answer. "Pamela, uh…when I crashed, a woman in one of those houses that was destroyed was an old woman. The kid that died in the Inn trying to kill us.….That was his grandmother. He has no other parents."

"Oh God! Are you sure?" She asked.

"Yes."

There was silence as Pamela started to cry. JT held her hand. After a few moments she stopped and he let her hand go; found a towel, wetted it and gently wiped her face.

"Thanks sweetheart. How sad. Don't feel bad Hannibal. It wasn't your fault. JT did you apologize to Hannibal?"

"He did Pamela." Hannibal answered for JT. "I would have done the same thing had I been JT. You're a beautiful a woman and when

I saw you lying on the floor, I was angry as well. I love you just as much."

"Oh, well in that case, come over here and give me a kiss." She said.

Hannibal did.

JT felt like a voyeur. He bent down and opened his shopping bag.

"Hey babe, guess what I got ya?"

"What?"

JT pulled out the matching iPhone. "This is for you. Hannibal got one too, but not an iPhone." He said.

"I don't need a cellphone JT."

JT stalled. "Uh.. Pamela, Hannibal and I are going to Texas. There is something going on that Hannibal thinks might be associated with his job."

"Texas?"

"Yes dear. We're going down in the *ISKRA*."

"What about me?" She asked.

"That's the problem. You can't travel for a day or two. Even if you could, you couldn't handle the altitude changes. So what Hannibal and I are going to do is go down there and do some investigating. When we find something, we'll turn it over to the police.

He's going to stay and I'll come back for you. By then you should be able to travel. I promise not to do any barrel rolls on the way home. Meanwhile we have the iPhones. Yours is an Indianapolis 317 area code number. I checked and when we get back to BC, we can get a new SIM card so that it works in the 250 area code."

"You've got one too? Where is your old one?"

"Uh . .I broke it, when I tried to club the kid with it. I got a new one."

"JT?" she quizzed.

"It was a two for one deal. See!" He said, holding it up.

"Where's the receipt?" She didn't take the phone. To her a phone was a phone.

"Right here. See. I got yours free." JT said, dancing on his toes as she inspected the sales receipt.

After a few seconds she said, "Very good." Actually she cared less. She just wanted to see him sweat a little.

JT breathed a sigh of relief. Hannibal was secretly laughing.

"You're right, I guess I should just try and recover. I'll miss you but at least I can call you." She said.

"I'll miss you too. When was the last time I told you I loved you?"

"A few minutes ago before Hannibal came into the room." She said.

JT blushed.

Hannibal caught on and laughed. "You two get a hotel room."

In unison they answered, "We've got a hotel room!" Pamela was laughing so hard she started to choke. JT ran around the bed and poured water into a cup which still had a little ice. Her coughing fit stopped, but she still had a huge grin on her face.

CHAPTER XIV

TRUE TO HIS WORD, Officer Jerry Parker met JT and Hannibal at the hospital. Since there was only space for one in front, "Hey Hannibal, you're the criminal, you get to ride in back." JT cracked.

Jerry chuckled and opened the door.

Hannibal gave JT a killer look.

As he drove downtown, JT was fascinated by all of the electronics and would have loved to dig into the innards of the car. So intent was he on trying to see where all the wires ran, Jerry was soon parking the car next to the Indianapolis City County Building, headquarters for the Indianapolis Police Department and City Government.

Jerry took them up to the command center and into his office. On the way in, Hannibal was greeted by members of the Indianapolis police that had been on the arresting team. They offered apologies.

Hannibal just shrugged it off.

In Jerry's office they sat and were offered a cup of coffee. JT declined and asked where the nearest Pepsi machine was.

"We don't have Pepsi here, only Coke."

"Shit, how about a Sprite or 7UP."

"I think they're in there."

JT left in search of the soft drink machine.

Jerry went out and came back with a pile of papers. By then JT had returned.

"That report is in here someplace. He separated papers until he came across what he was looking for. He handed Hannibal what looked like an official document. Hannibal read, shaking his head and handed the papers to JT.

It was very quiet in the office.

When JT was finished he handed the papers to Jerry. "This doesn't say very much that you haven't told us." He said.

"That's what I told you. There were no names. I'll send intelligence an email to see if they have anything new." He walked behind his desk, powered up his computer and began typing. When he was finished, he waited. Several minutes later there was a Microsoft musical note, indicating he had received an email. There was an attachment.

Jerry opened it, grunted and printed it out, which he gave to Hannibal. He quickly scanned the printout and handed the pages to JT. His heart sank as he read that Abby had been killed. There was a JEG image of a body covered by a sheet on the ground, surrounded by Thai police and onlookers.

JT thought he saw a woman that looked like Cindy near the corner of the frame but wasn't sure. He didn't say anything.

"How well did you know her?" Jerry said.

"She was a Thai narcotics agent working with my girlfriend trying to find the source of the drugs coming into the country. We met JT and Pamela in Vancouver, British Columbia and spent the next several days just going about on a mini-vacation. We became very close."

"Looks they might have found them. People just don't get blown away like that." Jerry said. "It says your Cindy was OK. That has got to be a relief."

"I just hope she is holding up. Do you think this will hit the local papers? I mean if Pamela sees this she isn't going to take it well." Hannibal asked.

"That depends." Jerry answered. "If it does it will be back page stuff. "

"Yeah, I guess you're right. " JT said.

"Well guys, is there anything else I can do for you?" Jerry asked. "I've got a lot of follow up investigations to do."

"Jerry is Hannibal free to travel outside of the State?" JT asked.

"I don't see why not. Why?"

"Hannibal thinks there is a stateside connection in Texas. He wants to go down there and check it out. I have a personal Warbirds jet out at Eagle Creek. We can be down there tomorrow or the day after."

"Was that you I heard about buzzing the field?" Jerry said.

"Uh, I did a barrel-roll coming in if that's what you're talking about." JT said.

Hannibal had a smile on his face.

"I live out that way and was just getting out of the car when this unusual looking jet flew over upside down."

"Uh, yep I guess that was me." JT said.

"Tell you what, when you get back do you mind if I get a flight? I've always wanted to fly in one of those things." Jerry asked.

"No problem. Be glad to take you up." JT said

"Great! I'm looking forward to it. You guys take it easy down there. If you need any help, I know a few guys on the Dallas PD force that can give you a hand if things get rough." Jerry said.

"Hey Jerry, thanks." Hannibal said. "I doubt we'll need it, since we're only going down to look around. I just can't believe my company is involved in this."

"Well you be careful anyway. Have a great flight. I'll get one of my rookies to drive you back to the Inn or hospital; your choice."

"Hospital." JT said.

"Inn." Hannibal said.

They looked at each other.

"We have to go to the hospital since that's where we left the car, then we'll go to the Inn."

"Settled." Hannibal said. They shook hands and left.

JT and Hannibal were driven back to the hospital. JT wanted to see Pamela once more before visitors were not allowed on the units. Hannibal waited in the rental. To pass the time, he pulled out his cellular and started playing with the various functions. It was still too early to call Cindy. He was trying not to think of what she was going through to cope with Abby's death.

He dialed her number anyway and got her voicemail. He didn't leave a message.

JT went up to Pamela's floor and room. As before she was asleep when he entered, but this time he did not disturb her. She was in a deep, possibly sedated sleep.

He went down to the nurse's station and asked for a piece of copy paper and an ink pen. On it he wrote, 'I LOVE YOU' in fancy script. Then he borrowed a red ink pen and drew hearts in the upper corners. When he was finished, the nurse looked at him and smiled.

He returned her smile and pens. The nurse said, "I wish my husband would take the time to do that. Here," she said. "You'll need a safety pin so that it won't get lost. Attach it to her pillow."

"Thanks," JT said and took off for her room once again where he pinned the note to her pillow as instructed, but out of the way so that it would not interfere with the tubes and monitor leads.

He took a chance and moved her hair to one side out of her face. She continued to sleep with a slight snore. Once again he looked at her face and quietly said that he loved her and left.

Once downstairs and in the car, he told Hannibal, instead of going to their room, to go to a local lounge and have a couple of drinks, which they did.

They drove east on I-465 to the I-69 exit and then into the Castleton Square Shopping Center area. There were plenty of places to eat and have a drink.

They chose one.

When seated, and dinner ordered, JT said. "OK man, what was this you were saying about something happening in Thailand? If we're going down to Texas to shake things up, I need to know what I'm putting my ass on the line for."

"I didn't say we were going down to shake up anything," Hannibal said.

"Well I can assure you that once whomever find out that the kid is dead and their plan failed, and that you are down there looking around, someone is going to try and whack you, and possibly me again." JT said.

Hannibal looked at his friend and said, "JT I'm responsible for this mess. You've got a lovely wife to live for. I need to do this on my own."

"Bull. Will you stop thinking that you're alone in this? OK, so maybe Pamela and I were innocent bystanders, but this attack made it personal. Also you've got Cindy to consider. You act as if you don't care if anything happens to you. You've got a life now. If you don't care I do. Just as you told Pamela, I love Cindy too. I loved Abby as well. Somebody has to pay. We have to make this right and get even."

Hannibal took his time to respond. "Look JT, I love Cindy. I just don't know how to handle this. Before if I had a problem it was only me I had to worry about. I'm scared for all of us."

"OK, so you're scared. I'm scared too. So let's plan this right. We need to get as much information about this place you work for and the people that are employed. Jerry said he knew a few Dallas police officers; maybe he can get that information for us."

They had to wait to continue as their food and drinks had arrived. Once the waiter left, JT said, "You still have to tell me about this thing in Thailand."

"In 1968 before I met you, we received word that several returning fighter aircraft had returned to the US carrying drugs." That got JT's attention.

"I don't know how it was discovered, but I guess several aircraft had already made it through, but one aircraft was discovered with the electronics bay stuffed with heroin. Remember that was the big thing before cocaine. After that a quiet search was conducted on returning aircraft and several aircraft were found to be dirty, so a surveillance task force was planned. Some Airmen was rounded up and arrested. From them, they were able to get information about the ring leaders, and then TET came.

Anything that was not associated with the recapture of the US Embassy and or the recapture of key locations in Nam was forgotten. So no information was released about the findings."

"One day I caught an Airman taking measurements of an F-4 electronics bay. At first I didn't think this Airman was capable of being a member of a drug gang. But a couple of days later, I had put on my flight suit and found it saturated in fire ants"

"Holy shit, no way." JT shuttered at the thought.

"I shit you not." Hannibal said.

JT said, "I saw something like that on the Army base. One night it was so hot a dude took his mattress outside and accidentally laid it on an ant hill. He was covered with them in seconds. He was screaming so loud they heard it all the way over at company HQ. We threw him in the shower after ripping his clothes off. He was covered in bites. In the morning we declared war. We dug a small trench around the hill and filled it with lighter fluid. Then someone brave enough would jump up and down around the hill. A horde of ants would come out and we'd light the trench.

Poof! They went up in smoke.

We did this several times and I guess the ants got wise and fewer and fewer of them came out, so we poured what must have been three cans of fluid down the top and set it on fire, at least that's what we tried to do. There was a small underground explosion; the top blew off and burning ants came flying out.

It was every man for himself. Someone found more lighter fluid cans and you'd have thought we were refighting Iwo Jima with all the fire torches. Everyone had their own battle going. Dudes were jumping up and down, yelling. Eventually we won; 15 to a zillion. We never had a problem with that hill again."

Hannibal laughed at the image and continued, "I was bitten so badly, I was rushed to the hospital. When I got out, I was sitting on my bunk and noticed a ball of tissue under my locker. I also found some in my uniforms and boots inside my locker. There were ants everywhere.

I took the tissue to the hospital to have it analyzed. They were covered in Honeydew melon juice, which had attracted the ants. This was not something you found every day. And then it hit me that when I had caught the Airman in the hanger, he had a lunchbox on the workbench and a Honeydew melon was sitting next to it. Still this was not enough evidence to go on, so I pulled his records. He was forced to join the military after getting caught with a small amount of drugs. He also had a buddy from the same hometown."

"I was the duty officer that night, so I had the driver and I load up a pistol, and we picked up a Thai MP, who had a loaded M1A1 Carbine and .45 sidearm. We raided the hangers and caught them red-handed."

"How come you didn't tell me about this back then?"

"I didn't think it was that important, especially since it was an Air Force thing. Also I'd only known you then for a couple of months, and was still feeling you out."

"Oh, that hurt."

"Sorry, but that's the way it was. Anyway the dudes were sent to make small rocks out of big ones."

JT sat in silence.

"There is still a lot about that situation I can't tell you. I will tell you this. A lot of things are starting to come together and you didn't hear that from me."

"What the hell are you talking about?"

"Nothing."

"Bullshit. My wife gets shot and you can't tell me?'

"It's not like that JT. Honest. I was told some things back then and sworn to secrecy. If I told you I'd not only have to shoot you and then scatter your body parts across the Nevada desert."

JT stared at his friend in a different light. What did he know that was so hush-hush that he couldn't share with him; his family, his brother?

"That is why I have to go down and finish this myself."

JT continued to sit in silence.

"Come on man, this is killing me. Say something."

"I'll see you in the morning. Have your bags, or should I say bag packed. You pay for the fuel. I'm going and there isn't much you can do about it."

Now it was Hannibal's turn to think.

"Pamela needs you."

"My family will look after her and she'd not going anywhere soon. The sooner we get down there the sooner we can surprise these assholes."

Hannibal sighed, "Yeah I guess you're right."

"Then let's do it. See you tomorrow early.

CHAPTER XV

Indianapolis, Eagle Creek Airport.

"**Hey JT,** can I fly some? Sort of see what this baby can do?"

"It's your quarter for the fuel, be my guest."

"You OK?"

"Aw, just a little pissed at you."

"For what?"

"For not trusting me."

"Come on man, you know how it can be in the military. You aren't some dumbass civilian that doesn't have a clue. You even told me you held a secret clearance, so you know what you could and could not say."

"Yeah, but I've never been on the receiving end from a friend before."

Hannibal turned to JT as he was performing the pre-lube of the engine bearings. "Hey man, when this is over I'll tell you everything. Down to the last detail. I promise. I'll even tell you the color of my shorts when they told me."

"Fuck that. Get in and let's get this thing airborne."

Knowing that Hannibal was watching his every move, JT executed a perfect takeoff and cleared Indianapolis airspace.

"Hey Hannibal?" He said over the intercom.

"What?"

"It's all yours. You have the controls." JT let go of his.

"Do you have your barf bag?"

"Do you? You can't do anything I haven't done before."

Bad mistake.

"I've got it," Hannibal said. He cleared the surrounding airspace with a series of "S turns and proceeded to show JT what it was like dodging incoming missiles in Nam.

"Hot damn! Not as good as my Phantom, but passable," he yelled.

He pulled back on the collective and went into a climb, performed a half-turn, flipped the *ISKRA* over on its back and went straight down.

"See that red building down there?"

"Yeah." JT said, barely hanging in, trying to keep his breakfast of Granola and tea down.

"In Nam, this is about the height we came in from and right about here....We'd drop our load."

Hannibal imitated the sound of bombs being released and pulled up into a hard left turn. JT wasn't ready for the maneuver and his helmet hit the right side of the canopy. Hannibal laughed.

"Right about here we'd check our 6 to see if we're about to get jumped."

Hannibal then slammed the control to the right, making a spiraling climb back up to altitude.

"OK, buddy you can have the controls back."

"JT?"

JT had pulled his mask off and was leaving the remains of his breakfast in his barf bag.

"Sissy."

In between heaves, JT held up his universal salute.

"OK, I've got the controls until you're finished."

It took JT five-minutes of breathing oxygen before he was back to somewhat himself.

"I've got it," he said.

"You sure?"

"Yeah. Man, how could you take that shit every day?"

"That's the secret. You do it every day and you get used to it."

"Oh man, I'll never be able to look at a granola bar again."

"You did OK pardner. Most people lose it at the first dive."

"I was lucky I guess as I had an F-16 pilot fly me in his T-28 Texan and did the same thing. I've done dives before but nothing so tight, pulling all those G's."

"There's hope for you yet."

"Gee, you think so?"

"Maybe. Nice plane. It won't win any wars, but it sure is stable. I like the feel of the controls. They're a little too stable, but I guess for the civilian market, you don't need something that will kill the pilot on his first flight. Heaven help us if they start letting civilians fly F-4's or F-15's."

"I've got it," JT said feeling much better. "You know what's odd?"

"What?"

"I needed that. It sort of cleared up my mind. Got my mind off of Pamela, and what we might be heading into."

"Yeah."

"Sorry about this morning. I knew you had your reasons."

"That's OK man."

JT was silent.

They continued to fly southwest and landed in Memphis, Tennessee where they refueled.

JT purchased a Pepsi and drank it in several gulps. He always felt that it was the only thing that cured him when he felt ill.

The Pepsi did its magic.

Hannibal had a bottled Five Alive.

"Sissy."

Once again they were airborne and crossed the mighty Mississippi River.

They watched as Arkansas crept by far below and soon entered DFW TCA.

CHASING ROXANNE

CHAPTER I

Dallas Love Field, Dallas, Texas.

JT and Hannibal exited the Iskra; JT unzipping his flight suit immediately after removing his helmet.

"Damn! I forgot how hot it could get here!" JT made a strangling noise as if he was going to kneel over dead. Hannibal just watched, lost in his own thoughts, but laughing. Yeah it was hot. Just the way he liked it.

"Beats the piss out of your Canadian weather."

"I didn't say I didn't like it, I said I had forgotten how hot it could get."

JT opened the small storage locker just behind the passenger seat and pulled out the wheel chocks, tossing them on the ground. Looking around taking in the sights, he had chosen this airport during his flight planning, not only because it was near multiple highways but well out of the way of the DFW air traffic. It was also close to downtown Dallas and seeing the rising towers to the southeast brought back memories of a long ago time.

A fuel truck met them. "Regular or premium?"

"How about just plain jet fuel; aviation grade?"

"Got that too. Fancy jet you guy got there. It must be one of them warbird things. What country?"

"Poland. It's a *PZL TS-11 ISKRA* or Spark in English"

"Nice. Never seen one before, but then I never enjoyed going up in planes. Like working around them though. You know the Confederate Air Force moved over to Midland and changed their name to Commemorative Air Force. Must have been a bummer getting people to join with a name like Confederate Air Force. "

"Never heard about the name change, but they only fly the WWII stuff. There is a factory over in Ft. Worth that rebuilds the WWII German ME-262 jet. Next door is a company that collects modern jet warbirds. Hannibal here flies for them."

"No shit! Well I'll be damn. Nice to meet you sir." The driver shook Hannibal's hand. "So do you own this one?"

"No he does," pointing to JT. The driver shook JT's hand. "Please to meet the both of you."

"Here comes the tow truck. You can pay for your fuel inside once you got everything put away."

With the *ISKRA* fuelled and hangered on pristine grey floors next to multi-million dollar corporate aircraft, JT pulled out his credit card to pay for the services. Hannibal pushed it aside and gave his card. To the beautiful redhead he said in a ghetto dialect, "He's all po' an everythin darling. Why he hasn't changed his combat boots since he was in Vietnam. He can't even afford a new pair of shoes. I let him hang around as he's such a good buddy an all. So I'll be making the payment for him." She returned his smile.

JT kicked Hannibal in the back of his knee causing his leg to buckle but he recovered. The redhead pretended to not have noticed. JT pretended to watch a large flat panel monitor displaying the latest news from around the world.

As they left, with what little baggage they had, Hannibal gave the redhead an overly friendly wave goodbye. "Oh man, wait until I see Cindy. You are dead meat."

"Ah come on, I was playing with her and she knew it."

"Sure you were. Hell I thought you were going to jump the counter and go for it right there."

"Come on JT. She was good looking but not that good looking."

"Yeah right. I'm still gonna tell. I liked her smile though."

Taking a shuttle, they arrived at the National Car Rental counter and once again Hannibal paid for the expenses.

"Doesn't look like much has changed since I was last here in the 80's," JT said as Hannibal exited the airport turning onto Mockingbird Rd. "Damn, there's that same service station I remember. You know Hannibal, the last time I was here, I heard of a corporate jet that couldn't get its landing gear down and was flying around and around Dallas burning off fuel. I didn't have anything to do so I drove over to see what the excitement was about. As I was watching from the fenced off area, I was taken back in time for there, just I had seen so many times in Thailand, was a helicopter making practice runs on several aircraft as they came in for a landing. It was obvious what he was practicing for. Fortunately, the corporate jet landed safely but it was eerie."

JT sat back and checked out his surroundings and lost in his thoughts.

"You know Hannibal, when I have the time I usually watch a cop show called *The First 48*. You ever hear about it?"

"Nope!"

"They show homicide cops in various cities solving murders and they have 48 hours to get the most information or the trail usually goes stale. Dallas is usually featured and each time, I keep looking to see if anything has changed in the skyline. You know after all of this time not one thing has. It's as if the surrounding communities have gridlocked downtown high rise expansion. I don't know if that is good or bad. Just looking at that service station back there reminds me of being in some sort of time warp. I bet I could drive these same roads and streets with my eyes closed."

"Not as long as I'm in the car."

"Hey Hannibal! See this!" JT held up his middle finger.

"One day you're going to do that and get it shot off. I have it on first-hand knowledge that on the LBJ someone did just that a couple of years ago. When are you going to grow up?"

JT changed the subject. "Where are we going?"

"There is hotel over in Arlington that I use when I'm in town as I haven't had time to find a place yet. Since I hadn't called to make arrangements, hopefully they'll have a couple of rooms available. It's a few minutes' drive to DFW and the office. We can stay there and wait for Cindy's plane to arrive tonight. You can call Pamela. Later we rest, eat and head to the airport. Until then there isn't very much to do but wait and develop a plan.

At the hotel they had two rooms available, which they checked into with adjoining suite doors.

"Hey man I gonna make that call to Pamela. After lunch we should go shopping and get a descent set of clothing too before we pick Cindy up."

"Sounds good to me too."

Anthony Parran

In his room JT set up his netbook and got into the hotel's wireless network. Checked his email for anything important: didn't find anything. Two-thirds was junk mail from Nigerian's flooding his inbox with offers of millions of dollars to export money out of their country.

He slipped out of his flight suit and changed into a pair of pants and shirt he had rolled up in a hurry before they left Indianapolis. When he had finished he called Pamela. Just the sound of her voice always made him feel good. She sounded in great spirits and was doing fine. His family had stopped in to see her at the hospital. She told him how they had brought her a home cooked meal to her room and promised when she was to be released; they would take her home with them and get her nice and fat.

When they hung up, he immediately went online to Facebook and issued a threat to his family to leave her alone. She was just the way he liked her. Not that they would listen. He only hoped she wouldn't get too fat from the high-calorie, high protein and carb meals.

He could have called, but for other reasons did not want to listen to his family talk about how his personal life needed to be examined and turned around. After several minutes as expected there were no replies back. What the hell at least she was in good hands and out of harm's way.

Tonight they would meet Cindy and tomorrow formalize a plan to take down those that had brought hurt and pain to his beautiful woman and the threat to kill Hannibal. Somebody was going to pay dearly for hurting Cindy and beautiful Abby. She didn't deserve to die. Not like that.

"I'm the judge, the jury and the executioner. No mercy." A heavy metal rock song was playing in his head. Something about death from above after he once saw an Iraqi war video where a Spectre C-130 was blowing the shit out of Iraqi's from above using nightvision and Infrared television; totally unseen and unheard by the Iraqi's running this way and that. At each turn they were blown to bits with cannon fire. That was some really cool stuff in a morbid way.

It did not matter that he did not have a visualization of faces yet. In his mind the bodies had none. He had blown them all off.

JT had to burn off the adrenaline rush he felt. So he did some exercises while he waited for Hannibal's call. He closed the blinds and sat in silence.

In his room, Hannibal just sat on his bed staring at the tall cabinet housing the television. The remote was on the table next to the bed. At first tempted to turn it on, he decided not to as with his luck the news about death and destruction would be on, which he had had enough of and maybe a repeat of the recent events in Indianapolis broadcast over again.

He looked over at the flight suit he had taken off and like JT had put on a pair of pants and a shirt. JT was right, he needed something a lot better to meet Cindy.

He made a telephone call to a Washington, DC area code and through a series of prearranged exchanges spoke with a familiar voice.

After several minutes he hung up and made another call to a Dallas number that was not associated with his work. He told them of his intentions and plans.

In return he received his orders.

After a short nap he called JT; he was awake. He opened the adjoining door and walked in.

They left the door open and took the elevator down. Ate a quick meal in the hotel restaurant and drove over to a Men's Warehouse and purchased some dress casual wear a a suit. JT refused to let Hannibal pay this time. Since he was the first to be fitted, he quickly ran over to the cashier and paid for his purchases.

Later after making it clear to the tailors that this was a rush job, they went in search of a decent pair of dress shoes. JT's Vietnam era boots and Hannibal's flight sneakers were not your standard going to meet and greet attire.

CHAPTER II

DFW International – Arriving passengers terminal

"OK, so how do I look?"

"Like a pimp." He said without pause.

"Man, one day I am going to break you in half."

"You do and I'm gonna tell." JT said referring to the redhead.

"Can't talk if you have a broken neck."

They never finished the banter; from the concourse arriving passengers exited. Like schools kids, they scanned the faces eagerly searching for Cindy's. The out flux of passengers ended and both looked at each other, asking the same question. Had she missed the flight?

Suddenly there was more commotion and Cindy finally exited, Hannibal had to do a double-take. Here was the most beautiful woman he had ever seen. She was dressed in a business suit and heels. Her hair combed straight down framing her face.

"Wow!" JT said.

Her arm was wrapped in a sling and he saw a few places on her face that appeared to have been bruises, but that only added to her attraction. Hannibal was dancing back and forth. He hadn't said a thing, but it was obvious what he as thinking.

Behind her she was followed by the flight crew, all male, all trying to vie for a position to carry her only one piece of carryon luggage, her purse.

"Damn Hannibal, she's really looks gorgeous."

Hannibal ignored him, walking towards her. In his outstretched hand was a single red rose. She ignored it, crushing it between them as she gave him a very passionate, X-rated kiss. The moans from the flight crew; very audible made it clear they were envious.

"OK everybody shows over! Keep moving!" JT ran around the couple directing passenger traffic.

To Hannibal and Cindy he said, "Will you two get a room for Christ sakes?" But he was happy to see them embrace.

When they finally separated, JT saw tears in Hannibal's eyes. "Come here you," Cindy said pointing to JT. She gave him a watered down version of the kiss but nonetheless just as exciting.

"I missed you guys." She giggled, and laced her arms in Hannibal's.

They walked towards the exit doors to the baggage claim area. JT politely stayed a discrete distance behind as they whispered to each other, stopping every once in a while to seal a comment with a kiss.

"I said get a room!"

A well hidden, extended manicured finger rose behind Cindy's back. JT snorted.

Downstairs, they retrieved her one bag and headed towards the main exit.

Once outside, they caught the shuttle limo to their parked car.

"Hey guys I famished, let's get something to eat."

"Naw, you guys go ahead. Just drop me off at the hotel."

"Come on, why don't you go with us? I haven't seen you or Hannibal for what seems like ages. "

"Cindy I'd love to but I have to check in with Pamela. My family is looking after her and the last I heard they were going to fatten her up."

"Oh my!"

"Yeah, that's what I said. Tell you what; let's meet for breakfast tomorrow morning and then we can catch up."

JT saw the look of relief in Hannibal's eyes. Hannibal would never say anything but tonight he wanted to be alone with Cindy. If he was in his shoes he'd want the same.

Later that afternoon Hannibal opened the door to their suite, barely able to keep his hands off of her once the door closed.

"Ouch!"

"I'm sorry sweetheart."

"What's that smell?"

"What smell?

Reluctantly breaking the embrace he turned on the lights. There on the table beside the bed was a large bouquet of flowers. Beside the bed was a chilled bottle of wine in a silver stand. Hannibal saw a note placed squarely in the middle of a pillow and read it. For several seconds he stared at it and pushed back a tear. He handed it to Cindy and she read, "I won't comma a knockin if the walls are a rockin. You be careful with her bad arm or I'll kick your ass."

"That is so sweet. Typical JT."

"Yeah, he can be that way."

CHAPTER III

The next morning JT, Hannibal and Cindy sat around a table, enjoying a cup of coffee and tea for JT.

"Damn, it seems like only yesterday we were sitting around a table like this."

"Only there was one more person."

"What happened over there Cindy? What happened to Abby?"

"You really liked her didn't you JT?"

"You know I did."

Cindy closed her eyes for several seconds, reliving the past. "We had information that the hanger we were looking for was closed as there was a Thai celebration going on. Something about a national Thai-boxing hero being in town giving an exhibition. That morning we had set up surveillance on the place. Abby had gone in and when she returned, she had somehow lifted an ID badge. We returned later to make sure the Intel was correct. It was, so we made our plan to come back after dark. We didn't see any over presence of security. Maybe they thought they didn't need it. I guess in retrospect that was true. Anyway, we came back later and decided the best approach was to just enter from the front. That way if we were caught we could say that our vehicle had broken down and we needed to use a phone. I had removed the ignition fuse and replaced it with a blown one. I had also left my Sat phone and netbook at the hotel."

"Abby felt it was best she go to the door first. I was to pretend to be a dumb Chinese. She simply stood in the door and swiped the card we had lifted. She didn't have a chance. The door blew outward taking her with it. That was the primary explosion. I was hit with debris in the arm and face. Then it was as if the world had ended as explosion after explosion went off. They were designed to take out everything in the hangers."

"When I came too I was in a hospital surrounded by all types of Thai security people including the local FBI agents. All wanted to know what and why we had been there. I didn't tell them anything as I wasn't sure who was who and what information I as allowed to give out.

"What about Abby's body?"

"Do you really want to know JT?"

He looked down and steeled himself for the news. "Yes."

Cindy sighed: her shoulders slumped. "There wasn't anything left JT. She was just....gone...."

Silence.

JT stifled a sob. Hannibal turned away, concealing a tear as well.

"Don't worry JT, she didn't suffer."

"People say that all the time. How do we know?"

Cindy reached over and grabbed his hand. "JT, she's in a better place. She's OK. They gave her a beautiful burial. Let her go."

"No way. If and when we survive this, I want to give her my own personal send off. We can do that, right Hannibal?"

"Yeah man, we'll all give her a beautiful send off."

"I had her blood all over me. I saw the body parts, the largest was an arm. By the way, I brought something back that I know she would have wanted you to have. Cindy reached into her purse and pulled out a small delicate looking ruby and diamond encrusted gold bracelet.

"This was on her arm JT." She said giving JT the bracelet.

JT took it as if it were the most precious thing in the world. With tears in his eyes, he tried to put it on his wrist, but had trouble closing the clasp.

"Give me your arm." Cindy said reaching over and closing the clasp.

"Thanks."

JT turned the bracelet around his arm marvelling at the simple beauty.

"It's beautiful, just like her."

"Yes."

"So what happened later?'

Cindy continued. "I was able to convince them that I was just there with Abby and had no idea she was a security agent. I told them Abby had stopped to help me when my car broke down and when she went to the door, all hell broke loose. I stuck to my story and was later given my passport back. They had searched my room but found nothing of great interest except my sat-phone and netbook. They couldn't understand why I had such high-tech equipment. I told them I was in Thailand gathering information for a documentary on the use of Camp Friendship after the Vietnam War; the present participation of Thai and US military personnel in simulated jungle exercises."

"I was followed for a bit but made sure to look like I was who I said I was. I asked about Abby and told the matter was a State secret and that I would not be allowed to see her remains. I'm so sorry JT that I couldn't do more, but I had to keep my ID a secret. Later I met with my FBI controllers and we felt that as unfortunate as the incident was, we did not want to scare the primaries away. Besides we had enough information to conclude that this was a large scale operation and that with what we were able to collect at the blown up hanger though our Thai contacts a few missing pieces of the puzzle."

"I hope it was some leads to here. Otherwise we are in the wrong place."

"As a matter of fact Hannibal it does lead to here. On one of the items found, there was a serial number, which had been photographed. I remember it, well not the number, but the sequence as being the same pattern that we were looking for. But everything fell into place was a charred bag with a Texas address on it. Bet you can't guess to where."

"AAR Headquarters, right here."

"Nope, to the Retired Transport Pilot's Association or RTPA headquarters in Los Colinas."

"What?"

"I did some digging around and found out that RTPA owns AAR. When you had your job interview Hannibal, who was it with?"

"AAR, so I thought. I met a guy, name of Hank Marshall. He looked over my resume. He said he'd get back to me after he looked into my references. Later he said that I came highly spoken for from a couple of his employees. He never said who."

"Well Hank Marshall is the founder of RTPA and later started up AAR as his personal project to preserve aviation history by searching all over Southeast Asia for any serviceable Jet aircraft from the Vietnam Era, bring them back, restore them and put them on display. His greatest finds were of all places, Thailand, Guam and Okinawa. But Thailand had the largest cache. Korat was a treasure trove."

"And that was all that was needed to open a smuggling operation again."

"Yeah Hannibal, but that means there had to be someone not only here that knew about the search for these aircraft but someone with connections in Thailand."

"Yes, JT and that someone also knew about the old ways of getting drugs onto aircraft and back into the States."

"I bet if we search the FBI database we could cross-reference names of people at RTPA and AAR that served in Thailand together."

"I thought about that too. But we need names and the only way to get that information is to either ask for it, which would raise all sorts of flags and send them to ground or sneak in and access their database. I'd start with the AAR operations as it is smaller and to be honest RTPA means a lot of people with a lot of professional and ethical backgrounds that would blow the whistle in a heartbeat if they knew drugs were being smuggled into the US on their watch."

"I agree."

"I agree too. So what do we do?"

"I suggest we meet upstairs and lay out a plan of action."

"Let's do it. I want these sons of a bitch. It's payback for Pamela and Abby."

"JT, take it easy. I want them too, but we can't go off half cocked."

"I ain't half-cocked. I'm ready Freddy. I'm the Thriller at Manila, I'm....."

"You're an ass."

"Oh God, what have I gotten myself into? Will you two stop that?"

"That hurt Hannibal."

"Shut up and let's go."

CHAPTER IV

A small table was now covered with hand-made drawing by Hannibal of the hanger layout where all of the aircraft and maintenance lockers were kept. As they sat, JT had also set up his Netbook with video camera. Pamela, a thousand miles away, was watching and participating in the session. Although there was very little she could do, it felt good to see her and have her part of the planning. JT missed her very much.

Cindy and she had spent the better part of 30 minutes catching up on things while JT gathered the materials they would need and Hannibal made the drawings.

Pamela was in an office room provided by JT's sister, using a desktop computer with a webcam.

The hotel suite rooms were large and since JT and Hannibal had chosen adjoining rooms, they were now in JT's room, going over the plans as the beds in Hannibal's room looked like a wild party had taken place. A partially concealed panty was on the floor as room service had not been around yet. JT didn't say anything as he was just happy to see his best friend's obvious love for each other.

So deep were they in going over the plans, they did not hear the knock on Hannibal's door at first. The next knock was louder and had a little more authority to it. The three of them looked at each other, and shrugged.

JT got up, went into Hannibal's room and opened the door. Having lived in Texas long enough to know when someone knocked on your door and that the person standing before you wearing a white Stetson hat, white shirt, tie and cowboy boots, you didn't have to ask for a badge. That person looked and smelled Texas Ranger. Such was an example standing before him now.

"May I help you Ranger uh, Ferguson?"

"So you know I'm a Texas Ranger?"

"Yes, I've lived in Texas before."

"Are you Mr. Washington?"

"Uh, no, but he's in the other room."

"Then you must be JT."

Uh oh. "Yes I am how did you know?"

"Can I come in please? I'd like to speak with Mr. Washington."

"Sure."

Stepping in, he said, "As you can read from my name tag, My name is Ranger Ferguson."

"Hannibal, you'd better get in here," JT said over his shoulder. "I don't know what you did man, but you're about to be busted."

Hannibal, followed by Cindy came in.

"Mr. Washington. My name is Ranger Ferguson," he repeated. "I am here on unofficial business."

"Uh, how do you do Ranger Ferguson. How can I help you?" Hannibal stuck out his hand which was taken.

JT stuck out his hand, which was ignored.

"Well, I've got a little problem. You see, I received a call from the Dallas police that had received a call from a friend that had received a call from the Indianapolis City Police. I was informed that certain individuals were coming down to investigate activities of a certain group. I was also informed that this group they were going to investigate has caused injury to loved ones of you Mr. Washington and you Mr. . . . . ."

"Travis, but as you have already noted, everyone calls me JT."

"Yes, Mr. Travis, or JT. Here's the problem. I can't let you come down here on a vendetta and take the law into your hands. Also, and this is not open for question or to be released, we too have been investigating this group. They came across our radar screen a couple of years ago when certain drug links started coming together, if you get my drift."

Ranger Ferguson walked around the room as he spoke. He looked into the other room and saw the table strewn with drawing and the netbook; Pamela's image still up.

He turned the papers over. "Howdy mam," He said to the video camera."

""Hi," was all that Pamela could say.

"I take it that you're Mrs. Travis."

"Yes"

"How're you feeling? Getting better?"

Not knowing what to say, Pamela said, "Yes, I feel much better."

"Well mam, you take it easy hear?"

Turning to JT, Hannibal and Cindy he continued.

"As I was saying we have been investigating this group and we're about ready to take them down; we don't want amateurs involved."

"Ranger Ferguson, Cindy here is an FBI agent."

"Yes I am aware of that, but she is out of her jurisdiction."

Nobody said anything.

"You have a lovely wife sir," looking at JT, "and you Mr. Washington have a distinguished career and reputation. Yes I know about your background as I have a father that was in Nam and he told me of your exploits. I'd hate to see that washed away."

"Ranger Ferguson, I, or we have no idea what you're talking about. We're just four people going over plans to purchase hanger space for our aircraft. If you already know about us, then you know JT and I flew down in a Polish warbird, and *ISKRA* TS-11. It is presently hangered at Dallas Love Field as we speak. Those corporate rental rates are outrageous, so we thought of putting JT's jet there. Besides I already work for them and had mentioned I could possibly get him a deal on hanger space."

Ranger Ferguson went back over to the table and examined each paper as Pamela watched a thousand miles away.

"Right. Anyway, I must go. Just thought I'd stop in. It was really nice meeting you folks and you too Pamela." He tipped his hat to the camera.

Before he reached the door he turned once again and said, "Like I said we have an investigation going. Hate to see someone accidentally stumble into a firefight. No need to lose, or see more loved ones get hurt."

With that Ranger Ferguson left the room. Only after the door was shut and they had counted to 30 did they feel relieved enough to breath.

"What the hell was that?"

"JT, I don't like that," Pamela said from the netbook window. "If he knows, then there is no way you guys are going to get anywhere near that place."

"How far do you think they'll let us go?"

"Not sure. We're probably already under surveillance. The thing is he didn't say we couldn't. He said that there was an ongoing investigation that we might screw up. So I have a feeling that we'll be given some room to navigate but that's about it."

"Do you think we should ask for their help?"

"To do what? I'm going to be honest here. My wife was almost killed. What about Abby? Are they going to just slap them on the wrists for pushing dope and lock them away for a white collar crime? No way man, I want blood!"

"JT?"

"What?"

"Calm down. We all want justice."

"JT?"

"Now what""

"I don't want you to go off half-cocked…."

"Thanks Pamela. We've already told him that."

"Well I want more than justice."

"And you'll get it."

"You're fuckin A right I will."

"JT?"

"WHAT!!!"

"Stop cursing."

They spent the next several hours going over their plan. JT's Netbook did not have the capability to pull up a Google map of the area and display it with meaningful information.

He jumped up and left the room. "Be right back." Was all he said.

Twenty-minutes later he returned with several sheets of 81/2 X 11 paper. Each with terrain, map and satellite images of the area they wanted. "Went downstairs and used their computers set up for guests. Made printouts of the area."

"You ain't so dumb after all."

"Hannibal?'

"What?"

"Bite me."

"I am going to take Hannibal's belt off and beat the carp out of both of you. Stop it!"

For the several hours they went over the printouts.

"OK, we've got all the information we're going to get here; we'll have to park someplace different than the hanger area, assuming Ranger Ferguson has the place under surveillance.

"What we need is some fire power."

"Yeah."

"I have my service weapon, but we'll need to get you two something. Hannibal is there a gun shop nearby?"

"I think so. This is Texas so that shouldn't be hard."

"Wait, I think I remember a place close by as I had gone there many years ago to get test a Desert Eagle." JT went over to this netbook and Googled Dallas gun shops and found what he was looking for.

"Right there, about two blocks away, let's go."

CHAPTER V

Near FT. Worth Naval Air Station, Advanced Aircraft Restorations

Hannibal and Cindy had just made a casual stroll across the street. Except for Cindy none of them had been recently engaged in covert surveillance and JT and Hannibal were too old to go hiding in bushes. Earlier they had driven to a bus stop about several blocks away and then took a bus tour that went right by the hangers. It was quiet.

Earlier the three of them had gone to the local gun range to hone up on their shooting skills. Cindy helped them in the modern techniques of handgun shooting. Whereas JT had once been an expert in rife and match pistols, this was for real and the targets could shoot back.

Using Cindy's credentials as an FBI agent, they were able to bypass the 14-day waiting period to get the weapons. JT's choice was a Desert Eagle. Hannibal chose a 9mm Sig Sauer. Each had extra clips, fully loaded and one in the hole.

"JT do you remember which end the pointy thing comes out of?"

"Oh, you are so funny."

"Hannibal what about you?"

"You gonna let her get away with that?'

"Look you clowns, I don't want to get my ass shot off."

"Cindy I was an expert in pistol and small bore rifle ….."

"Boring, are you ready to go?"

"Honest I was an expert, but yeah let's do it."

They exited the car. They had parked next to small office, about a block away from the hanger entrance, that way their vehicle would not look conspicuous. Watching Cindy as she led, they mimicked her movements and crouched, holding the weapons as she had instructed them in the 30-minutes they had had on the indoor shooting range.

Ex-military or not, people do forget how to handle a weapon and when the shit hits the fan, that was the last place she wanted to be; concerned for her safety in the front and back.

Each was alert but lost in their own thoughts as they rounded a corner.

WHACK!

Everyone froze; Cindy was the only one to hit the ground.

"What the hell was that?" Hannibal whispered.

There came the sound of footsteps on grass. Everyone held their breath and made themselves as tiny as possible behind the various array of decorative plants and objects. JT had to laugh as his only hiding place was behind a street lamp, straight out of the cartoons. He might as well have just stood out in the open but whoever it was, wasn't paying attention. He kept walking.

It was the paper delivery person.

Looking over onto the entranceway to the office that they had just left was a rolled up newspaper. The sound that they had heard was the delivery person throwing the paper hitting the door with a loud whack.

They waited until he had moved on before exposing themselves, breathing.

Getting off the ground, Cindy said, "I almost peed myself."

"You looked stupid hiding behind that pole, dumbass."

"What was I supposed to do?"

Just then JT started a muffled smirk, which became an almost uncontrolled laugh. Cindy thinking he had lost his mind looked in the direction he had had and she too started a low bellied laugh.

"What the hell's so funny?"

"Sweetheart, look at your shadow. Are you that happy to see me?"

"What the hell?"

Hannibal turned to look at his shadow, which was being cast by a decorative lamp onto to wall behind him. As he looked be soon broke out into a small giggle. There, on the wall was a fifteen-foot shadow with a somewhat huge phallus. Hannibal had hidden near a wall behind a plant with a branch projecting outwards at about his crotch level.

Grabbing the branch and shaking it he said, "Well baby you have always had the effect on me."

"OK, you two we're here on serious business." JT was trying to inject seriousness back into the mission, but was also trying to contain himself as well.

With cautious effort they moved around the decorative plants and made it to the entranceway. It was your standard double wide glass door with very little if any visible security.

JT saw a camera mounted on the wall but it was pointed at the reception desk.

Just as he started to swipe the card Cindy had given him, she grabbed his arm. He turned to see the look of concern in her eyes.

"JT remember what I told you about Abby?"

"Yeah"

"Well?"

"No way, this is civilized US of A."

"So? What if they really have something to hide and don't mind blowing things up to keep their secret hidden.

JT thought and looked at Hannibal. He too looked concerned.

"Hey buddy it's your call."

"Thanks for the support. You two go back around the corner and get on the ground. If this thing goes and least you can tell Pamela I love her."

"JT I should be doing this. I'm the trained expert."

"Not with one arm."

Cindy hesitated, but agreed.

"Be careful JT. The best information we had that there was some sort of pressure switch mounted on the inside of the entrance frame. It has to be pressed at the same time you swipe the card."

"OK, I'll feel around and let you know what I found." With that he waited until they had disappeared around the corner.

Texas Ranger blacked out GMC Suburban SUV.

"Sir, are you seeing this?" A radio crackled.

"Yeah what are they doing?"

"Not sure sir, but they must suspect something is wrong with the door."

"The report we have is that their location blew up in Thailand with some sort of sophisticated door bomb."

"They wouldn't do that here would they?"

"Not sure, but I'd be doing the same thing that they are."

"I sure wouldn't want to be the one to test the waters."

JT took cautious steps towards the door. "I can do this." He said. He started sweating. No way would they plant high explosives in the middle of an ultra-metropolitan airport and city. But what if what Cindy said was true? What if they had something to hide and didn't care what measures were taken to hide that information? "Shit!"

His hands were starting to shake as he felt the door frames, searching for a pressure switch.

Bingo! "Oh shit!"

"What?"

"There's a switch here"

"What?"

"Is there an echo in here? I found a switch."

"Don't move JT. Let me look at it." Cindy broke cover and with caution moved around to the door. When she reached the door, JT took her good hand and moved it to the location of the switch, moving out of the way.

"What's going on?"

"Stay there Hannibal. No use in all of us going up."

"Too bad, you aren't going to leave me alone." With that Hannibal also broke cover, bent over and scooted over to the door.

"Dammit Hannibal!" Cindy said, taking her hand out of JT's.

"Shut up and let's figure out how this thing works."

"Oh man, if we live through this she is gonna kick your ass righteously." JT said.

"You shut up too and let me see what this is."

A smirk came to Hannibal as JT moved out of the way, swapping places.

Texas Ranger blacked out GMC Suburban SUV.

"Now what sir?" The radio crackled again.

"Apparently they've found something"

"Sir, I think we'd better get them out of there and call the bomb squad people if that door is rigged."

"No, I think that Cindy FBI agent is trained to know what to look for. I'm not being careless, but if that thing goes we do not lose an entire department. I'm placing my bets on the agent."

"Yes sir."

"I want some people on the vehicles and move in closer. Protect yourselves but do not give yourselves away. Make sure your personal comm units are on the right channel."

"Yes sir."

"Yes sir."

"People, do not engage them. Let them continue"

There were several clicks of acknowledgement from the various persons

"Where is it?"

JT grabbed her good hand again and cautiously guided her hand to the switch.

"Go it?"

"Yeah."

"It's a square thing. Let me think this through. When we were in Thailand, Abby had stood in front of the door. When she swiped her card she didn't have a chance."

"I think what has to happen is we must press the switch first and then swipe the card. Sounds simple enough"

"Are you sure?"

"I guess we're going to find out. Give me the card JT."

JT gave it to her.

"OK, JT. Reach around me and press the switch."

JT did as instructed. There was a faint click. "OK Cindy, swipe."

She did. There was a buzz as the electronic lock disengaged.

"Told you so."

"What."

"They weren't that crazy to install explosives."

"Bet's off until we look later. I say there is."

They entered the building cautiously, gaining confidence as they moved towards the hanger doors.

Texas Ranger blacked out GMC Suburban SUV.

"They're in sir."

"OK, all units return to your vehicles and let them get on with their mission. I need to change my shorts."

A snicker came over the radio from an unidentified source.

"How about my rooftop teams? Can you see inside the hanger?"

"Nothing moving yet sir. The lights from the field are playing hell with the nightvision goggles."

"OK, just keep an eye on the windows for trouble."

"Roger."

Following Cindy's example, JT and Hannibal pulled out their various weapons, clinging to the walls as they made their way to the hanger. Instead of the two handed grip she had been taught, she was using one hand braced against her sling. They really didn't expect any trouble, but just in case.

Hannibal made it to the door first and looked through the glass into the darkened hanger area. A light was left on, maybe by accident in an office towards the back, but otherwise he saw no movement.

The light backlit several Vietnam era aircraft.

In the corner he saw his work area that had been reserved for the crates containing his Murphy Rebel.

Cautiously he signalled JT and Cindy to either side of the door with Cindy behind him as he turned the door handle.

Cindy saw a movement, turned and screamed. "JT!!"

"What!"

WHACK!

JT's vision was blurred, and he felt something wet running down his head. He tried to move his hands to feel what it was but for some reason they wouldn't move. Gradually he was able to make out sounds and as his vision cleared he saw that he was covered in blood.

His reaction was to jerk straight up, which only caused the chair he had been sitting in to topple over.

"Hello sleeping beauty. Care to join us?"

"Join what?"

"The living of course." Two sets of hands lifted his chair upright.

"Do I have to?"

"It would be nice if you did."

"JT are you all right?" This was from Cindy.

"Not sure yet. Wait a second….." He threw up.

"Sweetheart that was my nice clean floor you just puked on. I outa make you lick it up."

"Lick it up yourself."

"For a dead man you're very funny.'

"You got a Tylenol?"

"Not for you."

JT puked again.

"Wendell, get him some water." A voice to JT's right commanded.

"Ah come on, let him lick it up."

"Get the water."

Wendell walked over and filled a tiny paper cup with water from the water cooler, brought it over, pushed JT's head back and poured the contents somewhere in the vicinity of his mouth. The rest ran down his shirt.

"You with us now sweetheart?"

"Yeah."

The voice to the right said, "Now as I was saying, before you interrupted was how you three have completely fucked up my operation."

"By the way Mr. Travis, my name is Sam Foster. Mr. Washington and I go way back. A very long way back as in Thailand. Right Mr. Washington?"

"You OK JT," Hannibal asked JT, ignoring the question."

"Yeah, I'll live. Is this the motherfucker from Thailand you told me about? "

"Yep ."

JT turned his head to get a better look at his speaker. "Damn you're ugly. What ugly stick did you get beat with? Yo mama breast feed you from a monkey?"

A snicker came from across the room.

"Mr. Travis, your childish insults are beneath me. If you're trying to provoke me let it rest. Later I'll let Wendell instruct you on the proper form of addressing people, especially those that have control of your life.

"Whatever. Excuse me…." JT puked again. "Oops."

"Goddammit! Are you finished?"

"Not sure yet. I'll let you know. Wendell should have hit Hannibal in the head. His is tougher. You sure you don't have a Tylenol?"

"Mr. Travis you are interrupting my conversation. Wendell made an adjustment to your head with a crescent wrench as you were the one in the rear."

"Yeah and the rubber grip came off. You owe me a new one dude."

"Dude? Fuck you!"

WHACK! The crescent wrench once again made contact with JT's head. He saw it coming and was able to move, the side of his head and face and catching a glancing blow. The friction burn was worse than the lump.

"Wendell stop! Go see if there is some Tylenol in my desk. Look in the drawer on the lower right side."

"He sure is a smart ass for someone tied up and facing a short life expectancy."

"All you're doing is making him bleed and puke on my floor. Go look for the Tylenol. Where were we? Oh, yes, I was giving Mr. Washington a history lesson. Mr. Washington had me arrested."

"You had yourself arrested." Hannibal retorted.

"We had a nice setup too. At the time Captain Washington stumbled onto our operation and, oh, uh by the way, I need to apologize to you Mr. Travis."

"For what?"

"Your wife."

"What about my wife?" JT's voice rose .

"I'm sorry your wife was shot. Had Terrell done his job all right and proper, we would not be sitting here . Mr. Washington would be dead and you and your wife would be happily back in Canada. A little sad maybe."

"Fuck you."

Wendell had returned from his search mission holding a tiny white and red bottle containing Tylenol. He was in the process of swinging the wrench again.

"Wendell. Just give him the Tylenol."

Wendell lowered the wrench reluctantly. He aligned the two arrows on the cap and bottle; popping the lid.

Another person walked behind JT and untied one arm, which he held out to accept the medication.

"One lump or two?'

"Oh, and a comedian too?"

"Like I said, your wife I understand was shot but she's gonna live. I understand your family is taking real good care of her."

"How do you know?"

"I have resources."

"I was aware of your movements from the moment you left Indianapolis, your arrival at Dallas Love and thanks to Wendell here. He was the one that refuelled your jet."

This time JT raised his head to get a real good look at Wendell. He also saw Cindy and Hannibal tied in a similar fashion, seated n chair to his near right. The person that had untied his arms retied it and walked to the back of Cindy and Hannibal.

The speaker, Sam was more or less to his center left.

Behind Hannibal, Cindy and the unsub (unknown subject), he saw what looked like two executive corporate pilot types readying a Cessna Citation.

The stairs were down as they rushed to load several items onboard. They looked to be military transport boxes, painted in military olive drab colors and black letters. He could not read the writing at this distance. Each box had handles on the ends and sides for, as the military liked to call it, *easy humpin in the jungle by human transport.*

They would take one up and in, disappear and return for another one. He did not know how many had been loaded, but there was still two more to go.

The hanger doors were still closed.

Looking left and right he saw several aircraft of years gone by. To his left he saw a Cessna 337 Skymaster in the gray paint of an observation aircraft. A North American F100 Super Sabre, an F101 Voodoo and the wing of an aircraft, which he could not make out as the rest of it was behind him. To his right was the shark face painted on the nose of an F-4 Phantom.

The Mercury-vapor lights were bright.

"I told you I like fixing aircraft." Wendell said. "This wrench sure comes in handy. Nice and quiet but deadly."

Sam continued. "Regardless, we knew when you'd be here and we just waited. We watched you on the CCTV's but used infra-red thermal imaging. Cool stuff. Wendell was supposed to tap you on the head, not try to take it off. You look a mess Mr. Travis."

"Mike, go over and get some more water and a couple of paper towels. Untie Mr. Travis's hands so that he can clean himself up." Mike, the unsub, did as he was ordered.

"Let's get back to business."

While JT's hands were untied, Wendell made a point of slapping the crescent wrench in one hand. JT took the water and towels and gingerly padded his head down. He could feel the start of two lumps, but the bleeding from the facial laceration had slowed. He was roughly pushed back into the chair and Mike retied his hands.

"Mr. Washington as I was saying, you made a big mistake back in Thailand. I was fucked over for every possible military job opportunity. I received a General Discharge. Fortunately just like you, these people don't dig too deep into one's background. They only care if you can work or fly.

The job played right into our hands as we still had operations in Thailand. Things were going good your girlfriend started nosing around with that Thai security woman at the airbase."

"What do you think of our setup FBI agent Ng? You were supposed to die too and not just your friend."

"Fuck you."

"No wonder you three run together. We knew once you had lifted the ID, we had been compromised. The security measures we had taken worked as planned. By the way, that same plan is installed here as well with a few modifications. Can't go blowing up innocent people can we? Nice job finding that switch Mr. Travis. You missed your calling. You should be a demolitions expert."

"Fuck you." JT responded.

"Why didn't you just let us get inside and look around? If your operations was as good as you thought, we might not have found anything. You killed, no murdered, an innocent woman."

"That's just it Ms. Ng. We were not sure just how much information you had. We knew you to be FBI. The Korat one was our largest. We have others, but it will take time to get them to the level as Korat."

"Good for us. So what happens now?"

"Not sure about you two, but Mr. Washington and I have a little catching up to do."

"So let me loose and we can do some catching up. Let them go." Hannibal said.

"Nice gesture, but obviously they know too much and we just can't have that can we?"

"Then why don't you and me take it outside; just two old men in the dirt. I lose; you kill us, you lose; your men let us go."

"Very funny, but it is not that simple. Right now there is an SUV loaded with Texas Rangers and FBI Hostage rescue teams outside. Yeah we know that too and from the looks on your faces, I bet you knew that as well. We also know that on the rooftop next door is a sniper, with a sniper rifle. Don't get your hopes up; we had special lighting installed that would cause problems with nightvision goggles.

They can't see in here. In about 15-minutes we're going to load everyone into the Citation over there and just fly away.

I see the pilots have finished loading everything.

We've already been cleared for departure. We told DFW ATC that we were having some technical issues, but would have them solved soon and leave straight out as traffic at this time of night there is hardly any flights in our out. Besides that we control this airport.

The Citation is under a temporary false registration, so once we're out of Dallas/Ft. Worth airspace, we'll drop down in Oklahoma, wash the water soluble paint off and take off again to parts unknown, at least by the authorities. As for you three, you'll be excess cargo.

I hope you can fly without a chute. Two black birds and a yellow chick." He had to laugh at his own humour.

"Oooh you are so funny!"

Whack. Once again the crescent wrench made contact with JT's head.

"Stop it!"

"I'm going to take that wrench and stick it up your ass so far, you'll be called Ratchet Jaw."

"Oh now you're the one being funny."

"Stop it you two. Get them on the plane. We have very little time left."

With Mike in the lead, Cindy and Hannibal followed. JT was helped to a standing position by Wendell, who brought up the rear.

Sam kicked chairs out of the way, and moved a tool box back to clear a path for the Citation. He ran to the front of the hanger and hit the door open button.

"**Sir, I still can't** see inside and they have been in there a long time."

"I know, but we'll give it a few more minutes." Something about this just does not seem right."

"Your call sir."

"Yeah my call."

"Rooftop unit."

"Go ahead."

"What do you have?"

"I can't' tell yet sir. I can see some movement, but it is much distorted as if something is interfering with the image.

"Use your scope and look around the parking lots. See if you see any vehicles parked recently. Use your thermal imager on them and see if they radiate."

The sniper repositioned his weapon and did as instructed. His weapon of choice was a KART M-14 EBR Airsoft Sniper Rifle used by the US Navy Seals.

"Sir I've got heat signatures on several vehicles over by the hanger doors. There's a small door there as well. My guess is someone is already inside and they might be in trouble."

"Damn!"

"Sir?"

"Just thinking."

"OK, everybody listen up. I think they might have encountered a problem inside. Unload and make your way to both sides of the hanger and entranceway. Copy?"

"Copy." Each person replied."

"Be careful."

Two of the FBI Hostage Rescue agents went to the front entranceway. Not knowing about the switch, pulled on the door handle.

There was a flash of light and the sound of thunder as the explosions went off. The agents were thrown backwards as if they were rag dolls. The modifications to the setup did not blow the rest of the building.

"Everybody stop! Don't touch anything!"

"Sir, the hanger doors are opening and I think I hear a jet engine winding up."

"Everybody go around back. Go! Go! Go!"

Cindy was the first to be loaded on the Citation. Hannibal next.

Mike stood in front of them as JT was entering the door, followed by Wendell. The pilots had already commenced the start-up procedure when the front part of the hanger bulged inward from an explosion.

"GO! GO!" Sam yelled from outside waving at the pilots.

JT, seeing his advantage, leveraged his legs off the stairs and lunged backwards into Wendell, sending them down the short flight of stairs and onto the floor: the wrench clattering to the floor.

With hands still tied, he grabbed the wrench and rolled. He came up just as Wendell had regained his footing and swung.

SMACK!!!!

The wrench made contact with the side of his face. The end that had the pointy adjustment stuff on it. Blood and teeth flew to the side. Before he could recover, JT continued his turn to gain momentum and swung again. Wendell went down hard.

Standing over him, JT swung the wrench right into his open crotch making solid contact with his testicles. Wendell's unconscious body jerked.

"Can't stick it up your ass, but I guess that'll do." He hit him again and threw the wrench down, turned and ran for the still open door. To his left he saw Sam running towards him in an intercept course. The Citation had started its roll towards the doors, with the nose about to clear.

Using his teeth JT undid his knots, ran up the stairs right into Mike who had turned to see what the commotion was about.

While he was distracted, Cindy stood up and kicked him in the side , turning him so that Hannibal could head butt him.

JT reached Hannibal and untied his hands.

Cindy screamed as Sam entered the door.

Pushing her aside, Hannibal tackled Sam and out the door they flew to the floor.

JT turned and untied Cindy's hands.

"Go help Hannibal!"

"Naw, he's OK."

Suddenly the aircraft jerked and slew to the left, causing them to fall over the seats, across Mike's limp body and onto the floor. JT heard the report of what he knew to be an M-14.

Two HRT agents ran into the opening of the hanger doors right after the sniper shot the nose tire out on the Citation. The high-powered bullet ricocheted off the floor after passing through the tire and rattled around the metal beams.

The blown tire caused the jet to slew sideways. Its wings made contact with the F-101 and F-100 aircraft. Continuing it eventually make contact with the hanger door with a metallic crunching noise bringing it to a halt. There was a loud crack as the main wing spar broke. The self-sealing tanks kept fuel from spewing out onto the floor.

The pilots shut the engines down.

Hannibal was not interested in the events surrounding him. He and Sam; just two old men in the dirt, well floor, were trading punches.

"This is for Abby, you son of a bitch. This is for Pamela, you motherfucker. This is for Cindy." He continued to rain blows on Sam's face and head. He might have been a General, but in the hood of East St. Louis he had learned street fighting. Sam was no match.

"Kick his ass Hannibal!" JT yelled from inside the craft.

She pushed him aside just as the two pilots had opened the curtains separating them from the passenger compartment.

"Get back in there!!" She yelled. She followed up with a shove to the lead pilot who was shoved back into the co-pilot.

Dumb struck, and undecided until they saw JT wag his finger; they sat down.

Cindy leapt from the aircraft just in time to see Hannibal lift Sam once more and with a roundhouse kick nearly take his head off.

"Told you he had everything under control."

They heard Hannibal say, "And that motherfucker is for fucking with me."

"Everybody down...... Now!"

Two HRT agents in black ran over with MP-5's at the ready, joining the two that had come in from the hanger doors. They were followed closely by a Ranger wearing a Stetson. Another black clad figure with a wicked looking M-14 sniper rifle came running through the open hanger door as well.

JT, Hannibal and Cindy hit the floor. Sam and Wendell were already down and Mike was out cold in the aircraft.

"FBI!" Cindy yelled.

"Hands on the ground, straight out. All of you."

"FBI!" Cindy yelled again.

She was roughly turned over. Ranger Ferguson walked over and knelt beside her.

"You OK?"

"Sure, just a little sore from being tied up."

He stood up and surveyed the area.

"Help these three up." He instructed the HRT agents.

He walked over to Sam's body, kicking him over with his boot. "Get this piece of shit up."

"Yes sir," one of the HRT agents said and turned Sam over, setting him up with his head between his legs.

He then walked over to Wendell as he was coming too.

Wendell threw up.

"Hey Wendell, you'd better lick that shit up."

Ranger Ferguson's eyebrow rose a fraction.

"Hey Ranger Ferguson, you'd better watch out. Wendell lost his nuts to a wrench."

"Fuck you." Wendell groaned.

"Oh my, what a potty mouth."

"JT."

"What?"

"Shut up." Cindy said.

Turning around Ranger Ferguson instructed the HRT with the weird M-14, "Get the pilots out of the aircraft and set them over there." He point to some chairs that were overturned.

An HRT member came running in from the front of the blown away hanger.

"Maurice didn't make it sir. Carmella will be OK, but she's in some serious pain and has a lot of broken body parts. There's an ambulance outside now with paramedics looking after her."

"Thanks."

"Yes sir."

Ranger Ferguson turned preparing to give more instructions when he was shot right in the neck above his vest at close range by an HRT agent. His spinal cord was severed instantly. He went straight down.

"What the fuck!" JT yelled.

The HRT agent then turned and shot the one carrying the M-14.

"What the well is going on here?"

The remaining members of the HRT agents turned on their partners.

Everyone froze.

"What the hell are you doing." One yelled.

"Shut up!" the first HRT agent said pointing his weapon in the general direction of Hannibal, Cindy and JT.

"I bet you didn't expect that did you." The lead HRT agent said.

"Who the hell are you?" Cindy asked.

Without answering, the lead HRT removed his helmet and goggles.

"Well fuck me a new asshole." Hannibal said.

Cindy swung her head around to face Hannibal as she had never heard him curse before.

"Hello Captain Washington, or is it General? Nope it's Mr. nobody now. The Agent grinned.

"Who the hell is this?' Cindy asked.

"Cindy I want you to meet Airman Melvin Anderson."

"FBI Agent Melvin Anderson of the Hostage Rescue Team, to you Mr. Nobody."

"What?"

"You don't know how long I have been waiting to see that look of surprise on your face. And oh man did you deliver."

"Is this the other asshole from Thailand Hannibal?" JT asked.

Before Hannibal could answer, "Yes in the flesh."

"There ain't no way you're and FBI agent." JT said.

"Oh yes I am."

"How?" asked Cindy.

"This is so cool. I think I'm going to have an orgasm. First things first. Sam, my man, you OK?"

"Yeah, what took you so long?"

"Ferguson sent Carmella and me to the front door. I had to pretend dumb and ran around the side. Maurice took my place. "

"You let two of your agents die?" Hannibal said.

"Cut the odds down."

"You are one sick bastard." Cindy said

"I've been called that and a few others. Someone go over and put that fire out. I need someone to go outside and see how Carmilla is doing. Tell the paramedics everything is fine in here, but we need time to look for more explosive. That should keep them and DPS busy for a while until I decide what to do with these three."

"You aren't going to get away with this." Hannibal said.

"I already have."

'So you're the inside man?" Cindy asked.

"Well not really. There was one more above me. You'll meet him in a second. I was on the inside, and knew most of your movements Agent Ng, if that's what you mean. As you worked in a different department, I didn't have total access to your files or your whereabouts. I knew you were onto something regarding our operations."

"So how in the hell did you become and FBI agent?"

"The short version is this. Right after I was Dishonourably Discharged and sent to Leavenworth, my time was cut short. Sam's parents pulled some strings to get my sentence reduced. Just as they had made Sam's records disappear, they had mine changed from Dishonourable to Medical. A fact made true as I have a pinched nerve. For the most part it does not bother me. Anyway it was already in my records so it was not hard to find a person willing to make the changes for a cause."

Over the years I kept my nose clean and saw a job opening for a local sheriff. I applied and was accepted. For the next three years I worked narcotics and with the help of Sam, we gave up a location or two with minor operations. Well you can guess that suddenly I was the person to go to when it was about busting drug operations.

Unfortunately when we increased our operations of Roxanne, the FBI needed help trying to locate this new source of almost pure cocaine with such a low street value. Guess who they recruited?

Nobody answered.

What made it even more unfortunate was the plastic bags we were using. They couldn't take the vibration and started breaking open in flight of which Agent Ng is all too aware of. We thought we had the problem licked. But nobody can predict the turbulence an aircraft has to fly though, especially a military aircraft."

Before he could continue there was another commotion from the front of the blown out area of the hanger. The HRT agent that had been sent outside was returning with another man in an expensive suit.

Melvin straightened and said, "Good evening sir."

The man nodded, and surveyed his surroundings.

How much of the product is on the aircraft?"

"All of it sir."

"Damn. OK, I've spoken to the Dallas Police and they let me pass. We only have a few minutes before they get curious and wonder what is going on in here. Take these three around back. The rest of you unload the airplane and stick them outside next to the SUV's."

"And you are?" Cindy asked.

He ignored Cindy and walked over to Hannibal. "Good Evening General."

"What?"

"Cindy and JT, I'd like you to meet retired Major- General Mathius Peterson."

"Let me guess, he was in Thailand too." JT said.

"Well not quite Mr. Travis. I was in Guam. I was the Inspector- General for US Air Force bases in Southeast Asia.

"Ah man, this is way too good to be true." JT said. "Cindy you are looking at the head man. The IG. The man who can change personnel records. The man that can travel from base to base unnoticed unless he wants too and the man that can change aircraft serial numbers."

"Very good Mr. Travis."

"I'm not following." Cindy said.

Hannibal said, "An IG can go from base to base and implement instruction on the proficiency of how a base is run. He can write up infractions or he can ignore them, depending on who he is and what the infraction was. Things are different now, but back then when an IG was coming to a base, you would not believe the amount of shit that got trashed, hidden, or destroyed before he arrived. Every single unit in the Air Force…."

"And the Army." JT added.

"Did not want to be on the shit list of the IG." Hannibal continued. "You've heard of the saying shit rolls downhill?" Well if a base command took a hit from an IG, you can bet shit rolled down hill soon afterwards. Any base, or as JT pointed out, post that failed his inspection was made to feel the wrath in spades. And I do mean spades."

"We had an old warehouse on a main street when I first arrived in Thailand." JT said. " I had only been there for maybe a week, so I was detailed along with several others from my company to go through the warehouse. Anything that didn't have a serial number, part's number or couldn't be identified was loaded onto a truck and taken away. I can only guess to be buried. Once we came across a stash of old C-Rats, or rations that had spilled out of their cardboard boxes. We piled them onto another deuce and an half...."

"What's a deuce and a half?" Cindy asked.

"It's a 2 ½ ton truck. It's one of those trucks you see in war movies with the troops lining both side. Anyway we loaded them up and hid the stuff in the barracks. After the IG left we had a C-rats party about every night for nearly a month. A lot of it we gave away to the Thai's."

"So if I understand, correctly, you had the power to make or break a base. You had free reign over anyone and or anything. If your drug smuggling operations were in peril, you made the evidence disappear, or it was moved."

"Damn General, she a fast learner."

"And that Cindy is the inside man." Hannibal said. "There are very few positions within the US military where one can play God. The Inspector General is one of them.

"Is this the sonofabitch that had Abby killed?" JT asked

"Not killed JT. She was snooping in the wrong place at the wrong time."

"When was she supposed to have a right time? It was her job to snoop into your operations."

"She should have called and we'd have gladly shown her around."

JT ignored the sarcasm. "And because of you my wife was shot."

"Well, I had nothing to do with it directly. Our intention was to stop General Washington. You were just in the way."

JT smoldered. "Why would you want to stop Hannibal?"

"OK, enough of this history lesson. Somebody get those pilots off the plane. Sam do you have their pay?"

"Yes sir."

"Pay them off and tell them to get out of here. Nothing we can do about the Citation."

"Melvin let's lead these people out of here as if you're making and arrest. The rest of you finish up in here loading those cases. Let's go"

Anderson turned to Cindy, Hannibal and JT following the lead of Mathius. "Let's go." Anderson parroted the ordered. He followed Mathius's lead.

Hannibal followed slightly behind JT and Cindy.

Behind them an HRT agent followed loosely, weapon ready slung across his chest. Trigger finger outside the guard.

As Mathius and Anderson walked ahead of them, they passed near the spot where the M-14 had fallen on the floor. Hannibal dove towards it rolling, grabbed the M-14 while he was still rolling, brought the weapon up Jason Bourne style and fired right between Cindy and JT, striking Anderson in the back of the head.

The sonic path of the bullet caused JT and Cindy to dive for cover in opposite directions.

"Shit!" Cindy screamed.

"Fuck!"

The bullet's suction, took brain matter with it, grazing the head of Mathius.

It continued on and entered the previously undamaged Douglas A-1 Skyraider, the wing of which JT could only previous see, placing a bloody period at the end of the stencilled letters USAF.

Anderson just went straight down. His body was oozing blood, covering him and the floor.

Mathius fell to the floor moaning. He soiled his expensive suit as he rolled around in the blood and gore.

Hannibal continued to roll and was coming up into a kneeling position to take a bead on the trailing agent, but the agent was faster.

He shot Hannibal.

But Hannibal got off a round as well, although not as accurate before he went down. The impact of the 7.62mm round reaching supersonic speeds was enough to flip him backwards as it impacted his protective vest. His weapon flew to his side.

He was down for the immediate count.

"Hannibal!" Cindy yelled.

JT got up and ran for a fallen MP-5, brought it up as Sam was taking a bead on her.

JT fired first hitting him in the knee taking it out. His leg was whipped out from under him and he fell to the floor screaming.

Wendell, still trying to recover from his ball-dusting experience, tried tugging at the sling of the MP-5, the HRT agent Hannibal had shot. JT ran over to him and jammed the muzzle of the MP-5 roughly into his balls.

Wendell froze; the look of fear in his eyes. "Come on JT. Don't do it man."

"Oh so now we're begging?"

"Man I had orders. OK, I hit you on the head, but I didn't shoot anyone. I didn't shoot your wife. You've busted my balls already. Ain't that enough?"

JT hesitated and then kicked him in the legs. "......Get up you bag of shit!..... Slowly!"

To his right he saw Cindy running towards Hannibal, who was flat on his back.

"Hannibal!" She yelled again.

She almost made it.

"**Everybody down**! Let me see some hands......Now!!!"

"FBI. We need a medic over here immediately!" Cindy yelled.

"Aw, what the fuck now." JT whined.

Once again he hit the floor with the MP-5 stretched out in front of him. Wendell sat back down.

I said I want to see some hands, the voice yelled again.

Behind the voice a new set of MIB's, Men in Black, ran inside. Outside a shot rang out.

Behind the voice was another civilian in jeans and stripped dress western shirt.

"FBI. A man is down and needs immediate medical attention."

"Where?" The voice asked.

"Over here! FBI Special Agent in Charge Cynthia Ng."

"I know who you are."

"You do?"

"The voice walked briskly over to Hannibal and felt for a pulse from his neck. It was strong.

"You OK, Washington?"

"What?" Cindy questioned.

Hannibal's eyes fluttered and opened. "I think so sir. I don't think anything vital was hit. Just felt like the wind was knocked out of me."

"Get a medic over here now!" the voice ordered. "Where were you hit? There's blood everywhere."

"Who are you?" Cindy asked.

"In due time Ms. Ng."

"I think my right shoulder. I can move it, but it hurts like hell"

"Hannibal. Who is this man?"

The MIB's had taken the MP-5 from JT and helped him up. He too ran over to where Hannibal lay and caught the tail end of the question.

"Yeah, Hannibal, who is this man? Who are these people?"

"Cindy, JT meet Thomas Clayton of the Federal Marshal's office."

"The federales?"

"Yep."

"An honest to God, Federal Marshal?"

"Yes."

"Well bust my britches and call me Buckwheat."

"What? I'm sorry JT, but that was lost on me." Marshal Clayton said.

"Never mind."

"Hey old man, didn't anyone ever show you how to duck a bullet?

Hannibal held up his middle finger.

"I love you too. Can I have your Murphy Rebel since you won't be flying it for a while?"

"JT."

"What?"

"Shut up."

"Are you alright Washington?" This was from the civilian in the jeans.

"You ain't no Marshal are you?" JT inquired.

"Well my name is Marshall, but I'm not a federal Marshal. I own this place. I'm Hank Marshall. The president of Retired Transport Pilot's Association, thus the owner of Advanced Aircraft Restorations."

"Don't mind him Hank, That's JT and this is my soon to be wife, Cindy."

"I hear you're an FBI agent?"

"I am."

"You've got a good man there."

"Thank you."

"Here come the paramedics. Mr. Marshall I need you to identify these people." Hank and Federal Marshal Clayton walked away to make identifications.

"Hey sunshine." Cindy said.

"Hi."

"I thought I'd lost you."

"No way. Too old and hard to get killed."

She kissed him.

"I love you."

"I love you too."

"Will you two get a room?" JT said.

"Sweetheart?"

"Yes?"

"Where is that weird looking rifle?"

"Why?"

"I'm going to shoot JT with it."

Hannibal started laughing.

"Oh, so that's how it's going to be? You gonna treat me this way? I'm the one that brought the two of you together. You should be thanking me."

"JT."

"I know, I know. Shut up."

Moving Cindy out of the way, the paramedic began to take Hannibal's vitals. One of them had opened a large portable medical chest and prepared various medications and injections.

As JT walked away, Cindy caught with him.

"How did Hannibal know that Federal Marshal?" She asked.

"I don't know, but I have a feeling this is far deeper than you and I know and it goes a long way back, to like when we were in Thailand."

"You think so?"

"I'd say about 99.9% positive."

"Oh, God, I wonder if he knew enough about the Air base in Thailand could have stopped us from going."

JT stopped dead in his steps, and looked at her.

"I think Hannibal had a good reason for not telling us a lot of what was going on. But if he knew enough to have stopped you from going to that hanger, it would have tipped off whatever it was he was tracking.

I'm going to be honest, if he knew I'd hate him for the rest of my life. He didn't tell us so I will assume he didn't know. He sure as hell didn't act like he knew when we busted this place."

"You're right." Cindy replied.

"I might act silly a lot, but I'm not stupid. Hannibal once told me about the perils of having a military security clearance. My gut feeling tells me he knew about this operation a long time ago and was under strict orders not to say anything."

As they stood there, Dallas police, Federal agents, and paramedics made the hanger a surreal war zone. Blood was everywhere. The body of Ranger Ferguson was turned over and examined. Mathius was still groaning and rolling. He had to be sedated before they could get him on a gurney and moved.

Sam was leaning against a tool chest looking at his shattered leg while the paramedics stuck needles in him and bandaged his stump. They rushed in a chest of ice to freeze the leg. Maybe they thought they could save it. Only time would tell. JT felt no pity for his loss.

He found a spot and sat down on the floor. Cindy sat beside him as they watched Hannibal being rolled outside.

"Aren't you going with him?"

"I'll be there in plenty of time. Right now I'd only be in the way."

They sat quietly; islands in a sea of storm.

Cindy turned as she heard sobbing coming from JT.

"JT are you all right?"

"Yeah.......It's just..... Well it's just the adrenaline rush and of this, this mess.." JT waved his hands, "...has finally caught up with me. Sort of like jet lag."

Several weeks ago, I met two beautiful women and was reunited with my old friend. Had someone told me that later within 48-hours, our lives would be turned upside down; I'd have laughed and made reservations for them at the funny farm. Who would have thought it would come to this? I'm no stranger to unusual life changing experiences, but this has tested everything I know about life." JT wiped his eyes with the back of his hands. He searched his pockets and found the paper towel he had been given to clean up the blood on his face and wiped the tears away.

Cindy took the towel away and helped.

"Better?"

"A little, but yeah."

With her good arm she gave him a hug. She then placed her head on his shoulder and laced her arm around his. "I know what you mean."

JT smelled a mixture of perfume, sweat, and hair spray. He kissed the top of her head.

"Thank you." She said.

"So what happens now?" JT asked.

"I'm not sure. I'll have a ton of paper work. I guess Marshal Clayton will have a ton of questions."

"What about Hannibal?"

"That is a very big question that only he can answer. He obviously knew a lot and Lord knows he will have as much if not more than me of paperwork to fill out."

"Cindy, will you promise me something?"

"What?"

"Will you marry him?"

"Come on JT you know I will."

"I'm serious. Pinkie swear?"

She whacked him on the shoulder, "Dummy I am and I will."

"OK, just checking. One more promise."

"Oh boy, what is it?"

"That you'll let Pamela and me plan the wedding in Vancouver."

"Vancouver?"

"Yes, I know the perfect spot. We can even say a farewell to Abby there too."

"I'll have to check with Hannibal, but I think he'd like it."

"Good. It's settled." They heard footsteps and saw Hank approaching.

"Mr. Travis?"

"You can call me JT."

"Mr. JT, uh, JT I would like to offer my apology."

"For what?"

"I am the one that gave Sam the OK to travel to Indianapolis. He told me Mr. Washington was the one hiding things like drugs and could prove it."

Cindy and JT looked at each other.

"He said that if he went to Indianapolis, he could bring back the evidence."

I had reservations but I gave him time off to go. I wish I could take it all back now had I known he'd be so foolhardy as to plan a killing."

"I don't think that was his initial plan Hank. I think he was trying to scare Hannibal off the track."

"Off the track of what?"

"As Agent Ng and I have discussed, I think Hannibal had known about some things going on here than he has let on. Maybe they found out and were trying to mislead him."

"That still does not make it right in my books that your wife was shot as a result."

"You had nothing to do with it Hank. Only Sam is responsible."

"Just the same, here's my card. If you need anything, and I mean anything, just call. What about your wife's medical expenses?"

"We always take out travel insurance when we leave Canada, so we're fine."

"Humm. OK, but call me."

"I will. Hey you wouldn't know where I can get my hands on a used Cessna A-37 Tweety Bird would you? They had a lot of them in Thailand that were turned over to the Thai's for advance flight training. Just kidding, but if you come across one, let me know."

"Uh, sure."

"I'm kidding, honest."

"I think they're still in the US military inventory anyway. That makes it kind of hard to get one." Hank said and walked away.

"Maybe I should have asked for a Mitsubishi MU-2 or maybe a cool LearJet model 24."

"JT I have no idea what the hell you're talking about."

"Well, see this Mitsubishi MU-2 is a high-wing, really cool airplane........"

Cindy dropped her head between her legs. She should have known better.

"........and the LearJet Model 24 was built by Bill Lear. You know the guy that invented the 8-track player for cars and...."

"No JT, that was before my time."

"You didn't have an 8-track?"

"JT......Will you shut up. How in the world does Pamela put up with up?"

"Well, you see..."

She was saved by the bell.

Marshal Clayton walked over to where they were seated.

"Well we're just about finished here. All the bad guys are locked and boxed."

"You just made a funny." JT said.

"I know. You two look like you've lost your best friend and needed some cheering. Oops, bad choice of words."

"That's OK, but thanks for trying to cheer us up. We have a question for you, actually several."

"I knew you would. I'll make it easy. Let's go over to that office where it's quiet and I can talk without being overheard as this is still an ongoing investigation."

They got up, JT helping Cindy with her good hand and walked to the office. About halfway there they were interrupted.

"Sir you'd better take a look over here." An MIB's told him. They diverted to where the MIB was pointing to the multi-handled olive drab boxes. The lids were open on a couple of them.

Inside one box was plastic hundreds of plastic bags. Inside another one were bags containing a white powder.

"Bet we know what that is."

Another box contained circuit boards already cut to what one might assume is the shape of an electronics storage bay box.

"They were taking everything to a new location." Cindy said.

"Looks that way."

"Had we waited a day or two, there would not have been anything here what-so-ever."

"Yep. Melvin was on Ferguson's team and had the date of the raid, but not the exact time. You guys screwed it up."

"Hurray for us." JT said.

"Hannibal screwed it up." Cindy said.

"Nope. He called me in Washington. I jumped on the corporate jet down. I had only a few minutes to put together a team. He must have known that as he also called our office here. When I arrived, the team was in place and ready to go."

"So we really did screw things up."

"Let's go into that office now"

They each found a chair but Marshal Clayton sat on the end of the desk.

"Like I said there is still an ongoing investigation and Hannibal is free to tell you, especially you Cindy, may I call you Cindy what he knew. I'll let Hannibal trust his judgement about you JT."

"Don't you dare say it JT." Cindy said.

"What?"

"I know you well enough to know what you're going to say."

Marshal Clayton looked at the two of them.

"I can think it if I want."

"Go ahead Tom, May I call you Tom?'

"No wonder he likes you two so much. You sound like my brother and sister. When Hannibal stumbled across Melvin and Sam in Thailand, he accidentally fell into a can of worms. We knew about them, but we knew that they were not the real people running the operation. We actually let them make their shipments and tracked where each of them went. At the time they were small potatoes compared to some of the other stuff coming into the country from Mexico. They were led to believe it so that they would eventually reel in the man responsible. No offense Cindy, but back then, there were not enough high ranking women that had the kind of power a male officer had.

"No problem."

"The thing is, this person was so high up, he was totally invisible."

Hannibal was due to rotate back to the US. We asked him to extend his overseas commitment and he could fly any aircraft, not in combat, but anything he wanted. The excuse being he was testing them when in actually he would have unlimited access to any aircraft he wanted."

"So that's why he didn't come back to the States with me. I lost track of him and actually felt he'd forgotten me. But one day out of the blue he called and over the years since then from time to time he'd drop in for a day or two."

"I guess. What if I told you he was there snooping?"

"On me, I mean us?"

"No on where the shipments were coming and going to."

"But I was led to believe that trail had gone cold."

"Then he did his job. For a time it did. And then that aircraft landing at McChord broke the case wide open, thanks to you Cindy."

"Me?"

"Yes, you. You're the one that uncovered the serial numbers and when you sent your report to your boss we received a copy as well. Unfortunately so did Ferguson and his team."

"So they knew and contacted their boss, which was Mathius. How did you know it was him?" Cindy asked.

"Again we didn't, by accident we noticed that each time a shipment was getting close to being raided, there would be an IG inspection and the evidence went poof. Even today we have periodic inspections at bases such as the one in Korat as it is still used by our forces.

"I knew I had enlisted in the wrong occupation of the Army. Missed my chance." JT said.

"IG's are a special breed. Most, as far as I know, are honest and would never stoop to such levels, but it only takes one. We compared the times when Mathius was at each base and the timing of our raids. They matched. We only had circumstantial evidence. So Hannibal was told to get a job here as a start."

"So Hank was in on it?" Cindy asked.

"No. Hannibal got the job on his own merits, thank God. This way we could watch everyone, including Hank, and not feel his cover would be blown by some over achiever office busy body looking into things."

"I'm going home. This is far over my head. You spooks, MIB's, federales, Rangers, Police, FBI agents can have it." JT stood. "What about the pilots of the Citation?"

"They are the real meal deal. They were hired to fly a late night shipment, and told that they would be paid in cash. I would have had some concerns, but if someone is willing to pay cash for what appears to be a legal shipment, especially one in military hardware boxes from a hanger with military aircraft, who am I going to question?"

"One more question. Did Hannibal know that Cindy was at that conference in Vancouver?"

Marshal Clayton thought for a second. "Let me put it this way. He knew that there was a high level meeting taking place between Canada, the US and Thailand. He did not know who was in attendance. That was not his job. He was, as he said, actually there to purchase that airplane to make his cover story look good. The rest just fell into place. So if I am thinking ahead of you JT, he actually met Cindy for the first time and nature ran its course. They'll make a great couple."

"Told you so." JT said to Cindy. "I told her that Hannibal and she are made for each other."

Cindy blushed.

"Yeah you guys are all made for each other."

"Do you need me any longer down here? I mean in Texas?"

"My immediate answer is no. You were not a primary player in this. Cindy and Hannibal are. I know most of what Hannibal knows. We need Cindy to fill in the blanks. You're free to go."

JT started for the door and Marshal Clayton stood. "Thanks Cindy" He said and they shook hands. "I'll see you tomorrow. I guess you'll be at the hospital."

"Yes." She said. "I'll be there tonight too as long as they let me stay."

"I'll drop in before I leave tomorrow." JT said.

There was nothing more to say. They all walked outside into the hanger bay where there was still a lot of confusion but things seemed to be more ordered and controlled.

JT wandered over to the crates that he assumed were Hannibal's containing his Murphy Rebel.

God, to start over again building an airplane again. It takes years of dedication, cussing, sweat, and yes blood. JT could not count the number of times he had banged his knuckles, got burned, cut his hands, or spilled fluids on his clothing. Pamela had to throw away a couple of jeans and shirts because the epoxy had set into the fabric. The memory made him laugh. I'm too old to be doing that again.

Behind him he heard Cindy, Hank and Marshal Clayton whispering and decided to wander over. As he got closer they became silent. Obviously it was a conversation that he would not be privileged too.

He held up his hands in submission, "OK, I understand when my presence is not needed. I know when I'm being dissed. I'll just wander over there and see how Wendell is holding up.

Hey Wendell! How you holding up brother!?" He walked towards Wendell who was still sitting on the floor.

Wendell still looked pale as he was cuffed. He stared at JT flinching.

"That's OK brother. I'm not going to mess with you, but let me know if you need a set of new balls. I can get you a deal on eBay for a set of brass ones."

Against his will, the corner of his mouth turned up in a semblance of a smile. He was helped to stand by two MIB's. Together with the HRT agent who was stripped of his gear and flex-cuffed, both were led outside.

Marshal Clayton turned back to Cindy and Hank. "He's a strange one isn't he?"

Cindy could only laugh.

CHAPTER VI

Korat, Thailand, 1968

Captain Richard "Hannibal" Washington, with the aid of his crew chief, descended the stairs attached to the side of his F-4 Phantom fighter. He had just completed another bombing and strafing run in support of Operation Nigeria, supporting the US Marines pinned down at Khe Sanh. His flight had been called on alert and then scrambled when ground sensors had detected a large presence of some 2,000 North Vietnamese around the Marines. Although a Marine and US Navy operation, the Air Force had been called in to backup and destroy the enemy as they ran back into Laos.

Captain Washington had made a successful run, deepening on what one called successful. They had been called in on a trail with heavy jungle top-cover. There were some secondary explosions, indication some sort of ordinance had blown, but the extent of just what was hit would remain hidden until a US Army Special Forces, Navy Seals, or Marine Recon team was sent in.

As Captain Washington removed his gear, in the distance he saw a jeep, red dust trailing, headed in his direction. He went over the aircraft with his plane captain inspecting for damage. There were a few holes, but for once it was serviceable and would be back in operation soon.

The jeep he had seen locked brakes about 50-feet from his aircraft and a Colonel jumped out. His driver remained seated. "Captain Washington?'

"Yes sir." Captain Washington stood at attention.

"At ease. I'm Colonel Thomas Clayton. As soon as you finish your after-action report, I want you to report to my office immediately."

"Sure sir, just where is your office?"

"Over by the Base Operations Center. I'll send a jeep over."

"Can you tell me what this is about sir?"

"Not here, but you'll soon understand."

"Yes sir." Captain Washington relaxed.

Colonel Clayton got into his jeep and they drove away.

His plane captain came down from the ladder having insured all of the switches were in their safe position, "Wow sir, what was that about?"

"I have no idea, but I guess I'm going to find out soon enough."

"I hope it's nothing bad sir."

"Yeah, me too."

Captain Washington didn't have to wait long. True to his word, a jeep, driven by an Airman First Class, pulled up next to his aircraft. "Captain Washington sir, I was sent to pick you up."

Hannibal got into the passenger seat, throwing his flight bag in the rear. His driver took off, headed for the Base Operations Center.

They raced across the base, passing the rivets where several Lockheed L-1049 Constellations, known as Connie or Super Connie's; the C-121 bring the military version, were being readied sitting next to an above ground rubber fuel bladder.

Hannibal had always flown in fighters for his overseas deployment or the new Boeing C-5's that were replacing the Boing C-141.

JT told him that when he had finished his Basic at Ft. Leonard Wood, he flew a Trans World Airlines (TWA) flight from St. Louis to Indianapolis. It took nearly two-hours then, a distance that would later take only 45 minutes with the jet age.

Even in its military livery; it was a beautiful and graceful aircraft sitting high in the air on long landing gear legs. It was made ugly by the radome fixed atop the fuselage. The Connie's were used as Airborne Early Warning aircraft over the Vietnam theatre.

It had four- 18-cylinder radial Wright engines and had an unusual three-finned tail. When Dwight Eisenhower was president, this was his Air Force One.

Hannibal was brought back to the present. "Here we are sir."

"Thanks."

"Sir you'll find Colonel Clayton's office on your left." The driver reached into the rear of the jeep and handed Captain Washington his flight bag.

"Thanks again."

Colonel Thomas Clayton – Operations Intelligence, the plaque attached to the door read.

He knocked.

"Enter." A voice said behind the door.

Turning the knob, he entered.

"You asked that I report to you sir." Captain Washington stood at attention in front of the seated Colonel.

"At ease Captain. Sit down."

Captain Washington sat in one of the two chairs located in front of the desk. He placed his flight bag on the floor in front of the other.

"Sir, can I ask what this is about?"

"You can, but I'll get to the point in a second."

"Yes sir."

"Captain Washington I've gone over your career. Born in East St. Louis, attended the Air Force Academy after you were noticed by a senior officer. You've received good reviews from your peers and commanding officers."

"Well sir, I try to do my best."

Colonel Clayton continued. "You've had your share of missteps as well." He closed the file. "Enough about your past. I called you here for a special reason and special assignment. Captain Washington, what I am about to tell you is highly classified."

"Sir, I'm not cleared for Top Secret Intelligence."

"You are now. By the way, who is this Army Specialist you've been seen with?"

"His name is Jerome Travis sir.   He and I met the day the f-105 crashed. He saved my life. We've been friends every since."

"Kind of strange for an officer and an NCO to be friends."

"True sir, but life has a way of bringing people together. As you've noted from my records, I don't have family and JT, uh Specialist Travis is as close as I have had to family."

"I see.... Anyway, we've checked his background and he holds a secret clearance but what I am about to tell you must remain in this room and can only be shared with those I tell you."

"Yes sir.

"I understand you broke up a drug ring recently?"

"I don't think I broke up a ring sir. I might have stopped a shipment from going out."

"Captain, what if I told you, was a shipment of drugs going out goes much deeper the operation goes far beyond this base and involves a senior officer."

"Gee sir, at the time I assisted in arresting those two I felt those two were too dumb to have put together an operation of a larger scale, but felt that it would be taken care of higher up."

"Hump, well here's what you don't know. There is an Inspector General we suspect going around from base to base changing aircraft data on electronic bays."

".........I'm not following you sir."

"As you already know, the electronic bays have serial numbers assigned for each aircraft. When the Air Force changed over to the newer electronics, which I understand you helped design, we discovered a fighter returning to CONUS (Continental United States), from Vietnam, that the numbers did not match. Inside we found drugs.

The pilot was cleared, but his plane captain and several members of the maintenance crew were arrested. You might have read or heard about this in intelligence reports."

"Yes sir."

"Anyway, we thought we had it shut down until your discovery here."

"What has that got to do with me sir."

"We need someone outside this office to do some digging."

"Digging sir?"

"Yes, digging around. Because you saw first-hand what the operation looks like, we need you to look for other similar operations.. As you have mentioned, you don't have any family except for this, uh, JT."

"Yes sir."

You're due to rotate back to the States, where you'll ride a desk."

"I'm not looking forward to that sir."

"I didn't think you would, so what if I make you an offer you'll not refuse."

"Uh, that depends sir."

"Trust me, you'll like this one."

"What if you extend your deployment and get to fly some new aircraft in the inventory?"

"New aircraft sir?"

"Yes, we are upgrading the Thai Air Force to the Cessna T-37 Tweety Birds. Their T-6 Texan's are getting a little old. We're also getting some new General Dynamics F-111's Aardvark. We need someone of your experience to test and make flight evaluations. As a pilot you have a right to be around the aircraft.

Yeah, we could bring in another pilot, but that would look suspicious if this pilot didn't fly, yet was always in the hangers. What better way to investigate them than have an honest to God pilot the men trust in the hangers looking over the aircraft?"

"I guess that would work, but would I do if I find anything?"

"You report back to me; nobody else. In fact although you'll be listed in the same flight and squadron, nothing else will change. Your section leader has already been informed of your new duties."

"What if I'm away on a mission."

"As of now, you're grounded, well not grounded, but you will not be sent on any missions over Nam"

"Well, I guess that would work."

"Good. Captain Washington, I don't need tell you what would happen if we don't stop this ring. The US military is already receiving a black eye over this war. Can you imagine what would happen if it was discovered fighter aircraft were being used to smuggle drugs into the US?"

"Yes sir I can."

"Good. Also your friend, JT, or Specialist Travis is not to know about this either."

"Yes sir. Anything else?"

"No, you're dismissed."

Captain Washington stood grabbed his flight bag and left.

When his door closed colonel Clayton called the base commander. "Sir I just spoke to Captain Washington. He's agreed to come on board."

"Great job, great job."

"Yes sir." Colonel Clayton hung up.

Over the next several months, Captain Washington could not find any suspicious activity of drug smuggling. Now that he knew what to look for, he personally checked the serial numbers of the electronic bay equipment. They all matched. They had gone to ground at least in Korat.

CHAPTER VII

Retirement Day – Washington, D.C.

General Richard "Hannibal" Washington had just stepped into the shower. His dress blues he had laid out on the bed. This would be the last day of his long military career. His only family, JT and Pamela were in Canada. A mild wave of sadness came over him as he hadn't thought to ask them to come down. Besides it would be too expensive for this one-event, so he thought.

He let the hot water stream over his body. Finally after using the hotel brand soap, covering his entire body in white suds. He rinsed, turned the water off and stepped out of the shower. As usual, no matter how long the exhaust fans ran, the moisture overcame them and clouded the mirrors.

Taking a towel, he wiped it, but as soon as he did, it fogged over again.

Damn.

He opened the door slightly, and towelled off, killing time to let the steam out.

When the fog and moisture finally cleared, he looked at his face and body.

What looked back at him was an older version of himself, except he always found it amazing that the mind never saw a younger or older version; only the present.

He had to laugh at a thought. When he had done work in the ghetto, he took a young kid under his wing. One day he told the kid that he would never be able to see his face without the aid of a mirror. This blew the kid's mind and over the course of the next several days, the kid tried all sorts of ways to prove him wrong, but stopped short of taking his eyeballs out.

He never told another child that again.

Then Hannibal had a sad thought as he remembered the call he had received. The kid had followed his advice and said no. The drug dealer killed him.

He returned to the present and what he saw was a body still in good shape.

His chest had a few grey hairs. His head was salt and pepper. His eyes brown, and the white were clear. His muscle tone was still firm.

Although he sat behind a desk far more than he liked, for the past several years he found reasons to get up in the ratified air when he could, but it wasn't the same. No action. No looking for missile launchers. No one-on-one shootouts with the top enemy aviators.

Soon he would have to find a way to fly again. The idea of becoming a corporate or airline pilot didn't appeal to him. He wanted more freedom. He had saved nearly all of his money and invested. What else was he going to do? He had no one to leave his worldly belonging to.

The week before, anticipating his retirement, he went over them with his accountant he was shocked at his net worth. Well over $30 million.

What do you do with $30 million?

Hell of a long way from the ghetto.

He stepped out of the tiny bathroom and started dressing. The television was tuned to the local news channel; something about a gunman killing students at Virginia Tech. Why are people with a grudge always taking out their problems on innocent people?

There was a knock on the door.

It was too early for his driver to take him to the ceremony, which he had requested to be a quiet affair. The usual photographs with people of importance. No big parades or fly-bys.

He took a peep through the hole in the door and saw a male in civilian clothes. He opened it.

"General Washington? Remember me?"

"Yes sir, Colonel Clayton. How are you?"

"I'm fine. May I come in?"

"Sure. What brings you to the District?"

"Well I heard someone was retiring today. That wouldn't be you would it?"

Hannibal chuckled.

"Anyway, I'm here for other reasons"

"Oh?"

They walked into the living area. Colonel Clayton sat down. "Yes. Tell you what. Why don't you continue getting dressed. Can't keep you away from your ceremony and I'll tell you why I'm here."

"OK."

"I'm a Federal Marshal now. I'm out of the DC branch. Have you been keeping up with the local news?"

"Oh, I guess as much as the next person. Too much going on; very depressing."

"Yeah I agree with you on that. Your Secret Clearance is still active, so I don't need to repeat the rules. A couple of days ago we had an aircraft bust the McChord Air Force base airspace. It had lost commutations with ATC."

"A civilian aircraft?"

"No a Vietnam era Rockwell OV-10 Bronco."

"That's unusual."

"It is, but guess why."

"Hard to say."

"The aircraft was being flown by a retired Marine Captain and on its way to a place in Texas to be enshrined along with several other Vietnam era aircraft. A fine powder was found dripping out of the electronics bay. The powder had insulated the connections. Therefore the loss of communications."

"Uh oh. I don't think I need to guess where this conversation is going." General Washington had stopped tying his tie.

"Yep, it looks like our gang has resurfaced again. Now they're calling this stuff Roxanne. It is almost pure cocaine and selling below the other stuff out there."

"Roxanne?"

"I guess everyone has to have a brand name."

"The Captain involved?"

"The pilot? No, she was cleared by the FBI."

"A she?"

"Yeah, a Marine Captain Celina Majewski. She was arrested on the spot and underwent intense interrogations by an FBI agent."

"And she didn't know anything obviously, just like the rest."

"That's right. But the FBI agent passed on her information to her supers who passed in on to us. It landed in my lap as a result of my previous work."

"Let me take a stab at this. The aircraft was from Korat."

"You got it." Marshal Clayton looked at his watch. "You'd better finish getting dressed. Here's my card. Call me when you finish, but don't wait too long as this is important."

General Washington took his card, turning it over. "Nice to see you again sir."

"Haw! You outrank me now. I should be calling you sir."

"How about we split the difference? I'll be retired after today. I'll just call you Tom."

"And I'll call you Richard."

"I prefer Hannibal. It's my call sign and it's sort of grown on me.

"Hannibal it is. Good luck. I'll let myself out. Say is your friend, JT here?

"Ah no sir. He's married now and lives in Canada."

"Canada?"

"Yeah. He traveled all over the US after he got out of the Army, got tired of the company transfers, as it played hell with his personal life. He was offered a computer business in a small community up there. He married a local by the name of Pamela. I've met her. Very nice and lovely woman. She's good for him. Keeps him on the straight and narrow."

"That's interesting."

"Yeah and of all things he got his US and Canadian pilot's license and built himself a jet warbird."

""That's really odd. Should have joined the Air Force."

"He said he thought about it, but at the time felt his career was in computers and electronics."

"I bet he regrets that now. Back then computers took up huge buildings. Now every kid born that comes out of the womb knows computers."

"Oh, I don't think so, maybe the kids are smarter, but it still takes someone to support large operations and JT seems to be doing well. He landed a big contract. He has a big hanger that he operates out of. He said he likes it up there, nestled close to the Canadian Rockies and the vineyards. He hates the snow, but there he says you can see the season change, and the lakes are crystal clear."

Marshal Clayton reflected, "Yeah I hear Salmon fishing is very popular up that way. Anyway, I've got to get out here. Call me."

"I will."

Marshal Clayton got up and left.

Memories of long ago came flooding back as he remembered the sights and heavy humidity smells of the hangers in Thailand and the arrest of those two idiots.

Roxanne. What a name.

CHAPTER VIII

The Hotel – Ft. Worth, Texas

JT did not get a good's night sleep. After taking a shower he dressed slowly. Last night he walked through his and Hannibal's room. Room service had come and gone. Searching the credenza he found Hannibal's personal items. Cindy would be by later to pick them up. In the closet he found Hannibal's new suit hung up, Cindy's business dress hung up as well; the one she had worn on the airplane. Her travel bag was stacked next to Hannibal's small one.

It looked perfectly normal that their things belonged together.

He walked back to the credenza and opening another drawer where he found Cindy's panties, which he had spied lying on the floor the night before. They had been picked up and carefully folded on top of her other clothing.

Her other items; the Sat-phone, netBook, modem, were in another drawer.

The beds were made and looked fresh; the same for his room. The papers with the drawing and maps were stacked neatly beside his netBook, which was in screensaver mode.

He hit the enter key and entered his password when the login screen came up. Several seconds later, his desktop came up, but no image of Pamela. Instead, in the lower right corner a pop-up declared Microsoft had updated his Operating System, thus had shut it down. So the video cam program had been automatically closed.

He decided that it was too late to call her and didn't activate the program. Besides, with the blood, the cuts and bruises on his face and body he did not want her to freak out.

He went into his bathroom and washed the blood off of his face that he had missed during his confrontation with Wendell. Blood and water mixed; forming a swirling pink mess as it finally ran down the drain. He had gotten several spots of blood on the mirror and the counter top. So as not to scare the hotel service staff, he took some toilet paper and wiped them off and then flushed them down the toilet.

It was still early morning, but his head really hurt and it felt tender. Other than a possible vending machine, which he'd have to hunt down, he doubted there was a drug store close by.

He went back into Hannibal's room and searched through his things not finding what he was looking for until he opened Cindy's purse. There he found an almost full bottle of aspirin with Thai script.

He dispensed two and then eight more. He took the first two immediately, swishing them down after removing the plastic protection cover on the foam cups the hotel service had left. He then placed the remaining ones in the plastic and tucked them into a small pocket sewn into his netBook canvas protection cover.

He sat on the edge of his bed and then fell backwards, falling asleep.

It was a deep, but troubled sleep. As he looked at the lumps and bruises on his head and face, without the blood, they looked angry and his head still hurt like a sonofabitch. Rather than use the aspirin he had wrapped, he went back into Hannibal's room and dispensed two more from Cindy's bottle; taking a closer look at it.

Years ago he could make out some of the characters, but not now. He remembered the last time he saw one of these he thought he had caught the clap. He did not go to the base hospital as it would be reported to his company commander and he'd be placed on 14 and 14. A common military acronym for 14-days extra duty and 14-days restriction, he went to see a private doctor in downtown Korat.

Although times have since changed, even then it was a far cry from what he heard happened during WWII. The thought of a tube pushed up into his pee hole was not an inviting thought.

It turned out he didn't have VD, but for the next three days he had to hide pissing in the urinal as it was blue. All of the guys knew what blue piss meant and he'd never hear the end of it.

That was the good news.

The bad news was that the Thai women used the same facilities and would walk in unannounced, using the stalls right next to the men. Had they seen him pissing blue, news would spread like wildfire. It was one thing to be teased by your fellow soldiers but another thing entirely to be teased by the housegirls and the very young girls that brought over the soft drinks. They would never let him live it down.

He remembered a guy in the platoon called Sip-Loy, or number 10,000. Sip is bad (10); Sip-Loy was off the chart. His real name was Anthony and of all things was from his home State.

He was always pissing blue.

If the name Sip-Loy was brought up, everyone knew who the Thai's were referring to.

For some unexplained reason he had a run-in with him one day in the radar and radio repair shop, when Anthony confronted him, accusing him of some obscure infraction; the fight was on.

JT received a black-eye and Anthony a broken arm. Both were brought up before the squad leader, platoon leader, Top (First Sargent) and the company commander. JT said he had run into a door and Anthony fell down a flight of stairs from a radar van. They were taken into separate rooms and questioned again, but both stuck to their stories. No charges were filed.

JT shook his head at the long forgotten memory, placing the bottle back into Cindy's purse.

He ordered his somewhat standard traveling breakfast fare. Tea; lots of it, cinnamon toast and a side order of Canadian bacon, and a medium glass of OJ.

When he finished he cleaned up and placed the tray outside his door. He found the morning newspaper thrown there. He looked down the hallway and saw a paper had been placed at each door. He picked it up, opening to the front page. It didn't make headlines, but a full section had been dedicated to last night's fiasco. A picture was shown displaying the destroyed front of the hanger.

He scanned the article as he shut the door walking back to his bed. He didn't see anything new that he didn't already know. A lot of the information was watered down and the explosion reported as a ruptured gas main. Hell, JT thought, had the public known what had really been there; shit would have hit the fan big time.

He tossed the paper onto the second bed and walked over to his netBook, once again hitting the space bar to bring it out of screensaver mode. He entered his password and brought up the online NOAA weather charts and proceeded to file his flight plan. When he finished he sent an email to Pamela his plans, and like the newspaper, a watered down version of what happened. He started to close the email, but decided that he should add that he had bumped his head, that way she wouldn't go crazy when she saw him.

An hour later, he had packed his things. He had hoped Cindy would have made it back before he left, but when she didn't show he called the unit that Hannibal was on and informed that he was in OR . That was most likely where Cindy would be waiting. He called the waiting room and spoke to her.

"Her lady, how're holding up?"

"Oh, I'm tired. Hannibal was sedated but woke up several times. He's fine, or what passes as fine when you have a bullet stuck in you."

"Where did you sleep?"

"You really want to know?"

"If it's not 'R' rated."

"I slept in in his bed beside him. They made bed checks every now and then, but left us alone. I couldn't sleep in the chairs so I just curled up beside him. I can't say which was worse. Trying to sleep and avoid all of the cables and IV tubes and needles or the chair."

"I know I tried it once. So how long has he been in there?"

"Not long, maybe 45-minutes. They've been very kind and have kept me updated. He should be out soon.

"How is your arm?' JT asked.

"It's sore but fine. How's your head?"

"I'll live but I was looking for some aspirin and found some in your purse, I hope you don't mind."

"No, but don't' tell Hannibal about the condom."

"You had a condom in there?"

"Got you...." She started laughing.

"Ha Ha, maybe I should go back and look again."

"Go ahead."

"Naw, I know you don't."

"Anyway, I think I took four and wrapped several up for the trip home. Tell Hannibal I don't think I'll be coming over. I've already filed my flight plan. It will be a lonely flight back to Indy."

"I understand. Look at it like this, you'll see Pamela soon."

"Yeah, that's something to look forward to, and you had better keep your promise."

"Promise?"

"Yeah, the one you pinkie-swore on."

"I didn't pinkie swear but Pamela and you can plan our wedding."

"OK, anyway I have to go. Tell butt-ugly I love him. And I love you too."

"JT… if you weren't Hannibal's friend…..Yeah, I love you."

JT smiled. "Bye." He said and hung up.

He made one more sweep of the room after placing everything in his specially made bags. He went over to Hannibal's room, made sure the door was locked, and then locked the door between his and their room. He walked around his room once more, to make double sure he hadn't forgotten anything, and walked out into the hallway, waiting for the latch to engage locked.

He took the elevator down, gave the desk clerk his key and presented his credit card.

"Will your friend be checking out too?"

"Naw, he's getting some rest."

"Oh, do you want me to tell room service not to bother him?"

"That's OK, he's at a friend's home, but he'll be back later."

"OK. Sir that will be $237 on your credit card

"$237? Where were the hot babes?"

"Pardon me?"

"Nothing. $237 for one night stay? Sheez."

JT handed over the card as if it would be the last he'd see of it. She swiped it, punched a few keys to enter her code and a printer behind her cheerfully spit out the receipt.

She turned, and with a practice one can only get from working at a hotel desk, plucked the printout from the tray and presented him with it and his card at the same time.

"Have a nice day. We hope you enjoyed your stay and will be returning." She said in a cheerful voice and smile.

"Not if I can help it," JT muttered, looking at the printout on his way outside.

Outside, he saw a taxi stand to his left and took the first cab he came to. "Dallas Love." He said to the turbaned taxi driver.

The driver tossed his partially completed cigarette out the window, closed it and turned the air conditioning up full blast. He was wearing a Bluetooth receiver in his ear so that when he called in his fare, JT did not have privilege to the dispatcher's side of the conversation.

Anthony Parran

A non-smoker, JT gagged slightly as the strong tobacco smell was blown his way. The driver fastened his seatbelt; put the car in gear, pulled a level which activated the toll meter and drove away.

The starting fare was $2.25 and they hadn't moved yet.

"Crap."

CHAPTER XIV

Considering that it was still early morning, they made good time and was deposited at the door of the corporate hanger. The toll meter read $83.11. Once again JT handed over the credit card and the driver swiped it. He handed the data terminal to him. He rounded out the fare to $90 and pressed OK.

Several seconds later, there was a cheerful beep from the data terminal. He gave the data terminal back to the driver.

"You want receipt?"

"Yeah you'd better give me one. Maybe my wife can include this as a business expense."

Slowly the driver fished out his business card and on the back, where there was a pre-arranged toll column, entered the data, and gave it to JT.

"Thanks." He said; retrieved his bag from the seat and got out.

He entered the doors and behind the counter was same redhead that was there, what…Just yesterday?

"Where's your friend?" She asked.

"Ah, he's a little under the weather."

Disappointment shown on her face.

"He was so funny. Will he be coming back this way?"

"He was funny?"

"Oh yes, I knew he was playing with me."

"I'll be sure to tell him. How much do I owe you?"

"Nothing?"

"Nothing. The bill has already been paid for."

"Does it say from whom?" JT asked astonished.

"Let me see. She shuffled some papers and pulled out a printout. "It says here RTPA. A Hank Marshall?"

"Well kick me in the ….. Sorry."

"No problem. There's also a message here for you."

"Now what?"

The redhead handed him another 8 1/2 X 11 printout.

Take care JT, Tell Pamela we said hi. We'll make our way up to Canada when this is all finished. Love you.

Your friends,

Hannibal and Cindy.

"I bet he's nice to have you as a friend. Who's Cindy?"

"You read it? Cindy is an FBI agent and his future wife."

"Hard to miss when it comes off of our printer. So I guess I'm too late?"

"Uh yeah, we're more like family, but I'll be sure to tell Hannibal what he's missing."

"Well you have a good flight Mr. Travis." She said.

"Just JT please."

"OK JT. I'll have someone take you out to your aircraft. It's already outside the hanger and fueled."

"Thanks." He said, folded the printouts and opened his canvas bag, placing them next to the netBook.

Once outside, he looked once again to the southeast to the Dallas skyline. Just like the day before, it hadn't changed.

CHAPTER XV

Indianapolis, Indiana – Crown Hill Cemetery

Once again Reverend Allen Michaels stood before a casket and offered God the soul of its contents. There was no choir; there were very little people in attendance. There wasn't a camera crew. Terrell "T-Boy" Jefferson was just another street junkie gone bad and thus old news. Reverend Michaels finished with a small prayer. Terrell's uncle was the only family member in attendance. As the casket was lowered, only the grounds people were around to throw what little flowers had been arranged into the grave. Within minutes, the ceremony was over and once again the Cemetery quiet.

"**Indianapolis Center,** *ISKRA* Charlie-Charlie-Delta-Yankee is with you at Flight Level two-three with information Romeo."

"*ISKRA* Charlie-Charlie-Delta-Yankee, Indianapolis Approach. Radar contact. What are your intentions?"

"Indianapolis Center, I have a visual on Eagle Creek. Request permission to descend for a direct in approach and close flight plan."

"Roger *ISKRA* Charlie-Delta Yankee, cleared for direct descent approach into Indianapolis Eagle Creek, IFR cancelled. Flight plan closed. Contact Indianapolis Eagle Creek on one two zero decimal eight. Altimeter two niner decimal eight. Have a good evening sir."

"Roger, you too. Understand flight plan closed; contact Indianapolis Eagle Creek at one two zero decimal eight, altimeter two niner decimal eight. Charlie-Delta Yankee Clear."

To his left, JT could see the dark patch to the southwest of Indianapolis with a stretch of runway between two rows of trees; Eagle Creek Airport. Only a couple of days ago he and Pamela had flown here with so much happiness and laughter. Now there was only sadness in his heart.

The flight up from Texas had been lonely. He had too much time to think about the events of the days before. He had taken two more of Cindy's aspirin and drank from one of Pamela's water bottles still in the storage compartment.

To take his mind off things, he had plugged his iPhone into the audio mixer input and listened to music he had loaded via iTunes. That too had it consequences as some of the slower, mellower music only heightened his sad mood, so he skipped through a lot of songs until he found something more upbeat.

Pamela had called just before he took off. She had received his email and was glad that he was well and on his way home. She wanted to know when Hannibal and Cindy were coming back. He made up a little lie and said that Cindy had things to clear up and would be following in a commercial flight a couple of days later. She said his family would take her to the airport to meet him.

"**Indianapolis Eagle Creek,** *ISKRA* Charlie-Charlie Delta-Yankee."

"*ISKRA* Charlie-Charlie-Delta-Yankee."

"Indianapolis Eagle Creek request permission for landing, runway three."

"Permission granted, you're number one in the circuit. Altimeter two niner decimal eight."

"Number one in the circuit, altimeter two niner decimal eight."

As JT started his setup to make the mid-field approach, he saw several vehicles near the edge of the parking lights in the parking low a crowd of people.

He couldn't resist.

"Eagles Creek request permission to amend my approach and make a low flyby with zoom climb over runway three."

"Charlie-Delta-Yankee, permission granted. You are clear for zoom climb within airspace. Your family is outside waiting."

"Roger, Eagle Creek, I can see them."

Making a minor course adjustment, JT turned the nose of the aircraft to the right to go away from the airport, but not too much and enter into the Indianapolis TCA. When the runway was at his 45 degrees, he turned left for runway three and dropped down to 500 feet AGL, kicking in the throttles.

The *ISKRA* surged forward and when he was at the beginning of the runway, hauled back on the stick, going straight up, did a double barrel roll topping out at 5,000 feet, flipped it over onto its back and went straight down the same way he had gone up. At 1,500 feet he lined up with the runway and went straight out.

He came back around in the circuit and this time dropped down to 200 feet and flew straight down the runway. Over the end of the runway, he climbed once more to pattern altitude.

As he flew past an apartment complex a mile away he reduced power, banked left and entered a normal downwind circuit over the Eagle Creek Reservoir. The late afternoon sun glistened off sailboats.

The landing was uneventful. He turned off onto the taxiway, opened the canopy allowing the afternoon heat and humidity in. It felt and smelled good. It must have rained earlier. He could smell newly cut grass, something he missed dearly as he had not experienced that mixture in Oliver, BC.

As he turned into the aircraft tie-down area, he saw Pamela in a wheelchair. He felt sad and happy at the same time. His family was pushing her chair towards the aircraft. She waved. He waved back.

They patiently waited as he completed his shutdown procedures.

As he climbed out of the aircraft, he heard a commotion and turned. His family was trying to get Pamela to sit back down into the chair. She wasn't having any of it, broke free and with a heavy limp, made her way to him.

He dropped his bag back onto the seat and ran to her.

"Welcome home flyboy," she said and planted first a tiny and then a huge kiss on his lips. He felt the start of an erection as she pressed her body to his.

"Uh, baby, my family is here."

"So let them look." And she kissed him again.

From the corner of his eye, he saw that his family was staying a discrete distance away. Finally she pulled away. "I'm so happy to see you. Oh, JT what happened to your head?" She said looking up. JT had taken his helmet off when he ran to her.

"I ran into a wrench. I'll tell you about it later."

"My God, it must have been one big wrench. But you ran into it twice? You look terrible."

"You should see the other guy."

"What other guy?"

"Wendell, but like I said I'll tell you later. You get back into that chair young lady."

"I can walk, well a little. I'm tired of sitting in that thing anyway.

"Yeah, but it's only been a day or two and you might open the stitches."

By now his family had come over to meet him. They each gave him a hug and to his relief demanded that Pamela sit down, which she did as she was outnumbered.

Once she was seated, they followed him back to the *ISKRA*.

He took out his canvas bag and placed it on Pamela's lap. Then he took out his small luggage bag and gave it to his brother.

He pulled out the engine plugs and chocks, closed and secured the canopy. Next he went around the *ISKRA* and at each tie point, ran the rope through the eyelets and secured the aircraft.

"Hey JT, you and Pamela will be riding with me," said his brother.

He took over the duties of pushing his wife to his brother's car.

He helped her into the front seat and he got into the back.

He placed his gear on the open seat beside him.

Dinner was a cheerful affair. Everyone had something to say and kept asking him questions about what had happened in Texas. They had heard about an explosion at an airport and wondered if he had been there.

He skirted the deeper parts of the events, filing in a little more than what had appeared in the paper. He told them about Roxanne and how it had its origins in Korat, Thailand; that his friend Hannibal had been wrongly accused of smuggling it into the country. They now had it straightened out but Hannibal was slightly injured. He was OK, and in a hospital.

"And I'm going to ask once more, what did you do to run into a wrench?" Pamela asked eating a BBQ rib covered in BBQ sauce. JT cringed as he looked at her plate. The edges had disappeared as it was covered in mashed potatoes, coleslaw, cornbread, BBQ and greens. That surprised him as greens are a black staple. In a bowl next to her plate was peach cobbler, still steaming hot.

Yep he had to get her back home and soon.

He thought for a few seconds and gave them a cleaned up version of the events. "When we went into the hanger a guy was waiting for us. He hit me with a wrench to knock me out. I guess my head was too hard and he hit me again."

"Told you so," his mom said. "I always knew you were hard headed." The rest of the family chuckled.

Pamela looked at him knowing it was a lie.

After dinner and everyone helped clear the dishes, JT rolled Pamela into the family room, where they sat without saying anything. He had placed her on the sofa and sat next to her just glad to be so near to her again.

On the coffee table, JT eyed the evening paper and reached for it. Before his hand touched it, Pamela beat him, taking it away.

"What was that ?'

"You don't want to see it."

"Why?'

"Trust me. You don't want to see it."

Now that his curiosity was raised, he playfully pulled her hand away, which she had placed under her hip."

"Ow! My hip!" And she and punched him on the head

"Ow! My head!"

"What's going on in there?" His mom asked.

"JT pushed me."

"She hit me."

"She won't give me the newspaper."

"JT. Please trust me." She begged.

"What is so important that you don't want me to see the paper?"

He read the headlines and collapsed back onto the sofa next to her.

"NASA FINDS COCAINE IN SPACE SHUTTLE HANGER"

"No way!"

"Apparently so dear."

"Oh my God, I thought we had them all!"

"You can't fight them all JT. For you and Hannibal the fight is over sweetheart. Let it go. Let the people that know how to track these people do their job. They might ask for Cindy's help, but she's a professional. Rest JT, you need it."

JT continued to read and his heart sank even more. They didn't have any suspects. He took the paper and without ceremony began tearing the pages apart, crumpling them into a heap. When he was finished he gathered them up, went outside to the BBQ pit and stuffed the paper inside. He found a box of matches and struck one. He placed a flame to the corners, watching the flames grow. The light cast his shadow onto the outside brick wall.

As the paper burned, he found a small stick and stirred the ashes until the whole thing burn until there were only embers. A slight breeze fanned the smoke.

"JT come inside and let's go to bed." Pamela said. "We have to get some rest for the flight home.

"Yeah."

Inside, he helped Pamela up the stairs to the spare bedroom. He undressed her and walked her to the bathroom, where he started to close the door.

"Aren't you going to come in?"

"Here?"

"Yes, here."

"This is my sister's home and after what you did the last time I was in a bathroom with you, we might get thrown out."

Pamela laughed at the memory. "I promise to be nice. Besides I want you to help me bathe this time and not your sister."

"Now that's an Idea I can live with."

Later that night as they lay in the bed, her head on his shoulder she asked, "JT tell me what really happened."

He did, not leaving anything out.

"JT there is no way someone would put explosives in a civilized area."

"They did."

'My God, they were monsters."

"Yes."

"And that guy Anderson is dead?"

"Yes."

"What about Mathius?'

"I can only guess he is going away for a very long time."

You kicked that guy Wendell's ass right?"

"Yep."

"To think Hannibal knew about all of this."

"He only knew so much sweetheart. Even I still don't know all of the facts, but Marshal Clayton knew Hannibal back in Thailand."

"Did Hannibal know about Cindy's role?"

"No, I asked."

"That is wonderful. I'd hate to think he knew her and didn't warn her about the setup in Thailand."

"Yeah, but Hannibal didn't. Let's go to sleep."

Pamela took his hand to place on her breast. As she did, she felt the bracelet still on his wrist. "What's this?" She asked as she held his arms up.

" You know that Abby was killed when the blast went off. Cindy said that they only found her arm, with the bracelet. She took it and gave it to me."

"Oh, JT that is so sad."

"Yes, it is and as long as I am alive, I will wear it and never take it off. I hope you don't;' mind."

"You know I don't. God, what a way to die."

JT thought. "I hate saying it because I don't believe it, Cindy said she didn't suffer."

They laid in silence.

"Can you turn out the lights?"

"Sure."

"Did I ever tell you that I loved you?" Pamela said.

"Yes, and I can't get enough of it. I love you too."

She moved her head, bumping his.

"Ow!"

"Sorry."

The next morning JT asked his brother if he could use his car. He said he had to do some errands, but was free to use his wife's. Pamela was still in bed, but he woke her briefly and told her where he was going and what he had to do.

He drove downtown to the Indianapolis City-County building, parked and entered the police entrance. He approached the desk Sargent, "Hi, is Officer Jerry Parker working today?"

"Yes sir, can I ask what this is about?'

"I was here a couple of day ago. I had a friend that had crashed a jet on the Westside..."

"Oh, yeah, now I remember you. Just a second."

JT waited as he called upstairs.

"He said come on up. You can take the elevators to the right." He pointed.

When the elevator doors opened, JT was greeted by Jerry Parker and led to his office.

"Well it is nice to see you again. How's your head?"

"You knew about that?"

"Told you I had friends down there.'

"I'll live. I'll have to stop off someplace and get some more aspirin. So how much do you know?"

"Well I guess more than the public and that which I was cleared."

JT gave him the quick fill-ins.

"So do you think they caught everyone?" Officer Parker asked.

"Did you see yesterday's headlines?'

"Do you think it has anything to do with your Roxanne?'

"Maybe yes and maybe no."

"I don't follow you." Officer Parker said.

"If it's Roxanne, then the investigators have leads and people to torture and get answers."

"They don't torture people any more JT."

"Sure they don't. Anyway, if not Roxanne, they will have to start all over again."

"I can see your point. So why are you here?"

"I made a promise."

"What promise?"

"You asked if I'd take you up in the *ISKRA*, well here I am."

"Thanks, but no thanks."

"Huh?"

"Was that you yesterday afternoon buzzing the airport again?"

"Uh yes, I think so."

"I'll keep my feet planted on the ground thanks."

"I wouldn't do anything like that with you in."

"I know you wouldn't. If you did, remember I'm in the back seat and I'd pull my gun and shoot you. But then I have to ask myself, who'd fly the damn thing."

JT had a big laugh.

"Honest, I would keep it on the straight and narrow."

"Naw that's OK JT, I believe you. But seriously I like looking."

"Well if you ever change your mind, call me. And if you're up near Vancouver stop in."

"I will."

"Goodbye Jerry.

"Goodbye JT."

CHAPTER XVI

Oliver, British Columbia

As the *ISKRA*'s engine spooled down, JT said only one word. "Home"

"Yes," said Pamela.

JT did not unlatch the canopy immediately. He sat there and felt an enormous feeling of relief and sadness wash over him. All of the events of the previous week at once a heavy weight dissipate.

"JT are you OK."

"Yes, just thinking."

"Let's go home. We can think there. I need to get some rest. You too. We both could use some rest."

"Yeah, you're right."

He released the canopy and climbed out. He turned to Pamela and helped her out taking care not to dislodge the bandage on her hip under her flight suit.

She sat on the ground as JT unloaded the aircraft. With care she started to take her sneakers off as JT had given up and agreed she looked much better in them than the boots. She replaced them with her ever present sandals.

He ran inside, grabbed a chair and ran back outside where he picked her up, placing her in it.

With the *ISKRA* tucked away this side of the Oliver was in shadow as the sun set. On the opposite of the lake the mountain tops were bathed in a reddish glow. The glow turned the inside of the sides of the hanger red.

He wrote down some numbers for entry into his log books and aircraft log books, closed the canopy and as he went to get the two-bar, his attention was caught by the GPS he had not learned to use yet, which triggered another thought.

With Pamela in the Jag, he said, "I need to make a couple of calls."

"You did that before we left."

"I know, but I still have one more call to make."

"OK, but hurry. I can't wait to get home."

He walked over to her and planted a kiss on her lips. "I promise to hurry."

He made a call.

CHAPTER XVII

One Week Later

JT was antsy. Today he told Pamela he had no service calls, which he didn't, and was going to stay around the house, which annoyed her. She too did not have to work today, but she just wanted to sit for awhile by herself. She loved JT but enjoyed her moments just sitting on the deck, drinking her herbal tea and looking at the distant mountains.

A Purolator van pulled into the driveway. JT shot out of the house.

"Where are you going?"

"Be right back," was all he said.

The driver met him halfway, handed him a portable terminal for him to sign for the package. It was large and awkward.

"Can you help me with this?" The driver asked.

"Sure."

Together they managed it through the door which was being held open my Pamela.

"And what is this flyboy?"

"You'll see."

With the box inside, it was obvious from the markings and logo what was inside.

"JT, where did you get the money for this?"

"I didn't pay for it."

"What?"

"You'll see."

The driver left and came back with a smaller package and a box containing roses.

When he left, JT turned to his wife.

"I have loved you more than any man could love a woman. When we were in Indianapolis I thought I had lost you for good. I would not have been able to continue my life without you.'

"Oh, JT you would have."

"Maybe Pamela, but it would have been hard. You are my life. I'm not perfect, and sometimes wonder how you put up with me, but without you I'd be lost. Remember last week at the airport I said I needed to make a phone call?"

"Yes, but you never told me what it was about."

"When I was in Texas and the dust had settled, I met Hannibal's boss; a guy by the name of Hank. Nice guy. He apologized for having sent that guy Sam to Indianapolis and said if there was anything he could do, let him know. I couldn't think of anything at the time until I was putting the *ISKARA* away. I remembered I had promised you an HD television, so I called him up."

"JT that was stupid."

"Not really. He felt guilty about what happened. Not that he has anything to feel guilty about."

"I don't see your logic, but thank you sweetheart. Where are we going to put it?"

"We'll work something out."

"The flowers are beautiful too, but what's this?"

"I don't know, maybe a note from Hank."

Pamela, with her nails opened the small express package. Inside a note fell out, a check and a letter. She turned it over and read it.

Dear Mr. and Mrs. Travis:

It is with great pleasure I am sending you the HD television JT requested. I know it will never replace the suffering you went through, and the hurt my actions have brought on you Mrs. Travis and friends. You will find enclosed a check in the amount of $20,000 and tickets. The tickets are for the opening of the Vietnam Era Aircraft Museum, here in the Dallas/Ft. Worth area. The money you can use however you like, but I hope part of it is to come down and spend a week or two as my guest.

Sincerely,

Hank Marshall

Pamela turned the check over in her hands, held it up to the light to see if it was real.

"You can't check it that way." JT said.

"I can't believe it." She marveled at the paper. "$20,000 dollars and it's in US dollars. That's about what, $26,000 Canadian? Wow!"

"Yeah and it's from Hank you can bet it's real. I didn't expect that."

"Maybe I should get my ass shot off more often."

"Very funny. Ha Ha. No you won't. Look at what I had to go through."

"Well I'm the one with the hole in my ass. You only have a headache."

"Here let me look at the hole." JT raised her skirt. It wasn't a hole but more of a healing scar.

She slapped his hand.

"JT stop!" He pulled her skirt up again. She pretended to resist, but did not stop him. He kissed her hip and her legs. He stood up looking into her eyes, pushing her backwards towards the sofa. She dropped the box of flowers on the floor, but placed the check on the coffee table.

They spent the rest of the afternoon on the sofa.

CHASING ROXANNE

EPILOGUE:

The Celebration of life.

Above North Vancouver in the mountains to the north is Capilano Lake and further northeast is Grouse Mountain Ski Resort. Below these picturesque landmarks sits the Park Royal Motel, along the Capilano River, which flows out to the Burrard Inlet and from there into the Pacific Ocean.

The hotel staff had done its usual superb job of setting up the wedding arrangements. JT stood with Cindy inside the small restaurant door leading outside into a small clearing of green grass surrounded by tall trees, which blocked the sounds of the busy North Vancouver. A table had been set up to the right with a white linen cloth and a wedding cake in the center.

Although Pamela has planned most of it, Hannibal and Cindy made it clear that this was to be a small affair, to include the size of the cake.

On either side of the cake were presents, and one large one that couldn't fit on the table. It was such a mystery even JT had his try at guessing what it was. It was heavy and had to be brought in by dolly that left tracks in the wet grass.

There was only one row of chairs; five to either side of a path leading up to a small Gazebo decorated in dried flowers and white ribbons. Pamela had spent the better part of a week with her friend Arlene putting them together.

Arlene's daughter, Amanda would be the flower girl.

A child JT had never seen before today was the ring bearer. Cindy told him that he was the brother of a child that had been killed by a drug dealer when he had refused to participate in being a mule.

Seating in the first row was Pamela, Arlene, her husband Daniel, Hank and his wife and Marshal Clayton. Hank and his wife had flown up in their refurbished Aero Commander 500 Shrike Commander. JT was itching to see it after the wedding.

He was playing double duty. Not only was he giving Cindy away, but he was also the best man.

Cindy was dressed in a white gown that came just to the ground. It had white eyelet lace over white silk. The top was strapless. She said she didn't want the veil, so Pamela had done her hair up with sprigs of baby-breath and white ribbons to match those on the Gazebo.

She was beautiful.

Hannibal was already standing on the Gazebo next to the minister.

JT had taken him to the best tailor in town in Richmond, British Columbia, not too far from where they had stayed before and had them make the best suit with the best materials they could find. Hannibal now looked like a Fortune 50 CEO.

JT had to smile as he danced from one foot to the other. A man who's life had been standing at attention on military parade fields and now he couldn't stand still on the most important day of his life.

To the left of the Gazebo was a small table where, after the ceremony Cindy and he would sign on the dotted line, their signatures validated and the registry papers counter-signed.

Another small table had been set up to the left of the door for the DJ. He was waiting on JT for the cue to start the music.

Hannibal and Cindy had dispensed with the traditional words and wedding March. JT was surprised at their choice of music, but it fit. The only problem was, whenever JT heard it, it went straight to his heart. It was Pamela's and his wedding song.

Pamela nodded her head and JT nodded to the DJ. Everyone stood as the strains of *"The Book of Love"* floated across the grounds.

The book of love is long and boring
No one can lift the damn thing
It's full of charts and facts and figures and instructions for dancing
But I
I love it when you read to me
And you
You can read me anything
The book of love has music in it
In fact that's where music comes from
Some of it is just transcendental
Some of it is just really dumb

"Damn I hope I don't start blubbering," He said.

The screen door was opened and JT led Cindy slowly down the stairs to the Gazebo.

They were followed by Arlene's daughter holding a basket of flower petals. She tossed them in trail on the on the ground.

But I
I love it when you sing to me
And you
You can sing me anything
The book of love is long and boring
And written very long ago
It's full of flowers and heart-shaped boxes
And things we're all too young to know

"I'm scared." Cindy whispered.

"Good, so am I."

They made it without a hitch and she didn't try to run.

At the Gazebo, JT held her hand as she stepped onto it. Once there, JT stepped back and stood behind Hannibal, The little ring bearer moved up to join them.

The only sound was the final verses of the music.

And I
I love it when you give me things
And you
You ought to give me wedding rings
And I
I love it when you give me things
And you
You ought to give me wedding rings
You ought to give me wedding rings

JT heard someone sobbing and realized it was he.

Crap!

But so was everyone else.

The newly married couple sat at the table taking turns signing the registry. JT had hired a friend to take pictures and video it, but to be on the safe side he pulled out his Sony 14 Mega Pixel, running around taking pictures as well.

Pamela still had a mild limp, and tired easily. She sat serving Champagne.

Hank and his wife had been introduced to her and then Federal Marshal Clayton.

As they were gathered around the table, JT shouted. "Hey Hannibal! Hey man, I almost forgot. Remember that redhead in Dallas?"

Hannibal's eyes went wide. His mouth dropped.

"You remember her don't you? You know the one at that counter in Dallas."

Hannibal was pleading with his eyes for JT to stop.

"Yeah man, she wanted me to deliver a message."

Pamela was bearing down; ready to strangle him.

"Yeah man she said she wishes you the best of luck on your wedding day and that she was happy for you."

Hannibal breathed a sigh of relief. "What redhead?' Cindy asked.

"Uh.....She was the woman at the counter when JT and I landed at Dallas Love. She took a liking to me, but I told her I was already taken by a beautiful woman."

Cindy thought about it for a second. ".......I just bet you did."

The look Hannibal gave JT would have melted glaciers.

"But seeing as how this happened before today, you're forgiven. And I know it will never happen again, right?"

"Yes dear."

A nervous laugh went around.

"Goddammit JT, what did you do that for?" Pamela punched him in the chest with her tiny fist.

"Just having fun. Trust me, nothing happened. He was an Officer and a Gentleman the entire time."

By now Marshal Clayton had walked up.

"Mrs. Travis, can I speak to you alone for a few seconds?'

"Sure, about what?"

"Your husband. Have you ever considered having him committed?"

Anthony Parran

JT wandered over to where Hank and his wife stood. "Hi Hank. Look I know you gave them the big present, but can I ask what's inside?'

"Sure, but then I'd have to shoot you."

"Sir, with all due respect, that does not sound funny coming from you."

"You're right, but since you asked, it's a hand-picked tool chest set with a special set of aircraft tools. I chose them myself. Everything Hannibal will need to get his plane built.'

"I knew it. I should have bet him."

"What did he think it was?"

"He said I had sent it to them as a joke."

"Where in the world would he get an idea like that?" Hank asked.

As the celebration was winding down, Cindy turned to JT and said, "It's time."

They had taken the reception inside into the small European style dining area.

JT clapped his hands to get everyone's attention.

"Hannibal, Pamela, it is time. If anyone wants to join us you may. This is a private ceremony to honor Ms. Pattanapongtak Apsara," JT had practiced it many times to get it right, "or as we knew her; Abby. This will be a celebration of her life."

Everyone wanted to join in.

They exited onto the small well-kept grassy area. Sprinklers near the road to the left had come on and were making zip, zip, zip, zzzziiiipppp sounds as water shot arcs across an unwatered area to the north.

Beyond the trees was a small asphalt bike trail. A sort of small entranceway had been made by repeated hotel guest traffic through a hedge row.

At the entrance stood a small contingent of Buddhist Monks, which had gathered and waited while everyone was inside.

They would lead them to the rushing waters of the Capilano River and although it was shallow, it was still deep enough for their purposes.

As they passed the monks, each was handed white gaily painted paper boats with tiny flower arrangements. JT was given a special boat on which held a picture of Abby; the only one that could be found in her personal belongings.

The Monks turned and started across the trail.

There came a tinkling of a bell and in a flash, a speedo clad biker flew by.

When it was clear the procession started again towards the water's edge. To the right one could see a steel bridge where everyday life continued with the hum of vehicles and the occasional blat-blat of a motorcycle. To the left, the river wound beyond more trees and was lost.

JT, Pamela, Hannibal and Cindy stood holding hands. Everyone else stood behind them.

Before them one of the Monks walked to the water's edge where he blessed it using Joss Sticks and many chants. When he was finished he moved to the side where the other Monks formed a sort of gateway to the edge through which Hannibal, Cindy, Pamela, and finally JT entered.

There they placed their tiny boats into the water, watching as the swift current grabbed each; taking them south to the inlet of the Pacific Ocean. Each boat was caught in the current, twisting this way and that. JT kneeled, placed his boat in the water and watched, finally it bobbed and shuttered as the current took hold and gathered speed down the river.

Abby's spirits were finally free.

They each watched its journey, lost in thought.

Finally he felt a gentle hand on his shoulder and then two more. He turned to see the people he loved the most.

He stood, taking one last look to where the boats had disappeared.

They were forever gone.

Cindy and Pamela were quietly sobbing. JT turned to his left to look where the hidden mountains were and could not forget the image of a beautiful woman and her first sight of the lights of the Grouse

Mountain Ski Resort; he was having a hard time holding his emotions in check.

He then looked down at the beautiful bracelet that had once been Abby's. By a trick of the afternoon sun, it seemed to dance and sparkle. JT raised his arm. The more he watched the merrier it seemed.

Pamela, Hannibal and Cindy must have seen it dance too.

For a while longer he stared and then broke into a smile.

Those that did not know what was happening just stood and marvelled at the refractions of light playing around them.

As the sun set lower, the bracelet was now in shadow, JT lowered his arm.

Pamela took and held it as they walked back to the motel.

As they walked back to the trail and started to cross the bike path, an Asian couple was walking towards them. Between them a little girl was skipping and singing. Her dark hair framed her face as she twirled. Everyone stopped in mid-stride and wonder.

JT was dumbstruck the most. Before them danced a miniature Abby.

"I told you she was in happier place." Cindy said.

"Yes you did. Yes you did."

The End